INSPIRE

CORA CARMACK

Also by Cora Carmack

All Broke Down

All Lined Up

Seeking Her (Novella)

Finding It

Keeping Her (Novella)

Faking It

Losing It

INSPIRE

Inspire

This is a work of fiction.

ISBN 978-0-9883935-2-3

For Amy-

For letting me spoil every book I ever write so that I can talk through it with you.
I can still picture the exact moment I first told you that I was writing a book way back when. We were shopping, and I told you about those characters as we flipped through clothing racks, and you made me feel like it was more than just a far-flung dream. You made it feel inevitable. And for that, I will never be able to thank you enough.
As far as sisters go, you're a keeper. :)

PART ONE

Kalli

"What nourishes me also destroys me"
Christopher Marlowe

Chapter One

Balloons.

There are balloons filling the entire hallway when I exit my English and Composition class. *And rose petals.* A trail of pink, delicate rose petals that draw my eye to…

Shit.

I cross the hall quickly, trampling petals as I go.

"Van, get up."

My ex is on his knees, blocking the stairwell and all the people trying to leave. All the people who are now staring.

Of course they're staring. I would be staring too, if it weren't me. It's like something out of a bad 80s romantic comedy (who am I kidding? There's no such thing as a *bad* 80s romantic comedy. Even the bad ones are *brilliant*). But this…this is bad.

"Hear me out, Kalli." Oh damn. I've heard that tone before. "I'm lost without you. I can't think. I can't sleep." Can't shave apparently, judging by the badger living on his face. I feel a little bad for that insensitive thought until he continues, "I can't *write* without you, baby." And *that's* what it always comes down to. Not missing me. Missing what I *give* them. "I haven't put down a single decent word since you broke up with me."

This is the thing about dating artistic types. They're fun and charismatic and passionate, but that *passion* easily tips over into obsession. Believe me, I've been with enough of them to be intimately familiar with that particular character flaw (along with their penchants for narcissism, mood swings, and a general disdain for a good haircut). If I didn't need them as much as they needed me, I would gladly avoid the whole lot of them. And as someone who has spent a *long* time dealing with the artistic types, I am entirely qualified to say that their peculiarities get old really fast.

It's hard enough when a relationship ends. But when a relationship with an artist goes bad, it goes *spectacularly* bad.

Exhibit A: Van Noffke.

Potentially brilliant literary mind.

Wildly creative.

Total momma's boy.

And apparently not above humiliating himself.

I take hold of his elbow and pull him to his feet. I tug him away from the stairwell so that people can get by, but it appears that we're more interesting than whatever classes these people have to get to, and almost all of them stick around for the show.

Gods, I swear.

"Van, we talked about this. I'm sorry that you're having trouble moving on, but we aren't getting back together. It just won't work out."

I know it's wrong for me to be frustrated with him. He doesn't know why we can't spend any more time together, or that I've already stayed longer than I meant to. But I find myself angry all the same. I am continually baffled by humans' complete and utter lack of survival instincts. You would think some voice in the back of their minds would fight to preserve their safety, their sanity, but if there is such a voice, it's drowned out by the wild beating of their hearts as they chase after their desires. Success. Power. Love. Sex. It doesn't matter what the desire is, they all blind just the same.

Van runs his hand through his tousled black hair and gives me a pleading look. I think he might actually cry, and I am *so* not good with tears.

"It could, Kalliope. It could if you gave me one more chance."

Ugh. He's the only person who insists on calling me by my full name. I'd dropped the 'ope' off *Kalliope* ages ago, after I got tired of the pronunciation being butchered by modern mouths. I got *Kally-ope*, *Kay-lee-ope*. Someone fumbled it so badly once they called me *Cantaloupe*. And after one too many times having to draw out my name as *Kuh-lie-oh-pee*, I just gave it up entirely.

Which is what I have to do with Van now. I need to cut him off completely. For his own good. Maybe one more nudge of inspiration will end this permanently.

I step in close, and Van's eyes search mine greedily. I place my hand on his cheek, and he immediately seizes my waist and pulls me against his body. His breaths come faster, and for just a moment, I'm swept away by the pleasure that comes from being wanted this much.

That's what my gift feels like, too. The inspiration. It's this heady rush, like I'm breathing through every pore of my skin, pouring out the energy that poisons me if I keep it too long. For them though, it's like a drug that activates all the dormant parts of their brain, opening them up to ideas and thoughts and visions that they could never have on their own. It's like being high, but sacrificing none of the focus or reasoning skills. But like with most drugs…there are consequences. Addiction being one of them.

I want to step away because I'm not exactly immune to Van either. I have a connection to all of my artists. And when energy passes from me to them…well, let's just say I enjoy it as much as they do. But it's my responsibility to make certain that neither of us gets *too* attached, and if Van's big gesture is any indication, he's on the line. Even so, I hold on for a few more seconds. Touch will make this last push more effective. And then we can be done with it.

I concentrate, let down my carefully constructed mental shields, and allow the energy to spill out of me. Like the first breath of air after too long spent underwater, the release consumes me for a moment. Relief. Pleasure. I force my eyes open before the sensation can sweep me away and focus on the task in front of me.

"Van, it's over, and for that I'm sorry. But we're not getting back together. We can't. I won't. Maybe if you write about how you're feeling, it will help you get past it…the writer's block and me." He tries to pull me closer, but I rip his hands from my waist and step back. It aches for a moment, stopping that exchange of energy, pulling it back into me. But it's necessary. "*Use this.* You'll be fine."

Then I break for the stairs and try not to meet the eyes of any of the students watching. No doubt we were sending off some serious soap opera vibes.

This is what it is to be a muse. I walk the line between want and need, between power and submission. And I make the hard choices.

Always with the hard choices.

Thank the gods it's my last class of the day, and I can just go home. Or better yet…the grocery store. Because ice cream makes everything better. Especially break-ups. And by my estimate, Van had the privilege of being, oh…my ten thousandth one of those.

∞

There's a small grocery store off the edge of campus. It's a little ghetto and just has the basics, but it's popular among the students for late night beer and food runs. I grab some chocolate chip cookie dough ice cream, plus some cookies (because it's not enough to *just* have the cookie dough in the ice cream). The Greeks might have been responsible for many of history's greatest accomplishments, but they would be *pissed* if they knew they missed out on the perfection that is chocolate chip cookie dough ice cream. I grab some soda and some gummy bears, too. You know, the essentials of life. Or college life anyway.

Major perk to being immortal? My body renews itself daily, so I can eat whatever I want, and I'll wake up tomorrow looking just as I did the day before. The way I've always looked. Same goes for cuts and bruises and hair dye and every possible change I could make to my physical appearance. Nothing holds. Nothing lasts beyond the start of a new day. Definitely a complication when you're trying to live among humans without revealing just how very different you are from them. There's no disguising who I am, no changing my appearance so people won't notice my distinct tendency to stay the same age.

As I wait in the express checkout line next to a wall of magazines, my eyes catch on a guy a little older than me (or a little older than I appear anyway) with a girl who must be around five years old. He's dressed in a white button-up shirt and a loosened tie, with blond hair that looks like he's run his hands through it one too many times. He's the complete opposite of the kind of guys I spend all my time with. He's put together and refined and mature with dark glasses across the bridge of a strong nose. The little girl's white blonde curls are even more out of control than his, and he's looking down at her like she's his whole world.

She tries and fails to sneak a giant candy bar into their cart. He laughs, deep and throaty, and returns the chocolate back to where she found it.

My lips split in a smile, but a dull throb moves through my chest a moment later, eclipsing it. Thousands of years, and I've never known what this guy has. I've never known what it's like to love someone, to build a life, to grow older…because loving me is dangerous. *I'm the drug.*

It may be my purpose to inspire people, but I ruin just as many as I help.

That's why I don't get to have what he has. I get short, passion-filled flings. I get excitement and adrenaline and creation. I get a new life and a new home. I get temporary attachments. Again and again, that's all I ever get.

Touching the lives of mortals, influencing them, *inspiring* them…that's the closest I ever come to really living. For a little while anyway. Brushing up against that kind of talent and genius…it's exhilarating. But the closer my artist and I become, the more involved, the less real it feels to me. They say such beautiful words, create such gorgeous art, and call me their muse without ever having any idea how right they really are. It's always the artist falling for me. And I shouldn't be so naïve, not after the life I've lived, but just once I'd like to let myself do the same.

My eyes are drawn back to the father/daughter pair. He's flipping through a sports magazine while the cashier ahead of us calls over a manager to help her with a problem on the register. The little girl looks up at him in awe, the way all little girls seem to do with their fathers. Then she picks up a magazine like him. When she holds it up high, I see that it has a dark-haired woman on the cover, barely covered by the skimpiest swimsuit I've ever seen (and I've been around a *long time*), her body posed in a way that is entirely not appropriate for a grocery store magazine rack. My jaw drops open just as she speaks.

"This one," she says, her small mouth transforming the

words into something adorable.

The guy is distracted reading an article, but looks up when she holds the magazine closer to him and says loudly, "I want THIS ONE!"

His face pales, and he snatches the magazine out of her hand, lightning fast. First, her lips form a circle, then the bottom one curls down. Her eyes squinch and her shoulders hunch, and only when her entire appearance has been transformed does she begin to cry.

"Gwennie, don't."

"But I want to read a magazine, too."

"Not *that* one."

She opens her small mouth, and the wail she unleashes reverberates around the checkout area. He scrambles to stuff the magazine behind a few issues of *Good Housekeeping,* but by the time he looks back, little Gwennie has already grabbed another from the same spot she found the first. But she's still crying.

"I said *no,* Gwen." He tries to steal it away again, but this time the little girl is faster. She backpedals, bumping into the older woman still waiting on the cashier and the manager to solve whatever is holding them up.

"It has a pretty girl on it," she says, sniffling, tears threatening to return at any moment. She holds the magazine up to the older woman behind her in an attempt to gain some allies, no doubt, but the old woman splutters a shocked, nonsense response.

"We'll get you a different magazine with a pretty girl," the guy tries.

"But she's pretty and she's going swimming. I like swimming, and I never get to do it anymore."

The magazine is indeed about swimming. Or rather...the best beaches to find sexy, single women. It's also about fast, easy ways to get your girl hot (direct quote), a definitive list of the world's best tequilas, and the manliest cars (whatever that means).

The guy kneels in front of his daughter and says, "Please…" But then he just sighs as she darts around him again, and this time she comes to me. But when she stands below me, the magazine falls forgotten by her side. This close, with her eyes impossibly wide, I can see the beautiful mix of blue and green in her irises.

"You're pretty," she tells me. "Are *you* on a magazine?"

"I'm not, no." I smile at her, and the one she gives me in return is brilliant.

An ache breaks through my chest like the sun through clouds.

History says I have children. Orpheus. Linus. Mygdon. More. But the stories are wrong. They've been twisted and mistold over the years.

And the only thing worse than not really having a life is hearing lies about one that can never be true. Like I said…my body renews daily. It doesn't ever change. Nothing about my existence *ever* changes. Not because of too much ice cream. Not hair dye. Certainly not something that would take nine months of changes.

I force the smile to stay on my face…because hey, at least that means I can wear the same clothes and shoes for as long as I want. Silver lining, right?

If only I could make myself believe that.

The little girl looks down at her magazine, considers the scantily-clad woman on the front again, and then switches her gaze back to me. With a very serious expression she says, "You should be on a magazine like this. Do you swim?"

The man pops up behind her. He tries to pluck the magazine away, but she pulls it tightly against her chest.

He says, "I'm so sorry."

My eyes resist leaving the little girl, but when they do, I'm not sorry.

The guy is younger than I thought from his profile. Early twenties, I'd guess. And I knew he was broad and masculine, but now I've got an up close and personal look at the way that his shirt hints at the slopes and curves of a muscled chest beneath. He wears a tie loosened around his neck, and the few undone buttons reveal a triangle of sun-tanned skin. He's not at all the kind of guy I'm normally attracted to. He's clean-cut and serious, and yet I see something now that hints at more. The glasses say stoic and sophisticated, but the hair…those not-quite-tamed curls are just begging for a pair of hands to mess them up the rest of the way.

It almost makes me think this is what my artists would look like all grown up. Only they'll still be working on "growing up" a decade from now, and he's already there. He's also outrageously, *handsomely* embarrassed. He rubs at the back of his neck with a chagrined smile, and I'm not sure that I've ever met a guy who can pull off uncomfortable and sexy at the same time.

You can't look at a guy like this and *not* picture him as a husband…a dad. He might not be like the artists I usually date, but he's the kind of guy I would want to settle down with.

If settling down were even a thing I could do.

When I go too long without answering, little Gwen says, "I don't think she likes you."

My lips pull into a smile, and I flick my gaze up to his face once more. And God, that's not true. Not true at all. And maybe my thoughts are in my eyes because his gaze sharpens, turns hot and hard, and it makes me think of ripped fabric, sweat-slicked skin, and bruised lips.

The pull toward him is electric, irresistible, like a siren's call, only it's not sound that's a danger to me…it's everything else. He might look clean cut on the surface, but I've looked into the eyes of enough men to recognize the spark of wickedness hidden in those pale blue depths.

"I like him just fine," I say, finally answering Gwen's statement, and the crooked grin he gives me makes something swoop in my belly.

"Just fine? Is that all?" This time, I do notice his voice, and maybe it's even more like a siren call than I thought. Low and musical, it slides against my skin, stirring the energy just behind my lungs that makes me what I am.

Only this man isn't the type to need a muse. In fact, I think the opposite might be happening. Something about this guy speaks to me. Maybe it's the soft blue of his eyes or the chiseled jaw or that loosened tie that I could use to pull him closer and closer…

Yeah. As improbable as it is, he's the dangerous one here.

And for possibly the first time in my existence, I can feel my nerves threatening to overwhelm me. I should be able to think of a flirty reply. That's what I *do*. I should be able to turn this guy's head so fast he'll have whiplash. Instead, I'm too bothered by his presence to even meet his eyes again.

I bend my knees until I'm level with the little girl. I tuck one blonde, disobedient curl behind her ear and touch a finger to her tiny, perfect nose.

Her cheeks pink, and I tell her, "I think you're much prettier than the girl on that magazine."

"Really?" Her eyes go wide, and she looks at me as if I hold all the answers. And I do have so many answers, so many insights about the world that are just fighting to break out of me. So many things I can never share. With anyone.

"I do," I promise her. "But the thing is…there are more important things than being pretty. "

"Like what?"

"Like being good and nice and happy. That's what will make people want to play with you and be around you." I reach out toward the magazine, and she loosens her grip, letting me take it. "Pretty only matters in pictures."

I rise and hand the magazine to her father. Unbidden, my mind starts spiraling out of control, picturing this little girl, this man who I can't help but notice wears no ring, and me. I start picturing what it would be like to have that kind of life, something I *never* allow myself to do, and the look he gives me and the brush of his fingers over mine don't help me shut it down.

I stick out my hand when I should be walking away. Running even.

"I'm Kalli."

His hand is big and warm around mine. The earlier brush of his fingers is completely eclipsed by the strength and surety of his grip. And the inspiration swirls in me, like a storm gathering on the sea, clamoring for him. His eyes trail over my face and then down. His perusal is quick, and his eyes pull back to mine fast. He's trying to be a gentleman, but that intensity is still there in his gaze, and I feel it burn through my veins. Desire engulfs me, and I can no longer differentiate between it and the unnatural energy that rests just behind my ribs.

"Wilder," he says, his voice deeper, raspier. And all I want to do is touch him, to know what he's thinking, to study just where the wholesome and good half of him gives way to the sin I see in his eyes.

I'm almost lost to it, almost ready to push inspiration into this complete stranger, because the buzz I feel around him is addictive. And the release, oh gods, it would be so good.

But I can't. Absolutely can't. I have to be careful even with my artists not to overload them, not to give them too much. And it's so much easier to pass that point with someone who's not already open to his or her creative side.

Too much and I could ruin him. Ruin this perfect life he has.

And I might do this kind of thing out of necessity, but I don't have it in me to be that selfish. The other gods might think of mortals as less than them, but I've walked among them for millennium. They are not *less* to me. In fact, I'm more jealous of them than I'll ever admit aloud.

I'm saved from the temptation when Gwen latches onto my wrist, pulling my hand away from his so that she can have a turn at shaking, too.

"I'm Gwen!" she says, not even really shaking my hand, so much as pulling it toward her, pulling *me* toward her.

"It's so very nice to meet you, Gwen."

This is too much.

Too hard.

I tuck that same stubborn curl behind her ear and say, "I have to go. You be good for your Dad."

I pull my hand away and stumble back. Wilder protests, says "No," followed by a series of other words that I don't hear because I'm already on my way to the door, leaving my ice cream and cookies and everything else behind.

I'm not normal. I won't ever be.

Dealing with artists does get old. And I hate that I'm living the same story on repeat. But better that than to rub salt in my millennium-old wounds by letting myself get close to the things I can't have.

Wilder and Gwen are coming out of the store as I pull out of my parking spot. Rather than crossing into the parking lot, they stop on the sidewalk and stare as I pull closer to them, toward the exit.

Gwen's little hand waves wildly at me, but it's Wilder's steady, piercing gaze that has me locking up behind the wheel. He lifts a hand, one side of his mouth ticking up in an almost smile that is somehow even more handsome than the grin he shot me earlier.

As I pull out onto the street, I resist the urge to glance in my rear view mirror.

Eternity has never felt quite as long as it feels right now.

Chapter Two

Swift and sure, my life course corrects back to normal.

History and poets have assigned many attributes to time.

It flies. It dies. It heals all wounds.

But for me, time is so much more. Sometimes she's a torturer. Others a reward. She's been a friend. A foe. A nuisance. A nobody. My relationship with her is an ever-changing cycle, but one thing is always certain.

Time is my surest constant.

The scenery changes. The costumes. The players.

But a second is a second is a second until the very end of it all.

Lesson #1 of Immortality:

Accept time for what it is. It can go no faster or slower. Only life can do that.

And my life goes back to its normal speed for nine days.

For nine days, I go to class. I go to the gym (mostly for something to do since losing weight and gaining muscle aren't really possible with my specific…peculiarities). I choose another grocery store to stock up on college essentials (re: ice cream). And I spend my lunch hours sitting outside various artistically-focused buildings on campus, scoping out possible candidates for my next mutually beneficial relationship.

Maybe *scoping* is the wrong word. More like eliminating everyone I come across. I need a break. I need some time to just be me before I have to ingratiate myself to another person, before I have to lie about my past and mold myself into some guy's vision of the perfect woman.

∞

By day nine, I know I'm being too picky. I don't get to take breaks. I don't get to just be me. Not without paying the price.

But even so, I continue discounting every guy I see.

Too much chest hair (*Dude, when it's peeking out of a crew neck t-shirt, it's time to suck it up and tame that beast*).

Pointy eyebrows (*Shallow, I know, but it made him look like a cheesy movie villain, and I just couldn't look at him with a straight face*).

Dickface (*By this I mean that the guy was a jerk…not that his face actually looked like a dick. Although if I had anywhere near the power of the greater gods and could mete out penalties and blessings whenever I pleased, I'd think that would be a pretty creative and deserved punishment*).

But still…in the back of my mind, *day nine* is on repeat, and I can feel the urgency clinging to me. Where the creative energy normally sits comfortably in my chest, I've gone long enough now since that last touch with Van that I'm starting to feel it in other places too. My belly. The back of my throat. The tips of my fingers. The top of my spine.

That last place especially. It sits there, coiling around my neck, creeping up into my head until I can feel the way it pushes at my mind, insists that I *do something*…or it will.

I can't explain what keeps me from choosing, except that I'm tired. So very tired. And for the first time ever, that outweighs my fear of the consequences. And I keep telling myself that I can go a little longer. I'm not cutting it too close. I know my limits.

Mortals used to think disease was caused by imbalances and overabundances in the body. They would bleed patients in an attempt to restore balance and fight off disease. Of course, as the world grew in knowledge, they realized how wrong they were, how barbaric and harmful the treatment really was. But that's actually how it works for me. The longer I go, the more the energy builds up in me, and in its raw state it's even more potent than when I push it into others. If I lock it up inside, if I don't reset the balance…

Well, it starts with the headaches. Those are my first warning sign. Then the mood swings. Then I start losing track of time, getting caught up in flights of creative fancy. My thoughts tangle and twine, and I can lose hours, days even, wrapped up in my own mind.

What happens after that? I don't know. I've never really let it get that far. But I've seen it. Roughly a thousand years ago, in the period history now calls the Dark Ages. It's named such for the lack of historical records from the period, but for me the name fits in better ways. We were all still together then, my sisters and I. There were nine of us, all muses, each with our own purposes and specialties. By the end of that century, we would all go our separate ways, scattered across the globe, but it would only be eight of us.

I'm not sure how long I've been singing softly to myself when I draw myself back to the present, away from lives past, but a handful of people at nearby benches and trees are watching me, slightly dazed. I clamp my mouth shut, but they continue to stare.

As muses, we have as much of an aptitude for the arts as we do for inspiring them. But it's an unspoken rule that we don't seek to create anything ourselves. It's hard enough to hide among humans and do what we do without being able to change our appearances. Any kind of notoriety threatens our ability to conceal ourselves and live in the world. There's a reason I'm trolling a college campus rather than finding my next relationship in Hollywood or New York or Paris. I find my artists when they're still finding themselves. It's better for me that way, feels like I'm actually making a difference and helping them. There's also no fame involved (not yet anyway), so I don't risk getting photographed or noticed or otherwise exposed.

I need the world, need the people in it. Muses can't survive without it. We can only expend our energy with mortals, otherwise we would have withdrawn with the rest of the gods. And they might have left us here, but that doesn't mean they aren't watching. Doesn't mean they won't intervene if one of us jeopardizes the rest.

They've done it before. And they won't hesitate to cut us down to seven if they must.

I gather my belongings and decide to skip my next class in favor of checking out the offerings of the music library (the people, not the music). On my way, I catch sight of the flashing red and white lights of an ambulance by the on-campus apartments between here and the fine arts buildings. I'm heading that way anyway, so I cross that direction until I get to the group of students standing, blocking the sidewalk and waiting.

I nudge a bigger guy next to me as he texts rapidly on his cell.

"What's going on?" I ask.

It's the curvy redhead on my right that answers. "Suicide."

"Attempted," the Hispanic guy next to her corrects.

"I don't know. I have a friend who lives in the building, and she said he hung himself."

"Pills," the guy with the phone finally answers. "I know the guy who found him. It was pills."

At that moment, the front door opens, and they wheel out a stretcher. One paramedic is rolling it toward the ambulance.

The other has one of those respirator things fitted over the guy's mouth, and is squeezing it periodically. The crowd begins to shift and whisper, pushing forward in morbid curiosity as the stretcher arrives at the ambulance. They lift the patient up, high enough that I've got a clear view, and for all my thoughts about time being a constant, I swear it slows to a stop then.

Because I recognize the dark, shaggy hair. The shape of the face. Even with that oxygen thing over his nose and mouth, and his unusually pale skin, I know with a bone deep certainty that it's Van.

My Van.

I've seen his face in the brightness of day, scruffy from not shaving, and clean and smooth. I've seen him in the low light of his room, sleeping and awake. I've seen him in the glow of his laptop as he sat up late at night tapping away at the keys while I tried to sleep.

I know him.

Maybe he didn't know me, and maybe he was just a means to an end, and maybe I was that for him, too. But all the same…

I know him.

My breath catches in the back of my throat, halfway between my lungs and the open air, and for a moment I can't get myself to push it out or pull it in. My vision begins to narrow, a lens zeroing in until everything else disappears but the boy being loaded into the ambulance.

This is my fault.

If I hadn't influenced him one last time to get him to go away…If I'd never smiled back at him in that bar six months before that…If Van Noffke had never met me, he wouldn't be on that stretcher.

I stumble back away from the crowd. I try to walk slowly, calmly. But I just can't. I put one foot in front of the other, faster and faster, until I'm running. My heart seems to twist between every beat, and I'm just waiting…*waiting* for it to twist so hard it tears loose.

And somewhere along the way, the image of Van on that stretcher blurs with the wild energy I can feel pumping through my body, mingling with my blood, the energy grappling for release. And I'm no longer sure whether I'm running from what I saw or who I *am*.

Maybe those two things aren't really that different.

Creation and Destruction.

These are the things I inspire.

∞

Six days later, I stop going to class. I wake up in bed, and it just doesn't even occur to me to go. There's so much energy still trapped in me because I haven't been able to bring myself to do anything about it, to expel it, not after seeing Van.

And I'm just so full, I can't think beyond the way it feels. There's a world inside my head, and it's so easy, *too easy*, to vacate my real life for the one in my mind.

There's a tempest there…

Churning

    Raging

        Flooding

It laps at me in waves, crashing high and then rolling away. It drags me a little farther away from myself every time, that irresistible tide.

And it's suffocating and extraordinary and glorious. And I no longer want to push it out. I want to drown in it, in all the colors and ideas and feelings it opens up in me. The thoughts…they're so big that they eclipse everything else. The past. The future. Emotions. They drown those out completely.

For the first time in many, *many* years, I know what it feels like to not have memories shackled to my ankles, holding me back.

I pick up a pen and paper to write down how it feels to be this alive, to be this free. It's beautiful. *Brilliant.* This must be how the other gods feel. I might not be human, but that doesn't mean I'm free from the mortal coil. I'm just not chained to it by life and death. I'm chained by need. But not now, not anymore. I don't need anything.

I write a single word first.

Need.

One word becomes two.

Want.

More words spill out of me then, springing to mind faster than I can write them.

hope   hatred   joy
*   fear   awake   freedom*
laughter lies   faith
*   beauty   wild   desire*
purpose
*   truth*
*   change   art*
pain happy regret
*   passion   grace*
*   strength   courage*
*   shame*
dream   life   wonder   power
*   sorrow   poison   peace*
mercy   wisdom belief   grief   guilt
*   time*
*   love*

The words shift, become sentences. Those sentences tangle and twine into paragraphs, my ideas grow legs and they walk, run, *sprint* across the page, and I can't stop. I write all morning, across every piece of paper I own until my desk, the drawers, my backpack are all empty. Then I write across the furniture and the floors and the walls. I write words I love and hate and feel so intensely that they bring tears to my eyes.

And the words…gods. They're everything.

All that I am and want to be and hate to be…it's all in them, and sometimes I sit and marvel at how a series of scribbles can mean so much, how words can hold so much meaning in the space between their measly letters.

INSPIRE.

I write the word across my living room floor in big, black letters. Then I stare at it, unsure whether I want to scratch it out or deface it or write over it.

It's a curse, that word. A purpose I'm tired of serving.

So what if I just…quit?

I know what it will do to me. Is already doing to me. Somewhere in the back of my mind, I can look around at my scribed walls and know it's not normal. I know that I've let this go entirely too long, and now the power I wield is stronger than I am. It flexes in me, fierce and hungry, and for a moment, I feel a spike of fear. Then it passes in a wave of euphoria, and I know now why people find me, *what I can give them*, addictive.

It makes me feel brilliant and aware and one with everything around me, and for the first time ever, I *understand.* Not just an idea or a person or a place. I understand *everything.* The world. The past. The present. My existence.

It's vast and complicated and I can't put it into words, but I just *know.* For the first time in my life, I actually feel like a goddess.

I come to a decision then.

I draw a D at the end of the word I scrawled on my living room floor.

INSPIRED.

Maybe this is my curse, but I don't have to share it. I don't have to push it on other people.

Mortals…they're fragile. They can die or break or ruin. And I suppose I'm not immune to those last two either, but I'm stronger than they are. And I've been so very selfish for so very long.

Some already mad part of me rejoices at my decision. Greedy for it, for the way I feel right now. I give in to it.

And when I stumble out of my house, my fingers smudged with ink, it's dark and I am so very alive.

Chapter Three

Since I had come to the States, I had lived in almost every major city in the country. They each have their quirks and specialties, but move around enough and they all start to feel the same.

Austin doesn't feel that way. At least not yet.

It is this eclectic mix of modern culture and southern charm and creative freedom. And the best part?

I had nothing to do with it.

All the imagination and uniqueness is entirely a product of the people who live here. And they are my favorite part. The people are all so different. Hipsters and old money and artists and cowboys and geniuses of industry and technology and musicians and actors. Nowhere else but Austin could they (or would they) all fit together...*interact* like there are no differences between them.

Keep Austin Weird, as they say.

I weave through the crowds along Sixth Street downtown. It's a mile or two south of campus, but now that I'm here, I don't even remember the walk from my apartment. Which should worry me more, but it doesn't. My mind and body are barely connected at the moment. Or maybe they're more intertwined than ever...so in tune that I don't even have to think about where I'm going or what I'm doing. Which frees up my mind for other things.

This section of downtown has been blocked off to traffic, and pedestrians teem through the streets, laughing and talking and singing. Neon signs glow in every other window, music drifts from doorways, and the smell from food trucks and restaurants wafts through the streets. I soak it all in, revel in it. I hear a catcall or two, but my focus is on the lights, the colors. When something catches my eye, I turn and follow.

An older man busks on the street corner, his guitar slung over his shoulders and his case open before him. The glint of the coins catches my eye, and then the music curls through my mind, lifting me up and onto a new plane. I stay with him for a while, sometimes dancing, sometimes singing along, until some new thing draws my attention.

Eventually, I find my way into a club, up a flight of stairs, and into the crush of bodies on a dance floor. This isn't at all the kind of dance I used to inspire, used to enjoy, but there's still something about it that makes me pause.

Sweat-slicked limbs.

Bodies pressed close.

Bass thrumming right through my skin.

There's a strange kind of poetry in it. Raw and animalistic and desire in motion.

Once upon a time, I considered myself Greek, so I know a thing or two about hedonism. These days I don't really claim any place as home. I belong nowhere, so nowhere belongs to me.

When I'm in the middle of the crowd, I stand still, picking out shapes and lines in the writhing bodies around me. It really is something to see—the way people interact. Whether they're friends or lovers or strangers, everyone is connected on this dance floor. One body touches another that touches another without any insecurity, and I wish I weren't the only one to see the beauty in it.

That gives me an idea, and I draw in a deep breath. *What if they could see it? What if I could make them?* Stretching out my arms, I push that breath out, expelling some of the energy swirling in my chest with it. My fingers graze and drag along anonymous skin.

For a second, the whole room shudders, contracts and expands like a heartbeat. The crowd seems closer, bodies tight against mine. Hands settle on my hips, and a warm body presses at my back. But I barely feel that through the rush of power leaving me.

Now that the floodgates are open, the swell of pleasure that comes with the energy release overwhelms me. I don't focus, I can't. Heat rushes up through my skin, and my head spins in a way that feels simultaneously alarming and brilliant. All I can do is ride the wave as it leaks out of me and spills across the room. Sound. Touch. Sight. Smell. It's all somehow heightened and muted at the same time.

Long minutes later, the bliss begins to fade and my head starts to clear. Too late, the horror dawns and I try to throw up my walls, try to pull back the energy, but my wits are scattered, and I'm exhausted.

I don't realize how much all that energy had eclipsed my own thoughts and emotions until it begins to disappear. Suddenly panicked, I whip around, scanning the room, and my stomach heaves in fear. On the surface, the only obvious difference I can see is that the once frenzied movements of the crowd have begun to ebb and flow in a way that's almost in sync, almost choreographed.

But the people nearest me, they're the real problem. A few just seem manic, their eyes dazzlingly bright, smiles wide, laughter pealing from between their lips. Two have begun to dance so intensely that the crowd has stepped away, forming a circle around them, watching. One woman is sobbing, and her friend next to her is staring on in a mix of wonder and horror and fascination. The guy behind me, the one who'd had his hands on my hips, now drags those same hands back and forth between his ears and his eyes, undecided as to which he wants to cover more.

It's too much. It's all too much. And all I can think of is Van on that stretcher. He'd been with me longer, but I influenced him slowly, artfully. There was nothing careful about tonight. I'd dropped my walls and the magic had flowed from me unharnessed, uncontrolled, a blunt force trauma of power. I have no idea what that could do to people. Especially people I've not carefully studied and vetted.

The guy behind me collapses to his knees, and no one around us notices. It's someone farther out who pushes through the people to get to him. I reach out a hand, to help or soothe or *something*, but then pull it back fast.

I shouldn't touch him again. I'm still giving off waves of power, less now, but even slight contact between our skin could push him over the edge.

I wrap my arms around my middle and do my best not to touch anyone as I shift my way through the crowd. A fight breaks out behind me, and I hear people screaming.

I squeeze my lips tightly together, clamped between my teeth, until it feels like I might cut right through the skin. I know I'm crying, have *been* crying, when I taste salt even through my closed lips. More screaming erupts upstairs as I stumble out the door and over the uneven slabs of concrete on the sidewalk. I barely catch my balance before I go sprawling out on the street.

A hand reaches out to steady me, but I jerk myself away.

"Don't touch me. Nobody touch me."

I limp away, shaky and sick and…oh gods what have I done?

I pass the same street musician, and he calls out for me to join him again, but I keep my head down, my thoughts focused on reconstructing the mental shields I'd all but demolished back there.

What have I done?

I think it again and again as I push myself farther and farther from that club, turning north, away from the crowds and the bars.

What have I done? What have I done?

I must say it out loud because a man with a grizzly beard leaning against a brick building answers, "You've been bad, pretty one. That's what you've done."

I jolt, edging sideways to put distance between us. There's a high population of homeless people downtown, especially because there's a shelter not too far from here. Many of them are lovely people that have the same kind of vibrancy as this city. But you can never be too careful, and this guy…something about him makes alarm bells ring at the back of my weary mind. He reaches out to touch me, and I try to jump away, but he's quicker than I expect him to be.

His hand locks around my wrist and no matter how hard I tug, I can't break his hold. He squeezes, and the pinch of pain makes me focus on him. His skin is weathered and tough, but clean. And up close, his beard isn't as gnarled as I expected, just full and long. It's not until I look into his eyes that I know for certain this is no homeless man.

Deep set and large, each of his eyes has two irises and two pupils, and I know if I were to search, I'd find more than those four eyes trained on me, more than four eyes *on him*.

"Reckless," he says, his voice graveled and hard. "I don't need to tell you what happens to the reckless ones, Kalliope."

"How do you—"

"Don't play dumb with me, girly. Your life might be all pretty things and pretty words, but you're not naïve."

Lead lines my stomach, and I want to run, but fear weights me to my spot.

"Son of Argus," I say, and he arches a brow. "Watcher."

There's not many of us left in the world from the old days, but even so, the greater gods don't trust us to live out here on our own. The Argus are said to have hundreds of eyes, and never are they all closed at once, not even in sleep. No one knows quite what they see and how much, but it's enough that the gods trust them to keep the rest of us in line.

He nods, and my gaze catches on his strange eyes again. They're a blue so light it borders on silver. Cold. Hard. "Right you are. And I don't particularly like having to venture out among humans because some little goddess can't control herself."

Indignant, I say, "I can control—"

"Can you? Do you know what's happening back in that club right now?" I shake my head hard, not sure I want to know, but he answers anyway. "Complete chaos. The cops are currently wondering if it was some kind of bad drug reaction." He pauses, squints for a moment, then adds, "Someone just suggested bioterrorism."

I wince, and my stomach pitches, nausea rising swiftly up my throat.

"I didn't mean to. It was an accident."

He takes hold of my other wrist, drawing both arms up between us until he towers over me. He seems larger, more intimidating than before, and I try not to appear afraid.

"No more accidents," he says. "Risk exposing us again, and the gods might decide this world has enough art already."

I open my mouth, to say what, I don't know. But I never get that far.

Someone calls my name, softly at first, then louder.

"Kalli? Is that you? Kalli! Hey, man, let her go!"

The Argus holds on tight for another moment. His grip doesn't hurt. Not really. But his gaze almost does. Like he's looking into me, through me. I hear footsteps coming fast, and then my wrists are free, and the watcher moves too fast for a man who looks so old. He slips around the corner and out of sight just as another person skids to a halt beside me.

"Hey, Kalli right?"

I look up, and I'm so stunned that I forget to flinch away when a hand comes up to touch my cheek.

"You okay?"

I don't know. Don't know that at all. But I know this guy.

This time there's no little girl, no grocery store, no magazines. Something leaps behind my ribs, but it's not power. It's something even harder to control.

Want.

"Hi Wilder."

Chapter Four

His hand is warm against my cheek and he tilts my head up, peering into my eyes. He's not wearing the glasses tonight, and a few days worth of stubble resides on his jaw, and he looks so different than the last time I saw him. No tie. No button down. Instead he wears a fitted tee, a black leather jacket, and dark jeans that hang off his body perfectly. Even so, I still get that same steady feel from him.

Though that could be because he has his other hand braced at my waist, keeping me upright. Either way, he makes me feel safer than I have any right to be after a run in with one of the Argus.

"Are you okay?"

I nod, pulling back from his hand at my cheek like I should have done the instant he touched me. I'm lightheaded though, and as soon as I'm free my knees quake, and I throw out a hand to steady myself.

"Easy there." He loops an arm around my waist, and I can feel it burning through the fabric of my dress.

He leans close, peering at my eyes, and the smell of him surrounds me, warm and masculine with a hint of spice.

He asks, "How much have you had to drink?"

I tense. "None. I'm fine."

He arches one perfect eyebrow and says, "Try again."

"Really, I swear."

His gaze dips down, and I think he's looking at the rounded neck of my dress, and my heart flips over, sending off a ripple of anticipation in its wake. Then he says, "You're barefoot," and that anticipation turns to horror.

I step back, and sure enough, he's right.

My feet are bare and dirty, and now that I concentrate, I can feel a few stinging cuts on the bottom.

"I—" I pause, completely at a loss for how to explain this without sounding like a complete lunatic. I lift up my hand, wondering if I'd left my house this way, or if perhaps I'd taken my shoes off at some point and had been carrying them. The last few days are kind of a muddled blur in my mind. I can remember some of how I felt and thought, but physical actions…not so much. I had been completely in my head, but now the energy that had consumed me is all gone.

Horror slicks my stomach. I'd poured it all out on that crowd. I can't feel even an inkling of it now. A slideshow runs through my mind then of all my failures, all the artists I kept too long or let get too close. I see their faces, both as they once were, and then how I left them—broken, shells of their former selves. Van wasn't the first of mine to do violence against himself or someone else. Some had done it in misguided attempts to win me back. Others let their loss turn to anger. Against me. Against the world. But mostly themselves.

That's another reason why my body renews itself daily. Not just so I'll stay young and pretty, but because there's an unfortunate tendency for the affected to lash out, to try to destroy the beautiful thing that had once brought them success or motivation or joy.

I'm not saved from that kind of violence. No, the gods enjoy others' pain too much to give me that kind of gift, but at least I don't wear the marks of it forever on my skin.

For the most part, my entanglements are simple and short with just the right amount of give and take to leave the artist happy and on his or her way to a well-led life. But there are the exceptions. The ruined ones. The ones whose personalities pull too close to obsession; those who can't deal with my absence. They're rare. As are those who turn to violence. And I know it's not healthy or fair, but I've come to accept that when the violence turns to me, it's the world's (perhaps the gods') way of seeking balance.

Wilder's sigh brings me back to the present and he asks, "Where's your car?"

I swallow and look around, unwilling to tell him that I walked all the way from my place up by campus. Because that will make me look even crazier than I already do.

"What are you doing here?" I ask instead.

I get that same almost smile he gave me as I pulled out of the grocery store parking lot, and it hits me just as hard this time. His half smile is more charming than most peoples' full out grins.

"You're bossier than I remember." When I try to pull away, he appeases me by saying, "I was out with some friends, and I saw you leaving a club. You looked…"

He doesn't finish his sentence, and I'm glad for it. I don't want to know what I looked like.

"You followed me?"

"I tried to. I lost track of you in the crowds for a bit. I was crossing the street to keep searching down Sixth when I looked up by chance and saw you with that homeless guy."

"Oh."

Oh. That's all I've got to say right now. Even if I weren't completely addled by the events of the night, I don't think I would know what to say to this guy. He isn't one of my potential partners. I'm not luring him in to satisfy the necessities of my curse.

But I want to lure him in all the same, and that makes me feel guilty and sick and excited all at the same time.

"Why?" I ask.

"Why what?"

"Why did you follow me?"

He turns his head, looking down the street, and for a moment I don't think he'll answer me. Then he laughs. "I'm still trying to figure that one out. Give me a few minutes. I'll think of a reason that's not at all creepy. I promise."

Carefully, he eases back until his arm is no longer around me, and just his hand is left bracing me at my waist. I'm sure he doesn't mean for it to be suggestive, but I'm still coiled tight from the club, from the way it feels to use my ability. The simple touch of his hand sliding across the thin fabric of my dress is enough to set my nerves on fire, and I shiver.

He immediately sheds his jacket and hands it to me. The leather is worn and smooth, and for a moment I just hold it against me. It smells like him, and the warmth and scent is so comforting after the night I've had that I feel tears prick at the back of my eyes before I manage to get a grip on myself.

"Put that on. November in Texas might not be that cold, but I can't believe you left the house in just that dress. Or did you lose a coat too?"

I tilt my head to the side and survey him with a frown before tugging the jacket on. "And you called *me* bossy."

He smiles for half a second, but then his expression turns serious. "But really, what happened? Are you okay? Your face as you left that club…Are you…Did—"

"I'm fine. I swear. Just a weird night."

He reaches forward and pulls both sides of the coat together, cocooning me inside. His hands slip up, and I bite my lip, wanting him to put just a little more pressure behind that light touch. He lifts the collar, so that my face is blocked from the wind, and his knuckles graze my cheek.

I can tell he's not going to let it go. He's going to keep digging, and I have no idea what I could possibly say. "Where's Gwen?" I ask quickly, and it's such a stupid question, but it's the first thing that pops into my head. Like he would bring his daughter out for a night on the town. God, I don't even know what time it is. Sometime before two when the bars start to close, that's all I know. She's probably at home with her mother. His girlfriend, maybe. My stomach turns, and his hands drop from the jacket, making the sensation worsen.

"She's at home with my mother." I feel an inkling of relief before he adds, "Our mother. She's my little sister." That almost smile drives me *almost* mad again. "I tried to tell you, but you bolted out of the store. Left your ice cream and cookies behind."

Oh gods. Could I have made a bigger fool of myself? Why is he even standing here with me? He should think I'm crazy. All I've done is act it around him.

"Sorry, I had to go."

"Yeah…you said. You seemed a little spooked."

"I wasn't *spooked*. I just remembered something I had to do."

His expression tells me he doesn't believe me, and I fight not to blush. I must fail because his hand goes back to my face, a thumb dragging over the exact spot where I can feel the heat rising on my skin. His eyes are big and dark as he scans my face, and when he leans in, his body comes incredibly close to mine. "Is it strange that I wanted to go after you? I think I might have, if Gwen hadn't been with me."

I swallow once. Then again. Because it's not strange. He's reacting to my ability, to the way I look. I don't exclusively influence men, but they open up a lot easier to a pretty face than most girls do.

He continues, "Though I think Gwen would have been all too happy to chase you too. I don't know how you did it, but she was a complete angel the rest of the day. Didn't throw a single fit. I think I might have to call you Saint Kalli if you continue to work miracles like that."

I shrug. "She's sweet."

He barks a laugh, dipping his chin toward his chest, and dropping his hand. "Sometimes. Yeah." He takes a few steps back; it's then that I notice what he'd been hiding beneath his jacket and the button down he'd worn the first time we met.

His skin is covered in ink, from his wrists, all the way up and under the sleeves of his fitted tee. I barely have time to take in the art or contemplate this new puzzle piece of this man before his eyes catch sight of my feet again. Then he's all business. The line of his jaw is hard, stern, and that almost smile is long gone. He looks angry, either with me or with himself for forgetting.

"You didn't tell me where your car is."

"I, uh, didn't bring it. It's still back at my apartment."

He frowns, and I hope he'll just assume that I caught a cab.

"And you don't know where your shoes are?"

I shrug and smile because I'm pretty positive I'm better off sticking to nonverbal communication at the moment. Just smile and look pretty, that usually works for most things.

He shakes his head and says, "I'll take you home. But my car is a bit of a walk from here."

"It's fine. I'll just catch a cab."

He lifts an eyebrow and says, "Do you have money?"

I glance down, and sure enough, he's right. I don't have anything with me. No purse, no wallet, nothing. I'm not even sure how I got into that club without an ID. I must have charmed the bouncer, but I don't really remember.

When I don't answer he says, "Right. My car it is then."

He surveys me again, then turns to the side a little and says, "Hop on."

I blanch. "*Hop on?*"

"It's about five or six blocks to my car. No way I'm letting you walk all that way barefoot. I'd carry you in my arms, but..." He trails off, and his eyes linger along the hem of my dress that falls loose around my thighs and would no doubt flash the world if he were to hold me against his chest.

He clears his throat, and when he looks back at me, his eyes are hooded and his gaze drops briefly to my mouth. He turns away quickly and says again, his voice clipped, "Hop on."

I step up behind him and lay my hands atop his shoulders. The muscles bunch and harden beneath my touch, and I know my assumption that day at the grocery store was correct. He might spend his days hiding beneath business clothes, but he has an incredible body beneath.

"How do I..."

"Jump," he answers. "I'll catch you."

I take a deep breath, and rather than jumping straight away, I move close and lift one leg up to wrap around his hip. He reaches a hand back to grip my thigh, and it ends up half on the fabric of my dress, half on my bare skin. I feel him suck in a breath, and before I can think too much about it, I dig my fingers into his shoulders and jump, lifting my other leg.

He catches me as promised, but my dress has ridden up around my thighs so his other hand curls around bare flesh. I wrap one arm over his shoulder, and down onto his chest so I don't choke him by wrapping it around his neck. I reach down with the other to pull at my dress and make sure all the necessary parts of me are covered. The fabric slides down a little, covering part of his hand, but he doesn't bother adjusting his grip so he's not beneath my dress.

I fold my other arm around him to hold on, and I swear I can feel his heart racing beneath my hand. My chest presses against his hard back, and he doesn't move for several long moments.

"Wilder?"

He clears his throat and answers, his voice strained, "Just…trying to remember which direction my car is in."

He starts walking then, and I'm all too aware of the heat that's burning where our bodies press together. He pauses to shift me higher, gripping my legs a little harder, and the friction of my front against his back makes a moan form low in my throat. I pause long enough to be thankful that he gave me his jacket, otherwise he would feel the way my nipples have tightened into hard little buds because of his closeness. Somehow, putting on a bra didn't occur to *altered* me.

"So," I say, trying to distract myself. "Gwen is your little sister. That makes you how much older than her?"

"She's five, and I'm twenty-three, so about eighteen."

"Wow," I say.

He laughs. "Yeah, we were all a little shocked when she happened."

"Are you close?"

"Getting there. I wasn't around much when she was born. I was already out of the house and on my own, but…well, things are different now. I've been trying to make an effort to be around more for the last year or so."

My head hovers over his shoulder, close to his ear and I reply quietly, "I bet she's glad to have you back. Your parents, too."

He nods, some of his curls brushing my cheek, but quickly shifts the focus to me. "What about you? Any siblings?"

I hesitate, my usual lie on the tip of my tongue. Normally, I start out from the beginning saying no family. It keeps people from asking unwanted questions. But this time…I don't know what's different.

"Sisters. But we're estranged. I haven't seen or spoken to them in…well, a long time."

"I'm sorry." His voice is low and sincere, and it makes me want to lean my head against his shoulder.

I do just that when I reply, "It's okay. I'm over it." Have had a long time to get there.

The road we're on begins to slope upward, and he grips me tighter. I do the same, feeling bad that he has to carry me all this way.

"Well, you know how old I am. What about you?"

I stifle a laugh. Wouldn't that be something if I told him the truth? He'd drop me off at the hospital for a psych-consult rather than at my apartment.

"Twenty-one." Perpetually.

I feel him shift, and I lift my head off his shoulder only to find him turned sideways toward me, our lips inches apart.

It takes him a moment to say what's on his mind, and when he does, his voice is husky. "You sure? You look…young."

I laugh, and my voice might be a little breathy too. "If you're worried about me being underage. I promise…I'm not."

He stops then by a dark SUV and says, "This is me."

He lets go of one of my legs to fish for his keys, and I tighten my thighs around his waist. He pauses, ducking his head and bracing an arm against the vehicle. After a shuddering breath, he unlocks the car with the press of a button and pulls open the passenger side door. He turns and leans until my backside meets the leather seat. For a moment, I have to resist the urge to squeeze my arms and legs around him, to not let him go, but common sense wins out, and I let them fall slack.

Rather than stepping away completely, he turns to face me, his hips still cradled between my legs. He towers over me, and I can't help but notice how gorgeous he is. Perfectly angled jaw, high cheekbones, and sinfully full lips. His nose is slightly off-center, but somehow that only makes him more fascinating to me. A gifted sculptor once told me that the brilliance of art lives in its flaws.

He leans down toward me, planting a fist on the seat beside me, and I tilt my chin up. My mind is filled with the mistakes I've made and the possible repercussions and the look in the Watcher's eye, but somehow his closeness cuts through all of that. And I want him to kiss me.

Immortality has a way of muting the world over time, blurring the things that used to matter, and stifling emotions that used to be clear and sharp.

I don't know why he's different, but he is. As his mouth hovers closer to mine, it's everything else that blurs, not him. When I can feel the heat of his breath on my lips, my eyes flutter closed, and his groan is the only clue I get before I feel his body move away from mine, and the cool November air takes his place.

I open my eyes, and he stands a few feet back, turned slightly away. His hand rubs at the back of his neck, and his chest rises and falls on a slow, steady breath. He grips the top of my door and waits for me to shift my legs inside. I do, and the door closes with a thud before he disappears behind the SUV.

I dip my chin when he climbs inside, suddenly nervous. He twists the key in the ignition, and immediately turns down the air while we wait for it to warm. I'm saved the trouble of deciding what to say by the ringing of his phone. It rings twice, and it's not until he says my name that I realize it's coming from the pocket of his jacket. The one I'm wearing.

"Oh, sorry."

While I search his pockets, he accepts the call on his car's Bluetooth.

"Wild, where the fuck are you man? How am I supposed to get some while I've got Bridget in my ear asking about you every five seconds?"

"Rook, hang on a sec." Then he tells me, "It's in the zipper pocket."

I retrieve the phone and say again, "Sorry."

The guy on the phone says, "Ohh. And who might that pretty voice belong to?"

Wilder switches the call to his cell and says, "Rook. Something came up. I'm sorry." He sighs at his friend's response. "Not that kind of something." He rubs at the bridge of his nose, and it makes me think again of the glasses he'd worn last time. I wonder which version of Wilder is more authentic. Leather or lenses. "I know. I'll owe you one." I don't have to hear the words to know his friend isn't happy he's ditching. "Tell her whatever you want. Bridget isn't my problem anymore." That gets a strong enough response that Wilder tilts his ear away from the phone. "Fine. I'll owe you two. Gotta go." He hangs up without waiting for a reply and tosses the phone into a cup holder in the center console.

"So, where am I taking you?"

It's then that I remember how I spent my day before I wandered down to Sixth Street. I have a vague memory of my apartment, covered in my delusional thoughts, and I know I can't go back there. I can't face that. Not now. Not with him in tow.

"Anywhere but home."

Chapter Five

I have to lie again.

I make up some story about a fictional roommate being home with her boyfriend and a bunch of his friends that I can't stand. I tell him they won't leave until late, and he can just drop me off on campus somewhere.

"I'll kill time in the library or something," I say.

"The library? On a Saturday night? With no shoes?" I wince. Gods, I sound like an idiot. "Why don't you just let me take you home? I'll go in with you if you're worried about those guys. I'll feel better if I know you're home and safe."

I absolutely can't let him into my apartment. Not until I see what damage I did earlier today and find a way to undo it.

And that's not something I have the energy or strength to do tonight. In fact, if he weren't here, I'm fairly certain I'd still be huddled on the street somewhere, bawling my eyes out.

And there's a very real chance I might do that even with him here.

"No. Really. I'm fine," I say. "In fact, maybe I should just catch a cab. I don't want to put you out."

I start to slip off his jacket so I can leave, but he grips my arm to stop me. My eyes go to his ink again, and there's a familiar figure there that captures me.

Atlas.

I survey him then, wondering what about this man would make him want a tattoo of such a figure, of a Titan with such a heavy burden on his shoulders.

"Buckle up. I'll take you to my place. We'll get you cleaned up, and you can stay there until I can take you home."

I hesitate, and the stern look he shoots me shouldn't make my thighs clench, but it does. "Kalli. Seatbelt. Please."

When I follow his directive, he puts the car in drive and pulls out onto the narrow one-way street. A few turns have him merging onto the highway and heading north. He's silent, which I don't mind. It gives me time to evaluate how I'm going to handle this moving forward. Maybe I'll get lucky, and he'll live close to me. I can just wait until he's distracted and then sneak out and walk home. But when the exits for the university area come and go, and he keeps heading north, I give up on that idea.

Okay. Worst case scenario…I spend the night. That is, if he lets me. Then tomorrow I'll just have him drop me off on campus for class or I'll take the bus.

Except that I'm not sure exactly what day it is, and based on the crowds on Sixth Street, I'm going to guess it's a weekend. Which means no classes. And even if I manage to find a bus stop, I have no money. Or shoes.

I let out a frustrated exhale and lean my head against the cool glass of the window.

"You okay?" he asks.

I nod in lieu of an answer.

"You need water or something? Are you going to be sick?"

I resist the urge to laugh. Because I do feel like I might be sick, but not because of alcohol. "I swear, I'm fine. I'm not drunk."

He doesn't look like he believes me, and I don't blame him. In fact, it's probably easier if I just let him think that I am. Less explaining for me to do in the long run.

"Why Atlas?" I ask on impulse.

"Hmm?"

"Your tattoo. Atlas."

He frowns, and from his expression I gather he's surprised I recognize the image.

"The myth interested me."

"Just interest?" The tattoo takes up nearly his entire forearm. "Must be a lot of interest to have it permanently etched on your skin."

He shrugs. "I can identify with him."

"His punishment? Have you done something deserving of punishment, Wilder?"

Oh gods, I'm flirting. Why am I flirting? What is *wrong* with me?

He laughs and shakes his head. "I just always thought it was interesting that out of all the Titans that betrayed the gods, he was chosen to bear the weight of the Earth."

"That's a misconception, actually. It's not the Earth that Atlas holds, but the celestial spheres. The heavens. He keeps them from colliding with the Earth. And the others didn't exactly get away with it. I would rather Atlas's punishment than spend eternity being tortured in Tartarus."

He lifts an eyebrow. "You like mythology?"

I smile. "Loathe it, actually."

"Okay then. There went all my plans for small talk." He throws me a wink before turning back to the road, and somehow...*miraculously*...I find myself smiling.

Then I immediately feel awful. I shouldn't be here with him. Not after what I've done tonight...not ever.

Exiting the interstate, he turns under the highway heading into a residential part of North Austin. I'd guess we're between three and five miles from campus, which might not be a completely unreasonable walk if it came to that.

After a few turns, he pulls up in front of a simple duplex. It's boxy and gray and not anything special, but I'm suddenly overwhelmed with curiosity for what I might find inside. He pops open his door and turns off the car.

"Hold on a sec."

His door slams shut, and I watch him jog around the front of the hood. He pulls my door open and then his eyes dart down to the floorboard.

"How are your feet?"

I swallow and shrug. "They're fine."

He gives me that already familiar expression of doubt, and I laugh. "Why do you bother asking me questions if you're not going to believe what I say?"

"Because maybe one time you'll slip up and tell me the truth."

"My feet *are* fine, and I'm *not* drunk." I slide out of the car to prove my statement, but I know it's a mistake the second my sore feet hit concrete. I try to hide my wince, but it's not exactly something one controls with conscious thought, so instead my face ends up doing this weird twitch thing, and he gives me a knowing smile that makes me want to punch him. Or kiss him.

Maybe a little of both.

I keep my chin up and take a few steps past him, enough to push the door closed behind me. I turn, intending to head for his door with whatever dignity I can manage to scrape up. I take two hobbling steps before he's at my side, sweeping me up into his arms.

Dignity is long gone when I squeak and try to hold onto him with one arm while desperately yanking on the hem of my dress with the other.

"No one's around but me," he murmurs. The side of my breast is smashed up against his chest, and the vibrations when he speaks move through me, distracting me from my panic. "And I promise not to look."

I don't even answer him. I haven't the slightest clue what to say.

Me. At a loss for words. I've spent centuries learning how to speak to men, how to capture their interest, how to maneuver in their world, and now I'm undone by this dichotomy of a man and his not quite smile.

"Hold on to me," he says, and I wrap both my arms around his neck in answer. He drops the hand at my back to search for his keys, and I tighten my arms around him, drawing myself closer to his chest. I catch my breath at the sensation, glad for the thickness of his leather jacket that hides the way my breasts have become swollen and tight and gods…this is wrong. So very *wrong.* But I'm not sorry.

I hear the jingle of keys, but I don't know how he manages to get the door open because his eyes never leave mine. Our faces are so close together that when he leans forward to push the door open, my lips accidentally brush his jaw. He sucks in a breath and closes his eyes. Stepping over the threshold, he shuts the door behind us, and I don't think. I just act.

Before he can lower my feet down to the gray carpet below me, I tilt my chin up and touch my mouth to his. His arm returns to my back, his fingers curling around my side, but other than that, he doesn't move. Doesn't kiss me back.

I press a little harder, willing him to respond because if he doesn't…if I read all of this wrong…that would be the icing on the terrible fucking cake that is this night.

I pull back, already squirming in an attempt to get him to put me down.

"I'm sorry. I—"

He drops my legs, but loops that arm around my waist too, keeping me up and against him, my toes still off the floor. I don't look up at him and he says, "Kalli."

His voice. It's so smooth and warm, and I just want him to keep talking to me. I could forget everything about tonight, ignore it all to listen to his voice.

"You're really sober?" he asks.

He must take my scowl as truth enough because as soon as I open my mouth to reply, his lips slam into mine, hot and hard.

He pulls my bottom lip into his mouth, sucking and nibbling and driving me crazy. I thread my fingers through his hair like I've wanted to do since the first time I saw him. One of his hands slides up my side, grazing the curve of my breast before trailing up to my neck. A thumb runs along my jaw, and he tilts my head back, taking control.

Passion.

It comes from a Latin word that means *to suffer*. And that's what the slick thrust of his tongue against mine is—a suffering so sweet that my head spins.

His mouth slants over mine, rough and possessive, and all I want is to be closer to him. Slipping a hand beneath the back of his shirt, I follow the slopes and valleys of his muscled back with my fingers. When he drops to my neck, grazing his teeth and then tongue over my pulse, I dig my fingers into his lower back. He groans, and the feel of his hot breath where my neck meets my shoulder pulls goose bumps across my skin. So, of course, I do it again, slipping my hand farther up and then dragging my nails down.

He says my name, and I say his back.

"Wilder."

He traces two fingers over my swollen lips and groans. "This mouth has been driving me wild since the first time you smiled at me."

I do just that, pulling my lips wide, and he kisses me, frenzied and so, so good. He takes a step forward, then another, moving toward a plain couch in the center of the living room. When we're almost there, he finally lowers my feet to the floor, sliding his hands down to the curve of my ass. I stumble a bit and wince when a sensitive part of my foot drags across the carpet.

"Shit," Wilder breathes, pulling away. "I forgot. I'm a jackass. Sorry."

It takes me several long seconds to stop staring at his mouth. His lips are wet and swollen, and I know I have a matching pair. "It doesn't hurt that bad. Really."

He scoops me back up, and this time I don't pay attention to my dress. I wrap my arms around Wilder and go to kiss him again. He shifts, placing a kiss on my cheek instead and says, "Feet first."

"Look at you," I say, dragging my mouth over his jaw. "Chivalry is alive and kicking apparently."

He groans when I close my lips around his earlobe. "Alive, yes. But definitely in danger of being put aside for a *better offer*."

He nudges open a door with his foot and says, "Light on the right." I reach out and flip the switch. The bathroom is small and sparse, one of those where all the necessary items are crammed into as little space as possible. He has to turn sideways to get me through the door. There's no bathtub, just a standup shower, so I'm not sure how he intends for me to wash my feet. The sink is tiny too, so there's no perching up there.

Carefully, he sets me down in front of the shower. "It's cramped, I know."

I open the glass door, and then laugh. "Handheld showerhead, huh? Well, isn't that…helpful."

His eyes fix on me, and I swear I can almost see what he's picturing. Mostly because I'm picturing it, too. He takes two steps back, putting him out of reach and out of the bathroom.

"You're single-handedly trying to kill off what's left of my control."

I shed his jacket and hang it up on an open hook on the wall.

"Maybe control isn't all it's cracked up to be."

Stepping inside the shower, I leave the door open so I can see him slide down the wall to take a seat in the hallway. His broad body and long limbs look so good posed there. If I were in the business of making art, rather than prompting it, I wouldn't hesitate to snap his picture, to capture that look he's giving me. As I reach for the showerhead, he says, "So your name is Kalli. You're twenty-one. You're *not* intoxicated. You have an incredible knowledge of mythology even though you despise it. You have a sweet tooth, and a tendency to misplace your footwear. What else should I know about you, Cinderella?"

"Not drunk. Sweet tooth. Hates mythology. That's about the gist of it."

I turn on the water, and jump at the first spray of ice-cold water. I adjust the heat, directing the nozzle at the wall while I wait. I look back at him, and my stomach clenches. I want him. Badly. I can't explain why it's happening or why it's him, but my body knows even if my mind doesn't. But now that there's distance between us, and warm water stings against my abused feet, my mind is firmly in the driver's seat.

This guy isn't my type. Or at least, he shouldn't be. In my head, I keep seeing that guy from the grocery store. He looked all business. And typically that kind of man isn't exactly open to artistic expression. That doesn't mean I can't influence him, but it does mean that his reaction to me would be unpredictable. The more ordered and analytical the mind, the more likely that my abilities will cause adverse effects.

So for all intents and purposes, I should be nowhere near this guy. I should clean up my feet, maybe borrow a pair of flip-flops or something, and get the hell out of here.

But I'm not thinking of him like one of my artists.

No, he's something altogether different. Not to mention his appearance tonight has left me questioning all the assumptions I'd made in that grocery store. I was already wrong about him being Gwen's father. What else am I wrong about?

I don't like being wrong. Not about people. My ability to read them and analyze them is a skill I need in order to maintain the line…that damn line that I cannot cross again.

"You're in school?" he asks.

I nod, leaning over to get a better angle on my feet. "You?"

"Yeah."

"You graduating this semester?"

He rubs at the back of his neck, a nervous habit of his. I want to replace his hand with mine, soothing whatever thoughts have him troubled.

"No. I got started late. I'm in my second year now."

Hmm. Maybe that explains the tattoos. Perhaps they came before all-business-Wilder.

"I figured you were already out. Don't see many college guys wearing ties."

"That's just for work."

"Where do you work?"

"An office that would bore you to tears. I work part-time for a friend of the family. Accountant."

"Accountant? And is that what you're planning to do after school?"

He shrugs and instead turns the question back on me. "What about you? What's your major?"

I smile and switch to my other foot. "Undecided."

He stands and steps into the bathroom. He pulls open a medicine cabinet and removes a box of band-aids, setting them on the sink. "Is that because you don't know what you want to do?"

If only things were that simple. I've had lifetimes to chase whatever career or hobby I wanted. Those wants are superficial though. They're ornaments meant to pretty up existence. What I want...it goes far deeper than that. And it's completely untouchable.

"Sometimes the last thing that matters is what we *want* to do."

He crosses until he's standing just outside the shower.

"I get that. I used to think I could do whatever I wanted as long as I wanted it bad enough."

I stand up straight, holding the showerhead at my side.

"What changed?"

He shakes his head, tangling his fingers in his hair for a moment.

"Everything changed. All of it."

I don't like the way the lines of his face transform, turn defeated. Now I see Atlas in him. I don't know what it is he's holding up or how long he's been at it, but I can see the fatigue. It's a feeling I know like the back of my hand. I want his almost smile back.

I ask, "Do you ever just want to say fuck it all? Screw common sense and go after what you want anyway?"

If possible, his expression grows even darker. Defeat overlaid with guilt.

"Every single day."

All I want to do is wash that away. I can inspire genius works of art, moving music, writing that pricks the soul of humanity. I can elevate a person to the kind of success of which they've never even dreamed. But at the moment, I feel like none of that means anything if I can't make him smile.

I reach out my hand, and after a moment's hesitation, he takes it. Then I hold tight and turn the showerhead on him.

Chapter Six

The shocked look on his face as the water sprays up his chest draws a laugh from my throat. I'm not completely psycho, so I don't turn the water on his face, but he wastes no time taking advantage of my hesitation.

He steps right into the shower with me, and I jump back, slamming into the tile wall. In my surprise I get a little wild with the water and end up catching him in the face anyway. I cover my mouth with my hand to stop myself from laughing, and he takes hold of my other wrist, using my own hand to spray the water back on me. It hits me in the neck first, then as I try to pull away, sprays down my chest. I gasp as the water soaks through my dress, and if he didn't notice my lack of bra earlier, it won't take much for him to notice now.

I fight back, trying to regain control of the nozzle, and instead I end up pointing the stream of water straight up and it splashes down on both our heads. I squeal, and try to squeeze around him, thinking maybe I can get out of the door. My feet slip on the wet floor, and he catches me around the waist, laughing. "Oh, no you don't. You started this."

Another jet of water comes toward my face, and I manage to turn just in time so that it only catches my hair and neck. I look down, and can't control my laughter any longer. He'd stepped in still wearing his shoes, and they're soaked now. As are his jeans and the bottom of my dress. We probably look ridiculous.

In my complete and utter delirium, I forget about keeping a tight hold on the showerhead, and Wilder succeeds in wrestling it away from me.

"I've got you now."

He steps back, lifts his arm to aim, and I squeeze my eyes shut. I raise my hands to cover my face, but the spray doesn't come. Hesitantly, I peek out from between my fingers to find him staring at me, his eyes dark and piercing. I'm aware then of just the way his soaked shirt clings to his toned body, and I have no doubt that my own clothes are plastered to my wet skin. Heat pools between my thighs, and I squeeze them together to ease the sudden ache there.

He moves in close, and I catch my breath. He circles one arm around me, and greedily I pull my own arms up to loop around his neck. But he doesn't come in for a kiss like I expect. Instead he turns the knob behind me, shutting off the water and returning the showerhead to where it belongs. I'd thought to make him smile, but the look he gives me now is all hard angles and dark, serious eyes. I look past his shoulder to see that we'd left the door of the shower open, and water has collected in a puddle on the floor outside.

I swallow.

Shit. This was not at all a good idea. I made a giant mess and probably pissed him off, and I really, really need to just get out of here. This is what happens when I'm not thinking strategically. Normally, with an artist, I'm able to keep my head. I play on their emotions, while keeping mine rigidly in check. I read them, trying to decipher what they want and need before they ever tell me. It's my job to be their ideal woman, the one who'll motivate them and make passion burn so hot in their blood that it spills over into their art. But I don't need to be Wilder's ideal woman. I don't want that. I just want to be me.

The hand that had held the showerhead smoothes over my damp hair and down until he pushes the wet mess off my shoulder.

"What are you thinking?" he asks.

"That I'm an idiot."

A slight curve curls across his mouth.

"Because you started a fight you couldn't win?"

"Because I just am. For so many reasons."

His fingers trail from my shoulder down to the arc of my collarbone.

"God, do you have any idea how fucking gorgeous you are?"

I swallow and don't answer because I'll sound like a complete and total bitch if I say the truth. Beauty is the only attribute of mine that never changes, regardless of whatever guy I'm with. And it's a compliment to which I've grown callous.

"Kalli, I—" He stops and closes his eyes.

I reach up and run my thumb across a drop of water trailing over his cheek.

He releases a heavy breath and turns his face into my hand.

"What do you want?" he asks. "Give me the truth."

In a perfect world?

"You."

His hand curls around the back of my neck and he jerks me forward to meet him halfway. His kiss is wet and brutal, and I feel boneless in his arms. Incorporeal. Like the only the thing holding me together, the only thing tethering me to this existence is the drag and crush of his mouth against mine.

My back presses against cold tile, and his hand bunches up the wet skirt of my dress until he manages to peel enough of it away to slide a large hand against the bare skin of my thigh.

His fingers are slick against my leg, and my breath catches in my throat.

He breaks away from our kiss, and his mouth plays over my shoulder, dragging down the strap of my dress with his teeth until it falls to my elbow. The hand on my leg slips higher as his tongue teases at my collarbone. Then he moves lower to the drooping neckline of my dress. His fingers brush up against the edge of my underwear, and I can't stop the moan of anticipation that escapes my lips.

He hesitates then, pulling back slightly just before his hand or his mouth reach the places I really want him.

But I don't want him to slow down. I don't want him to think.

Because then I'll have to think too.

"Please," I whisper.

"Please what?"

I reach for him, plucking at the hem of his soaked shirt and pulling it up and away from a slim, toned stomach. When I keep pulling, he lets me tug it over his head. It slaps provocatively against the floor, and my body clenches in response.

"Please touch me."

He seems to war with himself for a few seconds longer, but when I trail one long finger down between his pectoral muscles, the indecision disappears. He wraps an arm low around my waist and pulls me up against him.

"You could tempt a saint."

"Are you a saint?"

He slides a hand down to cup my ass, pulling me forward against the hard ridge of his arousal and answers, "Not by a long shot."

Stepping out of the shower, his feet slap against the puddle on the floor. I wrap my legs around his waist to be closer to him, but then he has to angle us sideways just to fit us through his narrow bathroom door. I drop my head to his shoulder and laugh, and his own chuckle sends shivers racing across my skin.

He walks us down to a door at the end of a hallway. The bed is big and neatly made, and the room looks comfortable. Nothing fancy or expensive, but it's well taken care of, well decorated, and well lived-in. There's a window air-conditioning unit, and he must keep it turned down low because the room temperature is cooler than the rest of the house.

He leans back against the door, closing it behind him, and captures my lips once again. I don't know whether it's the drop in temperature or the change in his kiss that has me shivering. Gone is the frenzy, and in its place is a slow, steady exploration that kindles an already burning need at the juncture of my thighs. When his tongue has touched every corner of my mouth, he breaks away, resting his forehead on mine as we both struggle to catch our breath.

He crosses the room, and sets me on the edge of his bed. I remember my soaked clothes and protest, "I'm wet."

That draws another lazy chuckle from him and with a kiss to my forehead, he says, "I hope so."

I hide a grin, and then poke him in the chest. "Dirty."

He leans over me, until I have to lie back on my elbows to see his face. He braces his arms just outside my shoulders and lowers his mouth toward mine.

"Damn right. If you could see the way that dress is clinging to your body, you wouldn't blame me. Hell, even before the dress was wet, all I could think about was getting you out of it."

"Then why am I still in it?"

"Truth?" he asks, and I nod. He trails one hand over my waist and down to my hip, and his warm touch burns through the wet fabric. He says, "Now that I'm back home, I've been trying to clean up my act. Be more responsible. Do things right."

"And I'm wrong?"

"No. Jesus, no. You're…Fuck, I don't even have the words to describe you. And if you knew me, you'd know how rare that is."

"But we don't know each other."

We couldn't. He could never really know me.

"I'd like to know you."

Gods, I wish things were that simple. It's too easy to imagine myself with him. Imagine lazy days in bed. Discovering other ways to make him laugh. What I wouldn't give to be able to be with someone. No thoughts to my ability and how long is too long to stay. No lies about my past or what I am. If I could be normal, live like a normal person, I think Wilder would be a pretty perfect choice.

But I don't get normal.

And it's one thing to ignore that in the heat of the moment with his body flush against mine, but with him holding back? Not even I'm that reckless.

I place a hand on his chest to push him back so I can stand. "Maybe…" I don't even want to say the words, but I force myself. "Maybe this is a mistake."

I slip around him toward his door even though I don't have the slightest clue where I'll go or what I'll do. As soon as I touch the doorknob, I feel him behind me. He places a hand on the door, holding it shut.

"Tell me why first." He looms behind me, his body tempting and his breath teasing at the nape of my neck.

I sigh, but don't turn around to face him. "Because you're not sure you want this. That's reason enough for me."

He spins me around with surprising speed, and presses me back against the door. He leans his weight into me, not enough to be heavy, but so that I can feel the hard jut of his erection against the softness of my belly.

"First, you're wrong. *Want* doesn't even begin to describe how I feel about having you in my bed. You're sexy, intriguing, and you look damn good in my shower. Though next time I'd advocate we do that part without our clothes." I scoff out a laugh, but when he tips my chin up with his finger, he looks serious. "But I wasn't asking why you thought it was a mistake. I want to know why you look so exhausted, and why you're not wearing shoes, and what that homeless man on the street said to make you look so scared. I want to know why I couldn't take you home and do this in *your* bed. Those are the whys I want answered."

And those are precisely the answers I can't give him, so instead I rise up on my toes and kiss him again. He groans against my mouth, and his tongue delves inside, searching and demanding. When I've forgotten everything besides the heat of his kiss, he pulls back, resting his forehead against mine. I'm panting for breath when he says, "Don't think I've forgotten about those questions."

That leaves me two options. Leave before he digs any deeper…or work harder at distracting him.

The choice is easier than it should be.

Chapter Seven

I touch his chest, and push him back until he stands far enough away for me to gather the ends of my damp dress and pull it up and over my head. I'm not wearing a bra, so my nipples immediately pull into painfully tight buds in the cold room. His gaze drops down to take me in, and I fix my eyes on his bare chest in turn. I'm confident in my looks, but I also know that I don't necessarily meet modern society's idea of a perfect beauty. I was made for a time when men valued the curves of a woman. My breasts are plump and full, and my stomach slopes out into generous hips. Sometimes men would rather I be thinner, but that's another thing about me that I can't change. This is the shape I'll always have.

From the dark look in his eyes, I guess he's not the type to prefer stick thin girls. His face dips close to mine, and his stubbled cheek rubs against my jaw. Hot breath tickles my ear, and he whispers, "You're so damn beautiful it hurts."

This time I don't have to ask him to touch me. His hands reach out to cup my breasts, his palms rasping over my taut nipples. I bite my lip and close my eyes.

Sweet suffering.

That will be how I remember this night for the rest of my days.

I should walk away. I might make a point to avoid emotional attachments, but I know a few things about highs and lows. And Wilder is one peak that's guaranteed to come with a miserably low valley. But I also know that I wouldn't normally risk a dalliance with a non-artist. Too many risks. Too many complications. But tonight there's so little energy in me after that fiasco back in the club that there's almost no risk at all to take this one thing for myself, this one night.

"Look at me, Kalli."

I open my eyes and think *one night*. And I'm not sure which is more overwhelming, my excitement for what's to come or the dread for the moment when that one night ends. He lifts my breasts, dragging his thumbs over the tips; it takes all my concentration to keep my eyes on him.

"We might not know each other now, but I have every intention of knowing you after tonight," he says. "I'm going to know every inch of your body. I'll know what makes you breathe faster and what makes you feel like you can't breathe at all. I'll know what makes you close your eyes, and the sounds you make when something feels good. If there's one thing I am, it's determined, and I've decided to know you better than anyone ever has."

I must have been holding my breath during his speech because he leans down and kisses me before murmuring, "Breathe."

And I do. I drag in air desperately, and he smiles. "Well, there's fact number one. You like it when I tell you what I'm going to do to you, don't you?"

"Gods, yes."

He laughs. "One God wasn't enough for that one, huh? I'll keep that in mind."

With a hand on my shoulder, he maneuvers me to sit on the bed, and then he kneels in front of me. With a gentle hand, he picks up my foot and props it on his knee. He studies the scrapes for a moment, but they must all be minor because he abandons that foot to pull up the other. He looks confused for a moment and I say, "Don't you dare ask me if I'm drunk again."

"It's just…I could have sworn there were scrapes on your feet, but they look fine now."

I stiffen. Well, that at least tells me what time it is. We must have passed midnight sometime between the shower and now. Whatever might have happened to my feet was undone with the start of a new day.

I lie, "Just sore is all."

"And I still don't get to know how you lost your shoes?"

"Nope."

"Did something bad happen? Was there—"

"I'm fine." It takes all over my willpower to block out thoughts of the bad thing that happened tonight. He thinks of me as a victim when really, I'm the villain here. "A little cold though." I scramble back and tug his comforter down enough that I can slide between the sheets. They're cold too, and I shiver. "Take off those wet jeans and come warm me up."

He grins. "Yes, ma'am."

He undoes the button at the top of his pants, and I'm so eager to have him that I feel giddy.

"Wait," I say. Then I scoot back down the bed, still holding the blankets tight against me. "I want to."

He makes a sound low in his throat, but drops his hand away. I reach for the front of his jeans and seek out the zipper. I suck my bottom lip between my teeth as I drag it down. Since the denim is wet, it takes both of my hands to inch the jeans down his hips. Then I let him kick them off the rest of the way, along with his shoes. Underneath he wears black boxer briefs.

Boxer briefs are hands down the best invention of the last century.

I lift my eyes to his, and his gaze pierces through me as I drag that last item of clothing down his hips, too.

And suddenly, I'm nervous.

I've never slept with someone like this. Without knowing exactly where we stand, and how things will end with the other person. Every other time, I've been in control. But now, the balance of power is completely off because I want this with a desperation that puts too much out of my control.

I lift my hand and wrap my fingers around his erection, thinking maybe it will shift that balance, give me the upper hand. He utters my name with a low growl and smoothes a hand over my cheek, resting one callused thumb on my bottom lip. I tighten my grip and give a slow tug.

"Jesus, Kalli. You feel so good."

I kiss his thumb when it passes over my lips again, and he bends, taking my mouth in a bruising kiss. He pulls back the covers and grips my hips to slide me further up the bed. Back in the open air, I should be cold, but I'm not. In fact, I'm burning up.

Wilder crawls up my body, his limbs sleek and strong. He dips and places a kiss on my sternum, just between the swell of my breasts. He closes his eyes, humming under his breath and drags his stubbled cheek over the sensitive swell of skin until his hot breath skates over the tip.

I cry out, arching under him, and he's barely even touched me.

"I think," he says, murmuring just above my skin, "that this part of you will have to wait."

"Wait?" I ask, breathless.

"Mmhmm. I told you that I'm going to know all of you, but you're so fucking responsive. And so damn sweet. I know if I taste you here…" His teeth graze my nipple for just a second, and my back nearly bows off the bed. "I'll get impatient if I take your perfect breast into my mouth, and I won't be able to resist being inside you."

"So don't. You're not the only one who lacks patience."

He chuckles, moving over to kiss my shoulder. "I made a promise, sweet. And I keep my promises."

He hovers above me and presses his lips to my temple, then my forehead, followed by the tip of my nose.

"We'll start small," he says, moving over my cheek and down the line of my jaw. "You know, when I saw you in that grocery store, I almost thought I was dreaming. You looked…God, you looked unreal. So out of place there. Too beautiful for words." His teeth nip the other side of my jaw before he sucks my earlobe into his mouth. "Then you were so sweet to Gwen. Instead of spending the day telling me about her favorite Disney princess, all she could talk about was you. Kalli. And every time she said your name I wanted to kick myself for not getting your number, for letting you slip through my hands."

He moves then to my neck and at the first lave of his tongue, I grip his shoulders. I'm not sure whether I want to beg him to stop teasing me or to keep going. "Then when I saw you tonight, I thought…" He laughs and continues, "I thought I was crazy. I *acted* crazy, following you when you took off. And then when I lost you, I was certain I'd been hallucinating. That I had wanted to see you again so badly that my mind had gotten the better of me. Tonight I'm going to bury myself in you so deep that I'll have no doubt that every second of this is real."

I dig my fingernails into his muscled shoulders and give in to my instinct to beg. "Wilder, please."

In reward, he lowers his head and sucks the tip of one breast into his mouth. I gasp and wrap my legs around his hips, using all my strength to pull him down toward me. His length falls heavy against the damp fabric of my underwear, and we both groan. He pumps his hips, sliding against me, and I press up hard.

"You're trying to make me break my promise."

I tangle my hand in his hair until he meets my gaze, then give him an innocent smile. "I have no idea what you mean."

"Sure you don't."

He shifts back, pulling my legs from around his waist, and spreading them open. He slides down more, raining kisses over my belly and hips and thighs before settling that sinful mouth just above the line of my underwear.

"I'm going to know this part of you too, sweet. So don't hold back. If you like something, you tell me. Okay?" When I don't answer, he runs the flat of his tongue over the strip of fabric between my legs. I whimper and he asks, "Okay?"

I breathe a shaky, "Okay."

He brings my legs up and together long enough to pull the scrap of fabric over my thighs and off. Then he lays me open again.

He'd said he was determined, and if I'd had any doubt, I believed him then. He's meticulous and thorough and sinfully skilled with his mouth. My hips rise and fall with his ministrations, and I lose track of the number of times I call his name.

It doesn't take him long to know me at all. Within minutes, he's zoned in on my most sensitive spots, discovered which movements make my legs shake, and the pressure that makes me tighten my grip in his hair.

"You taste sweet here, too. So damn sweet."

He keeps me on the edge for so long that when I do fall over, it catches me by surprise. It lifts me up and then flattens me, leaving my head dizzy and spinning. The pleasure is so thick that my body feels heavy with it, like I might not ever be able to move again. And he's still going, easing me through it, drawing out my pleasure until the last possible second, until my hearing goes fuzzy, until it goes on for so long it almost hurts. Almost.

And I can't help but imagine if he'd be this dedicated to getting to know the rest of me. Not just my body. But my thoughts. My desires. My fears.

As my mind clears and the real world rolls back in, alarm streaks through me like lightning. Suddenly I am unable to keep all my thoughts at bay. Not about what happened tonight, or who I am, or all the reasons I can never see Wilder again after tonight. And the truth scorches me, burns me up, and sends tears pricking at my eyes.

Because I've never felt anything this perfect. Never been so overwhelmed by the need to touch someone, to hold tight and not let go.

And knowing that I can't? That I *have* to let him go…It's devastating.

It all catches up to me then, the lack of sleep, the exhaustion from all the energy I've expended. And that's when I pay for all the lightness I felt by holding on to the inspiration. I'd felt light and free, but now the full weight of all my years is back. Doubled even. Rather than lying sated and carefree in his bed, I feel as if I'm being crushed against it, pressed down by a mountain of stones.

"Kalli." By the way he says my name, I guess it's not the first time he's said it. "Where'd you go? Come back to me."

I take a gasping breath, trying not to let it overwhelm me, and Wilder rolls to lie beside me. Tears well in my eyes, and I want to scream because he shouldn't see me like this. I don't want him to see me like this.

"I'm okay," I answer, even though I'm not. And I know without even having to look at him this time that he doesn't believe me.

"Come here."

He pulls me flush against his chest, just drags me over as if gravity isn't fighting tooth and nail to pry me back. I cling to him—arms and legs and lips. I bury my face in his neck, kissing him there between gasping breaths. And somehow he makes it better and worse all at the same time. From the moment I laid eyes on him, he represented the life I would never have. But back then it had been abstract. A vague idea of family and love and *permanence*. But it's not vague anymore. I know the taste of his mouth and the weight of his body on mine. I know what it's like to give my pleasure up to another person, to give them complete control. I know what it's like to give that to *him*, when I've always maintained my head, my emotional distance with every other man in my life.

Then there's this…his arms around me and his soft words in my ear telling me that it's going to be okay, telling me it's fine every time I choke out an apology. He doesn't just tolerate my emotion, he welcomes it. How will I ever forget the feel of *this*?

Sometime between his stroking of my hair and the kisses he drops on my forehead, my thoughts thin and then go quiet. My tears dry up. I buckle under the weight of the night, and in his tight hold fall straight to sleep.

Chapter Eight

I wake to exquisite warmth, and for a moment it's thousands of years ago, and I'm lounging under a golden Greek sun. I remember the mountains where we dwelled for so long. I know that land like a lover's face. Each sloping feature is as easy to recall now as it was a millennium ago. Things had been so much simpler then, and the prospect of eternity had still seemed a blessing. Slowly, I become aware of a breeze rippling through my hair, but it's not the mountain wind that beckons me. This isn't cool and crisp, but warm and sweet.

I drag my eyes open, and instead of mountainous rock, I find soft, heated skin. I blink, confused because the body I'm draped over is not familiar. The chest is broader, dusted with fine blond hairs that reappear low on a taut stomach.

Van is long and lean with dark hair. I conjure his face, and it comes to me with an oxygen mask fitted over his mouth. Then the memories return in a rush, first pain and guilt and confusion, but they swiftly fade into horror.

I try to jerk upright, but the arm around my middle tightens, and I'm drawn further onto the body of the person lying next to me.

Wilder.

I blink. And those memories come back too, but slower. They tease at my mind almost as sensually as the actual events of last night, and now I'm practically on top of him. One of my legs is slung over his waist, and it's abundantly clear that we're both naked. Then I remember exactly how our interlude had ended. Or rather…the fact that it hadn't really reached its end. Not for him anyway. He'd completely flipped my world upside down, and then instead of reciprocating, instead getting to know his body as intimately as he explored mine…*I cried.*

I cried on him. While naked. Then apparently, I fell asleep.

Oh man, I *suck*.

I look up at his face, and despite my wiggling, he's still out. The scruff on his face has thickened even more overnight, and I have to resist the urge to drag my fingers across it. His chest rises and falls steadily with each breath, pressing his abdomen up against my breasts each time. His hand is positioned low on my back, fingers curling almost possessively around the curve of my bottom.

And for a brief moment, I think about shifting further on top of him. His erection is semi-hard, brushing against my leg, and it would be so easy to slide my hips over his, to rock against him. Would his hand slide further down my ass when he woke? Would he pull me down for a kiss? In his sleepiness, would he look more sweet or sexy? I could do my best to erase the way last night ended, and maybe he'd forgive me for crying all over him and leaving him unsatisfied in his own bed.

But to what end? It would be good, maybe even brilliant, but when it was over, there would be questions I couldn't answer. And while my actions yesterday had tamed the need to use my gift, I wasn't running on empty anymore. Not like last night.

In fact, I can feel the energy pulsing in me, announcing its presence, reminding me of who and *what* I am.

It would be stupid to start this again in the light of day. And I'd done enough stupid things in the last two weeks to last me for the next century.

No. I promised myself one night. And that night had already come and gone, so now I had to say goodbye. To this warm bed. To the heat of Wilder's skin. To my one night of almost normal.

Carefully, I peel his hand off my back, and place it on the bed. I shift up on my knees, trying not to jostle the mattress too much, and then slip off the bed. The floor is cold, and the air-conditioner is still on full blast, so goose bumps riot across my skin.

I find my dress on the floor, and it's still damp and cold. I glance back at the bed, and a traitorous voice at the back of my mind wants him to wake up. I want him to see me there, standing naked in his room, and I want him to stop me from running, to take away this choice I have to make.

For a moment, I entertain the idea of being with him. Would it be possible? Could I hold back the energy from him and expend it elsewhere? But how would I keep that balance? And what kind of relationship could I ever have with him when I had to run off to satisfy my needs with another person every few days? No…even if I was willing to risk it, it could never work. No matter how badly I want it to.

Who knew it would be this hard? It's not as if I'm as young as I look. I've been around the block a few (thousand) times. We didn't even sleep together. Not really. There are men that I've been far more intimate with, men who've known me better, longer. I should be able to file him away with the rest of the memories and move on.

I don't know why he's different. Sure, he's got the whole mystery factor with his odd ties and tattoos combo. And he's sweet. And he's caring. And he doesn't need anything from me.

But is that really enough to explain the tight pull I feel toward him now? It's almost as if there's…

My mouth goes dry.

A string. That's what I'd been about to say. I feel as if there's a cord between us, and no matter where I go or what I think, I can still feel its weight, the reminding pressure that he's there, that he's not going away.

I've never seen the fates, the three beings whose strings decide the life of every mortal and every god alike. They always remained separate from the rest of us. I think the greater gods didn't like the reminder that they weren't entirely in control of their own destinies, that in some ways they aren't that different than the mortals they place themselves so high above. But I've heard stories. I've heard that they appear both old and young all at once, their countenances shifting between one blink and the next. Some say that they are time. Others maintain that they're the only thing not affected by it. They are at once old and young, alive and dead. They are the past, present, and the future. Always.

I've never seen the fates, no. But I've felt them.

I clutch my damp dress close, but not even the cold fabric can keep me from tumbling into the memory.

Mel.

I don't think of her often. Not anymore. You don't live as long as I have without learning how to compartmentalize. And soon, you have so many thoughts stored away in so many boxes that they all sort of fade into the background.

Melpomene was one of my eight sisters. And for our early life, she was the chief muse of tragedy. The plays and poetry and music she inspired...there was a depth to it that wasn't rivaled by any of the rest of us. There was something about her that enabled the artist to dig deeper, to examine the darkest portions of the soul, but because of that she had...well, she had a higher rate of *incident* than the rest of us. Sometimes the artist would go so deep that she wasn't able to get them back. And while she might have dealt in tragedy, Mel wasn't swathed in darkness. She was light and brilliance and beauty. And she felt guilt. It clung to her more stubbornly than the rest of us.

Century after century, it weighed on her until her light began to fade. Somehow, even though she renewed daily like the rest of us, she began to look older. She had no wrinkles or graying hair or any other signs of age, but even so, we all saw it. Her eyes carried her years, the curve of her mouth was dragged down by the past.

In December of the year 557 A.D., we were in Constantinople. It was Brumalia, a festival for the winter solstice honoring the gods who held some connection to the harvest. By then, the gods had been re-christened with Roman names. Saturn. Ceres. Bacchus.

It was supposed to be a celebration. Wine and food and dance. But Mel wouldn't celebrate. By that point, I'm not even sure she could. She'd stopped taking on artists. She couldn't handle it anymore, and looking back, she'd lasted far longer than I had before the effects set in. She withdrew inside herself. I can remember looking across the room during the festivities, and she was standing by the wall, so still that she nearly blended in with the statues decorating the hall. It hadn't been like it was with me. When I gave in to the power, it had been a chaotic euphoria. Melpomene reminded me of a woman drowning. She'd been still, not struggling to survive; silent, not gasping for air. But even so...I could almost envision the way her hair would bloom around her in the water. I could nearly see her sinking down into a darkness where I would never reach her.

Then between one instant and the next, she collapsed. She writhed on the floor and howled, the noise a keening that was simultaneously desperate and furious. The energy hadn't just leaked out of her; it had exploded, filling the space until even I was choking on the potency. The gentle celebratory music swelled to a cacophonous roar. The room burst into movement and noise. Some reacted with glee, others malice, and still others in terror. There was going to be a riot. A stampede. A massacre. You didn't need to be an oracle to prophesy that future.

Maybe if I could get to her, maybe she would still have the strength to pull back. But I couldn't even see her on the floor anymore through the throngs of people. They rushed for the doors, uncaringly trampling over anyone who fell in their wake. I couldn't see Mel, but I could hear her, screams so melancholy they neared a song. A dirge.

Then between one step and the next, I felt something pull tight in my chest, constricting, making it hard to breathe. And though it wasn't a familiar sensation, I knew instinctively it had to do with Mel. Then whatever that binding was, it gave way, it tore loose as if someone had tugged hard enough to tear it free. I was so busy trying to steady my feet and catch my breath that it took me several seconds to realize that Mel was no longer screaming. And I suddenly felt as if gravity had lessened, as if there was one less thing holding me to this earth.

I suck in a breath, and cold air stings my lungs. I'm shivering, and maybe it's the memories or maybe it's my damp dress in Wilder's cold room. Either way, I force myself to pull back from the past. I don't want to think about the moment I found her, nor the fury who had been standing over her lifeless body, blood dripping from her sword. I don't want to think about the Earthquake Poseidon had caused to cover up Mel's…to cover up Mel.

The only thing that matters about that night now is that I not repeat it. Because that's what the Argus's threats mean for me. Step out of line, and it could be me facing the swift justice of a fury's blow.

And the string.

When I'd talked to my sisters afterward, we'd all experienced the same feeling, as if the cord binding us together, the thing that intertwined our fates with Melpomene's, had been cut.

I'd known it was fate, but I'd always assumed that those kinds of heavy ties only existed because my sisters and I were bound by blood, by purpose. Because we were immortal. I'd never felt it with another person. Certainly not a human.

I glance back at Wilder. The sheets are tangled around his hips. He has one arm folded behind his head and beneath his pillow. The other is sprawled wide where I left it. Bare skin gives way to inked designs on his arms and upper chest, and he looks...*sexy* doesn't do him justice.

I don't feel that kind of pull to him, do I?

I don't.

It's just attraction. The lure of the forbidden fruit. It will disappear with distance. With time. And I've got plenty of that. I sneak into his closet and borrow a t-shirt and a pair of gym shorts with a drawstring waist.

Okay, so it's not borrowing, since I don't plan on ever seeing him again. But my dress is wet, and what else am I supposed to do? It's not because I want something of his. It's necessity. That's it. And yeah, it makes me an even bigger jerk for stealing from him, especially after all he did for me last night, but...

Why am I reasoning this out with myself? I just need to leave before he wakes up.

I grab a cheap pair of plastic flip-flops that are way too big, but at least they're shoes. Add them to my tally of sins.

With one last glance at the sleeping man in the bed, I ignore the twist of my heart, and sneak out of his house into the pink early morning sky and begin my walk home.

I learn that it's Saturday morning when I get back to my apartment, which I'd apparently left unlocked the night before. Though if someone tried to rob or vandalize it, you certainly wouldn't have been able to tell. Not with the way I left it. It takes me the entire weekend of near constant working and cleaning to undo the damage of my dance with inspiration.

That word...*Inspired*. It's the last thing I tackle, and though I'm able to scrub the ink away, it appears I went over the word so many times that I scratched it into the floorboard. I have to settle for a slight rearrangement of my living room so that the rug in front of my couch now covers the carved word.

I sit on the floor, and place my hand over the spot on the rug that I know covers the word.

"Enough," I speak aloud to the empty room. "You can't change this. You can only live with it."

So, that's what I do.

I live with it.

With the guilt. With the memories. With the longing.

I bury it as deep as I can.

I won't be Melpomene. I won't allow myself to crumble under the weight of this life. So I box up those memories and seal them away. Wilder, too. I refuse to be like Mel, and it's not *possible* to be the girl I'd been with him last night, so all of it has to go.

There's only one thing I can be. The only thing I've ever been.

Someone's muse.

And if it stings a little that the very nature of my life, of what I am, requires me to be someone's possession, someone's tool, then it's a sting I do my best to ignore.

To live with.

PART TWO

Wilder

"Beauty is unbearable, drives us to despair, offering us for a minute the glimpse of an eternity that we should like to stretch out over the whole of time."
Albert Camus

Chapter Nine

It's a bleak fucking Christmas.

Mom spends most of the holiday working double shifts at the hospital. And I pick up whatever extra hours Mr. Gibson will give me at the firm. There's plenty to do as the year draws to a close.

It's necessary, and if I'm honest, I prefer that god-awful boring office to being at Mom's. That probably makes me a dick, but it's just a little too much for me to handle. Without the distraction of classes, I can't even pretend that I don't see how miserable Mom is. Gwennie, too. It's hard on her because she's still young enough that she doesn't quite grasp what's happened. Oh, she knows Dad's gone. I caught her playing prison with her dolls once too, so I know she gets that part, at least a little.

But she thinks it's all temporary. Like the bad version of a vacation. That eventually Dad will come back, and they'll move back to the old house with two floors and big rooms and a pool, instead of the apartment she and mom are in now. She thinks everything will go back to normal. To her, money is just the colorful sheets in Monopoly or plastic gold coins. She can't even pronounce the word *embezzlement*, let alone grasp what it means for our family, the mess Dad left us in.

Sometimes she'll say things…about how she can't wait until we have a pool again or she'll wonder what Dad will get her for Christmas, and I can see the way it affects Mom. She'd always appeared young for her age, but in the last year, her posture has changed, her shoulders curve downward. I don't know if it's fatigue or fear or the absolute fucking unfairness of it all that weighs on her, but it's there and I can't unsee it. And I'm doing my damndest to fix it, but I can't fill the gap Dad left. I can't even fucking fill the gap left in her bank account, but I will. I'll get this damn business degree, and then I'll get a job that pays decent enough to get back a little of what we lost.

And in the mean time, I'll do what I can to make up for the rest.

Like taking Gwen out to find a dress for Christmas, second hand of course, because we can no longer afford to buy her the poufy monstrosities that she loves to wear for every holiday and occasion. She's growing so damn fast that she doesn't fit into any of her old ones, a discovery which had led to a complete meltdown this morning when I came over to take my shift as babysitter while Mom went to work.

When Mom had told her that she couldn't take her shopping for a special dress this year, Gwen's sobs had been headache-inducing. I'd promised to work something out just so she'd stop, and so Mom could get to work without being late.

It's the day before Christmas Eve, so the last thing I want to do is go anywhere near anything that involves the word shopping, but I'd made a decision after Dad was sentenced to put my own wants aside for a while, and this is part of that.

We try the mall first, but as I feared, those tiny little dresses are fucking expensive. I don't even let Gwen try them on because I can already envision the chaos that would ensue when I had to explain that we couldn't get whatever dress she wanted. I go for a different tactic, and map out directions to a Goodwill on my phone.

But from the moment we enter, Gwen is pouty and stubborn, and nothing in their limited selection of little girl's dresses is what she wants. I'm reaching the end of my patience, and I have to work hard not to snap at Gwen as I take her hand and pull her back toward the front of the store. A middle-aged woman sorting donations at the front counter calls out as we near the door, "Try Caroline's Closet. It's north a few streets. Still second-hand, but I think she might find it a little more to her liking."

I thank her, and load Gwen into her booster seat in the back of my SUV. She complains when I try to buckle her in, so I step back and close the door. Sure enough, after a minute or so of trying to buckle herself in, she starts to whine that it won't work. I lean between the seats, reaching back to her, and click the thing into place.

I take a deep breath and clutch the steering wheel tight for a moment.

This is my life now. Not even now. Always. This is my life. Period. The end. I sigh and lift my glasses to rub at my eyes.

It's not that I don't love Gwen. I do. Even with that high-pitched cry she's so good at weaponizing to get what she wants. I love her, and I love Mom, and I would do just about anything for them. But when you think stuff like that…you think of grand, heroic gestures. Pushing someone out of the way of a moving vehicle. Standing between them and danger. Sacrificing something important. But it's not like that. Not at all. It's not one big moment, it's a thousand. It's every day. And you don't sacrifice just one important thing, you sacrifice a little more and a little more until you start to feel hollowed out. It's not the sacrifice that hurts so much as the thought that it will never end. That you're stuck in your fate, and nothing and no one can change it. You'll just keep giving and giving until you don't even know who you are.

"Ready to go?" I ask Gwen, even though it's me that's kept us parked here as I regrouped. I get a reply somewhere between a humph and a sniff. Probably the best I'm going to do.

I find the store that the lady mentioned on my phone, and it is just a few blocks north of us, so I shift into drive and pull back onto the street. I can tell just from the outside that Caroline's Closet has a much better chance at pleasing Gwen. The store logo is pink with flowers and butterflies, and it appears that the store is specifically focused on kids' clothing. We have to parallel park on the street, and Gwen nearly gives me a heart attack when she takes off running to the store as soon as her feet hit the ground. I slam the door shut, and lock it with my key chain while I take off after her. I swing the door to the store open, and nearly run over her as she stands in awe just over the threshold.

The place is like a little girl's paradise. It's not just the clothes, though there are a lot of them, it's the decorations, the space. Everything about it looks like a child's fantasy. There's enough pink to make me feel like I've overdosed on Pepto Bismal, but Gwen likes it, and I can deal with just about anything to make her happy.

She looks up at me silently, asking for permission, I think. And I nod. She disappears between racks of clothes that are taller than she is, and I scramble to catch up.

She's struggling to unhook a baby blue dress when I find her, and I lift it off the rack for her. I become her designated dress holder, and my arm is covered by the time an employee finds us and asks, "Can I help you find anything?"

She's short with black-rimmed hipster glasses that make her big eyes look even larger. Gwen is immediately infatuated with the giant flower on her headband. I can see her hand reaching toward it, and I take it in mine before she can accost the employee. Lennox, according to her nametag.

"This is Gwen," I say. "We're doing some last minute shopping for a holiday dress. For her."

Lennox smiles, and bends so that she's closer to Gwen's height.

"Yes, you'll look much better in one of our dresses than he would."

Gwen giggles uncontrollably, and Lennox asks her questions about her size, what colors she likes, and what kind of dresses she's had in the past. Then she asks me what I'm looking to spend, and she doesn't even blink when I tell her what I can afford.

"I think we can handle that. Why don't we go ahead and take these dresses you have"—she takes the scratchy things off my arm—"and we'll get you set up in a dressing room. While you start trying these on, I'll grab some others I think you might like."

I'm immediately glad we came here. I was an only child until Gwen came along, so I've not had much experience shopping for kid's clothes or dresses, and I don't realize how much pressure I'd been feeling until it eases.

"We've even got a nice, comfy couch for Dad to sit on while he waits."

"Oh I'm not—"

Gwen interrupts me to say, "My dad is in prison. That's just Wilder. My brother."

To Lennox's credit, her eyes only widen for just a second at Gwen's admission, and then she's back to normal.

"Okay then. Brother Wilder, it is."

The dressing rooms are just as intricately decorated as the rest of the place. There are pink cushioned benches, and ornate mirrors that remind me of Snow White, and soft cream-colored curtains cover each door.

The couch is an old-style. Victorian, maybe? And it's been reupholstered with black and white polka dots that make my vision go blurry. Lennox gets Gwen set up in a dressing room, and I take a seat on the couch to wait.

I've never really done this kind of thing before, and I'm hoping that Gwen can get these dresses on all by herself. She dresses herself every day, but that's usually jeans and shirts and skirts, not fancy dresses.

"You should take notes, so we can remember which ones are our favorites," Gwen tells me.

Lennox shoots me a smile, and I nod seriously before pulling up the notes function on my phone and holding it up for Gwen's approval.

"I look forward to seeing those notes," Lennox says before winking at me and heading off to presumably find more dresses for my sister.

I watch her go. She's a little funkier than my usual type. She wears these odd converse shoes that are a cross between tennis shoes and boots. They lace all the way up to her knees. She's got on tights beneath them, shorts and what appears to be two oversized sweaters. But she seems nice.

Not quite as…

I shake my head. I've been in an epic slump for the last month and a half since I'd woken up to find my bed empty of the most beautiful girl I'd ever seen in real life. I shouldn't still be thinking about Kalli, shouldn't be comparing every girl I meet to her. It was one night, and she'd been skittish and emotional the whole time. I can't say I'm surprised she ran out on me. She didn't seem like the kind of girl for a one night stand, and I've definitely had my fair share of those to know the difference.

But that's over too. No more wild life. I can't live like that and put Mom and Gwen first.

No point dwelling on things I can't have. My old life and Kalli both.

There's a rustling from the direction of the dressing rooms, and I look up expecting to see Gwen's first dress, but it's the curtain next to hers that slides open.

"Hey Len! Is this how you wanted this dress to hang?"

My eyes snag on the girl's hand as it tugs at a flowy section of fabric over her hips. And somehow I know…just from that voice and her slim hands…I know it's her.

I've spent weeks thinking about her, obsessing over the things I said and did, wondering if it was my fault she felt the need to run away, trying to understand what might have happened to her that night to leave her so on edge. And now she's here.

My eyes track up her body in slow motion. Smooth, olive-brown skin, generous hips and breasts, cinched in at the waist, dark curls spilling over her shoulders.

Then I get to her face. Kalli.

The sight of her hits me like a physical blow, and if I weren't sitting down, I might have actually stumbled back. She seems just as surprised to see me sitting there, and she blinks, like maybe I'm part of her imagination, and I'll disappear any moment.

I don't disappear.

Neither does she.

We stare at each other, and I swear, the hold this girl has on me after just two meetings is unreal. Fucking scary, actually.

She sucks in a breath, wrapping an arm around her waist in a gesture that's about either comfort or shock, maybe both. And I wonder if she feels it too. If she's just as intrigued and freaked out as I am.

Neither of us has spoken by the time Lennox returns, stepping between us and severing the connection. She tilts her head to the side, surveying the dress that Kalli's wearing. She tugs once at the dress, trying to get it fall in a different way, but nothing changes.

"Hmm…" she says. "I think I've put in too many pleats. If I do half as many and gather more fabric in each one, I think it will sit better." She steps back, looking over Kalli from head-to-toe.

Guilty. I totally do it, too. She's just as stunning as I remember her, and I don't know what they're talking about with the dress. It fits her perfectly. My mouth is actually watering looking at her, and Jesus, I've got to talk to her. Have to get her number. I can't go another month thinking about her after another chance encounter.

Fuck chance. I'm not leaving it to luck again.

Chapter Ten

"You can go ahead and take that one off," Lennox says. "I'll make a note on what to fix. Try the purple one next."

Lennox hangs two more little girl dresses outside Gwen's dressing room and asks, "You doing okay, Gwen?"

Gwen calls out a yes, then Lennox is leaving, and Kalli is turning to go back to the dressing room. Before I really think it through, I'm standing.

"Hey."

Her fingers tighten around the curtain, but she doesn't retreat inside. She tosses her head a little, just enough to get her thick curls to swing over her shoulder, and then she looks at me over her shoulder.

"Hey." Her voice is quiet, and I'm incredibly aware that my little sister is just a curtain away. All I want to do is push Kalli into that dressing room and press her against the wall and show her just what she missed when she snuck out of my apartment.

But I can't.

"I didn't realize this place has clothes for adults."

"It doesn't." Her body is still turned away from me, like she's going to bolt any second. "Lennox is studying fashion design. She's part of a showcase coming up in a couple months, and I'm her…" She pauses, as if searching for the word. "I'm her friend. I just play mannequin for her on occasion."

"Mannequin?" Lennox calls out from where she's flipping through hangers on a nearby rack. "I heard that! Mannequins are plastic. Mannequins are scary life-size fake people with curiously absent genitalia. Mannequins might one day come to life and kill us all."

The smile Kalli sends in her friend's direction is small, but striking. It's one of those moments where a picture is worth a thousand words. Ten thousand. I don't even know that it's something that could really be captured with anything other than the eye.

And there I go again. What is it about this girl that turns me into such a fool? Or maybe it's not her at all. Maybe I've lost some confidence over the last year. When you used to spend your nights in bar after bar with just about any girl you wanted, and you suddenly shift to spending your nights babysitting…it wrecks your head a little.

But still…it feels like more than that with her.

I've never had to think about what to say to a girl. I like to think I'm fairly charming, and I've always been good at stringing words together. With Kalli…I'm scared that if I don't reign myself in, I'll frighten her off as I wax poetic about her eyebrows or whatever part of her has caught my attention at the time.

"You are not my mannequin," Lennox says. "You're my *muse*. Seriously. I was totally stuck on this collection until you came along."

Kalli's eyes flick to mine, and there's something in them. Unease, maybe?

"I'm going to change," she says. And I don't know if she's saying it to me or Lennox or both of us.

Her curtain closes, and I strain my ears to listen for her movements. I think I hear the glide of fabric over her skin before it thumps against the floor. I rest my elbows on my knees and shove my fingers into my hair because now I'm thinking about her body, how it had looked against my sheets. All that smooth, unblemished skin. Perfect. It doesn't seem possible, but her body was the closest damn thing I'd ever seen to it. I remember the way her wet dress clung to her after our water fight in the shower.

Shit. *Shit.* I needed to stop thinking about this or I was going to make a fool of myself in more ways than one.

"Wilder," Gwen's high-pitched voice calls. And that's exactly what I need to distract me. I stand, moving closer to her dressing room.

"Yeah?"

"I need help."

I blew out a breath. It would probably make me a bad brother to ask if Lennox could help her.

"Can I come in?" I ask.

She doesn't answer, just pulls the curtain aside enough so that I can duck inside.

She's covered. Mostly. But it looks like the black and red dress she has on has some kind of wrapping mechanism, and she's tied it up all wrong. I unknot the bows she's made to start over, but then I'm not really sure how the thing is supposed to wrap either.

"It goes there," Gwen tells me.

"I don't think so. What about here?"

"That looks stupid."

We try a few more ways, and we get close, but something about it just looks slightly off.

"Maybe we should just try another dress," I say when my back starts to ache from bending down to her level.

"Need some help?" a voice asks outside the curtain, and it's not Lennox, but Kalli.

The fabric rustles, and she opens it just far enough to peek inside, but that's enough for Gwen.

"Kalli!"

Apparently I wasn't the only one impacted by that meeting in the grocery store. Gwen can barely remember things I tell her an hour later, but she hasn't forgotten Kalli's name. She shrugs off my hands where I've been messing with the ties to her dress and flings herself through the curtain onto Kalli.

Kalli's laugh puts her smile to shame, and it moves through me like electricity. She squeezes my sister tight, and as she looks down at her, I swear she's freaking glowing.

Hell, I think she's just one of those people who shine a little brighter than everyone else. The ones that always seem to draw your eye in public, the ones you find yourself looking at for a second time for no other reason than simply because it's where your eyes want to go.

And my eyes definitely want to go to Kalli. Not just a second time, but a third, and a fourth, and over and over again. She pulls back and gestures for my clumsily dressed sister to step inside the dressing room again, and she follows behind her, closing the curtain. I swallow.

The room had felt generously spacious a few moments before. Now I'm all too aware of the inches between us, and the space vibrates with something almost like static. Kalli kneels, putting her farther away from me and closer to my little sister. She undoes the ties I'd been wrestling with, and then she loops one side of the wrap through a small hole in the dress at my sister's waist that I hadn't noticed. There's one on the other side, too. And once she's fed both ties through, she wraps them again around her waist, hiding the holes, and completing a perfect bow in the middle of Gwen's back.

My sister twirls once, the skirt fanning around her, brushing against my knees and Kalli's stomach. She comes to a stop, her eyes meeting Kalli's in the mirror, as if seeking approval.

"Very pretty."

A blush sweeps over Gwen's apple cheeks and tiny nose. "Really?"

"Really. You look very special in that dress."

"This one!" Gwen cries, looking up at me.

"Are you sure? You don't want to get one that's a little easier to put on?"

She leaps forwarding, clinging to my knees, and says, "Please, can I have this one? Please, Wilder."

I try to surreptitiously check the price tag, but Kalli sees it. Damn. Nothing to do about that.

"Sure," I promise. "If this is the one you want, we can get it."

She starts bouncing up and down then, the fabric of the skirt bouncing wildly with her as she dances her victory. I smile, and my eyes are drawn again to Kalli, who's smiling at Gwen, too. Then her eyes lift to mine. They dim. Her smile falters.

And that shouldn't feel like a knife through my chest, but it does. I pull the curtain wide, and say, "You get dressed, Gwen. I'll wait for you outside."

Kalli steps out first, and I follow, my eyes taking in the new dress she's wearing. It's purple, black, and gray. And on the surface, it seems simple. It's loose and long, and her shape should be swallowed beneath it, but it's not. Instead, the looseness of it feels like a tease. Here and there are cut-outs that give a peek at the silk-lined interior and just a hint of skin. It feels halfway between something she'd wear on the beach and something she'd wear in the bedroom. And I enjoy the thought of her in both of those places.

I've forgotten how to be charming. Forgotten how to entice a woman. All I know is that I have to see her again, and now that Gwen has found her dress, there's nothing keeping me here. So, instead I just say the first thing that comes to my mind. "I've been thinking about you."

She hesitates outside her dressing room. "You have?"

I nod. Because if I actually voice how often I think about her, I'm likely to send her running again. I gesture behind me where Lennox is presumably moving somewhere through the shop and ask, "Is that your roommate?"

Her brows furrow. "Roommate?"

"The night we…uh, the last time I saw you, you said your roommate had friends over you didn't like."

"Oh. No. Lennox and I haven't known each other that long. That roommate…she moved out. We weren't a good fit. She was…reckless."

"Well, I'm glad she's gone then."

She nods. "Yep. She's definitely gone, and *everything* is under control now."

Again, I cut right to the chase. "Can I take you out sometime? Dinner?"

She leans toward me a few inches, then seems to realize what she's doing and straightens.

"I can't."

And…a knockout in one punch.

"You can't?"

God, I should shut up. She said no. I should take that hint and spare myself further misery, but I don't. Because there's something in her eyes, the way she tracks my movements just as obsessively as I do hers. I remember how vulnerable she'd looked that night when I'd started asking questions about what had happened to her earlier. I see that same vulnerability in her now, and I think she's hiding. I think that's why she said no, and I'm just enough of a masochist to attempt changing her mind.

"You should," I say. "You should go out with me."

"Oh, I should, should I?" Her tone sounds offended, but there's the barest tilt at the corner of her mouth that gives me hope.

"You should. You see, I know me. And I'm a pretty fun date."

"I'm sure you are."

"I'm also a good kisser."

"And how do you know that?"

I step closer, closing the distance between us, until she has to tilt her head up to meet my eyes.

"I've been told once or twice," I say. "Would you disagree?"

My eyes drop to her lips, and her tongue peeks out for just half a second, wetting her bottom lip.

"Wilder."

I close my eyes. It's surreal hearing her say my name again. I'd never thought it would happen.

"Kalli," I return.

Our eyes meet again, and that vulnerability is back tenfold. She looks scared. Of me? And before I know what I'm doing, I've reached up and skimmed my fingers along her cheek. I want to comfort her, take away whatever it is that has her worried. For a moment, she turns into my touch. Soft, warm skin against my calloused fingertips. I keep my touch light even though I'm dying to tunnel my fingers into her hair and taste that full mouth again.

Then she pulls away, and practically dives into the dressing room before shutting the curtain between us. I groan and press my forehead into the wall between the two rooms. This is all going so wrong, and I don't know how to make it right. What the hell is wrong with me?

I don't hear Lennox return until she says from just over my shoulder. "Hate shopping that much, do you?"

"No, it's not…it's nothing."

She surveys me for a moment; then her eyes flick to the curtain separating me from Kalli. She presses her lips together in contemplation. Then Gwen comes running out with her chosen dress in her hand.

"That's the one?" Lennox asks.

Gwen's nod is vigorous.

"You don't want to try on any of the rest?"

She shakes her head. "Kalli says this one is special."

Lennox's eyes shoot back to me.

"Okay then. Let's get you two checked out."

I don't want to go to the front register, but I don't have much of a choice. Lennox is walking away with Gwen's dress, and I'd look a little crazy waiting outside Kalli's dressing room just so I could talk to her again. So with one final glance at the closed curtain, I head toward the front.

While Lennox rings us up, she asks, "So. Do you know Kalli?"

"We've met before. But I don't think I'd say I *know* her."

Unless knowing the way she tastes counts. And the way her back arches when she comes. The little panting breaths she makes when she's almost there. I know those things. Fat lot of good it has done me today.

"Tell me about it. Girl has more secrets than *Lost*. She's hard to pin down."

So it isn't just me then.

Lennox moves to slip a plastic garment bag over Gwen's dress and says casually, "You should come to Christmas at my place."

"Uh. I'm sorry. What?"

"Not like…alone or anything. Jesus, I'm not crazy. I'm having an Orphan Christmas for all the people who can't afford or don't want to visit family. Kalli will be there."

"Really?"

She nods with a knowing smile. "Took me days of prodding to get her to agree to come."

I'm tempted. So damn tempted.

"I can't. I've got family stuff."

"So come after. We're doing a big pot luck dinner, and then we'll probably stay up late drinking and playing games and watching terrible holiday-themed movies."

"Yeah?"

In answer, she prints out some extra receipt paper from the register, grabs a pen a writes down her address. We exchange numbers, too. "In case you have any issues," she says.

She holds the paper out to me, and I take it. "Are you going to tell Kalli I'm coming?"

She scoffs. "Yeah, right. I do know one thing about that girl, and it's that she goes out of her way not to let anyone too close. And I'm just about ready to strangle her for it. But I think you're probably a more preferable option."

"So, you're helping me? You don't even know me."

She shrugs. "I don't see a lot of dudes come here with little kids. And of the ones that do, there are two kinds. The ones who would give anything to be somewhere else. And the ones who are here because they would give anything for their little girl."

"She's not mine," I remind her.

"Still applies. Even more so considering you're her brother. I have a brother. A good brother, but I guarantee he would *never* take me shopping."

I want to tell her that I'm not nearly as good as she's making me out to be. I might be here with Gwen now, but I was pretty damn absent for the first few years of her life. But I'm selfish enough to want her to like me, so that maybe I'll have an ally in whatever this thing with Kalli is.

Realizing I still haven't introduced myself to her, I hold out my hand over the counter and say, "Wilder Bell."

She takes it, giving my hand a surprisingly firm shake before adding, "Lennox Hastings. Does this mean I'll be seeing you for Christmas?"

"Yeah. I think you will."

Chapter Eleven

Mom's eyes meet mine from her perch on the couch. It's the first time I've seen her out of scrubs in weeks. Mom had been a nurse for nearly a decade, but she quit a few years back when Dad's business started flourishing. Or when we thought it had anyway. She went from staying at home to working as many hours as she could pack in practically overnight. Out of scrubs, she wears a red holiday sweater, and it makes the paleness of her cheeks stand out even more. Gwen is on the floor in Dora the Explorer pajamas, tearing through the wrapping paper on her present.

We're doing something new this Christmas. Instead of opening all the presents in the morning, we've been spreading them out throughout the day. Mom and I thought it might make up for the fact that there aren't as many presents under the tree as there used to be.

Last year's Christmas had been even more extravagant than usual. Dad had gone on a crazy buying spree, which had included my SUV that was parked outside in the drive. He bought it outright. We probably should have known then that something was up, but Dad had just convinced us that business was good. We should have questioned how his investment business was flourishing at a time when everyone else in the market seemed to be struggling, but when things are good like that, you don't want to go searching for problems.

Me, especially. Dad wasn't on my back to go to college or get a real job or any of that kind of thing. Then it all went away in the blink of an eye. If the SUV hadn't been in my name, they would have taken that too. I'd tried to give it to Mom after news about Dad had come to light, and the bank had repossessed both their vehicles. But she wouldn't have it. She bought a beat up old Camry from a friend at the hospital, and refused to even think about taking the SUV.

"Your father gave you that," she told me. "I don't know why he did what he did. Don't know how he could convince himself it wasn't wrong, but we've had enough taken from us. It might relieve a little stress to take that vehicle from you, but it wouldn't do a damn thing for the ache in my heart. The only thing that helps with that is having you back here. Having you and Gwen here makes me feel so full, I don't even notice what else is missing."

Except it's impossible not to notice what's missing now.

Dad is gone. So is the old house.

No more giant Christmas tree with an abundance of decorations. Instead, we've got one of those fake half-size ones, covered not in expensive ornaments, but just the more personal ones. Things I made in school, a few things by Gwen, some candy canes.

But for all the changes, Gwen doesn't seem to notice as she liberates a doll I recognize from some TV show she loves out of its packaging. I cross from my position against the wall, and take a seat on the couch by Mom. I wrap an arm around her shoulder, and pull her close. She leans all her weight into me, and I choke back the emotion building at the back of my throat.

"Christmas is Christmas," I tell her. "That hasn't changed. It won't change."

She reaches up to rest a hand against my cheek. Her fingers brush over my unshaven jaw, and she grips my face and looks at me.

"Thank you, Wilder. I know this hasn't been easy. And I know you've given up so much." Tears well in her eyes, but she presses on, her hold on my jaw tight. "I'm so sorry for that. I'm really close to being back on my feet, and then you can go back to—"

I cut her off by pulling her into a hug.

"Stop, Mom. I'm happy where I am. It was about time I grew up anyway."

It's one of my unwritten rules that I'll just keep saying that until it's true. One day it will be.

We pass the day together. Mom bakes cookies. We watch Christmas-themed movies on the small TV that came with the furnished apartment. Gwen starts playing with her toys, and Mom and I both get dragged into an imaginary tea party with a few stuffed Disney characters, a Spiderman figurine that Gwen unearthed from a box of my old toys, and a worn out old baby doll that is less cute and more Chucky.

Around nine that night, Gwen finally passes out with her cheek pressed flat against the carpet and Spiderman in her hand.

"I got her," I tell Mom, and then bend to scoop her up. She flails sleepily in my arms for a moment, fighting my hold before burying her head in my neck and going slack again.

I walk her down the hallway, and into her small bedroom. I balance her in my arms with one hand, and pull back her covers with the other. I lay her down on her mattress as gently as I can, but she still wakes up, peering up at me with bleary eyes. She whines for a second, as if she can't decide whether she wants to be awake or asleep.

"Are you gonna see Kalli?" she finally asks.

I stiffen, and then pull her covers up to her neck. I'm still out of practice at the whole brother-ing thing. I probably shouldn't let her get attached to the idea of seeing Kalli again, but hell, I'm not doing a very good job of keeping myself from that.

I finally settle on honesty. "I don't know. Maybe."

"You said you were. At the dress store."

"I know. I'm still not sure about some things though."

"I like her. You should have brought her to *our* Christmas."

Gwen's cheek is imprinted with the texture of the carpet where she'd fallen asleep, and I run a hand over the reddened skin. "You go to sleep," I tell her. "And be good for Mom."

She nods, and falls back asleep with an easiness that I envy.

I sigh, turning on the lamp by her bed that she prefers to keep on, and then leave the door cracked just enough so that Mom can see inside.

I'd been doing my best not to think about Kalli today. One, because the way I feel about her after just a few encounters can't be healthy. I keep telling myself that I don't know anything about her, and yet my mind always counters with images of her smile or the way she talks to Gwen or the mischievous and almost hopeful look she'd had right before she turned my own showerhead on me.

Maybe I don't know her. But I wasn't lying when I told her that I wanted to. There's only one other thing I've ever wanted this bad, and I gave it up for Mom and Gwen. So even though she ran from me, even though she's been skittish and distant, I'm still going to go for it. You don't get a shot at a girl like that every day. Hell, I doubted that most people ever got one. There's just something about her. I can't put my finger on it. She puts me at ease, like the way you feel around an old friend, as if there's no need to pretend, no need to worry about how you're coming off. And yet at the same time, I'm anything but calm around her. She's too gorgeous. Too perfect for it not to mess with my nerves.

As such, I'm restless when I re-enter the living room.

"You want some hot chocolate?" Mom asks. "I was thinking of making some."

I hesitate. I'd like to head over to Lennox's party now, but I don't know how I feel about leaving Mom alone. Maybe I should stay a little while longer. Until she's ready to go to sleep. I'm just about to say this when she continues, "Unless you've got other plans. With the boys?"

I smile. Ellis Rook and I have been friends since elementary school. We met Owen in high school. He was two years above us, and took us under his wing. We're all well past grown now. Hell, Rook is a full foot taller than Mom at 6'4". But she still calls them the boys as if we're little kids playing video games in the back room.

"Nah," I tell her. "Owen went on a ski trip, and Rook's family is in Missouri for the holidays." It's an unspoken thought between us that this time last year I probably would have joined Owen, but now every spare penny I have goes to Mom or school. "There's, uh, this party I was thinking about going to."

Her lips remain in a smile, but I can see the corners twitch down just for a second.

"Not that kind of party. It's for some people who weren't able to go home to see family for the holidays." God. She's going to think I'd rather be with the people who *can't* see their family, than to actually spend time with my own. "But that's whatever. I think I'll stay and hang out with you for a little while."

"No." She crosses and pats at my arm. "You go. See your friends. I'll probably conk out soon."

"Then I'll stay until you're ready to go to bed."

"Wilder Bell." I squint down at her, unsure why she's using the same tone normally reserved for when I cause problems. "You don't need to babysit me. You're twenty-three years old. You should get to live your own life. Go to your party."

I frown, and she pushes at my shoulder, turning me toward the door.

"Go. I'm going to take a bubble bath and relax anyway."

I hesitate. "You're sure?"

"Of course, I am. Now, get out of here."

I grab my leather jacket from where I draped it over the back of the recliner, and shrug it on.

"Call me if you need anything."

"Still don't need babysitting," Mom replies.

I smile and plant a quick kiss on her forehead. "All right. Point taken."

I grab my keys, and when I'm almost out the door, Mom calls for me again. I look back, and she's at the entrance to the hallway that leads back to her bedroom.

"Yeah?"

"Thank you again. For everything."

"Right back at you."

∞

Lennox lives in an apartment just off the highway. It's not the nicest neighborhood, and I'm a little shocked that she lives here. I hope she doesn't live here alone, and that Kalli doesn't visit often. The whole idea of her in this place makes me uneasy.

She lives on the top floor of a three-story building that has definitely seen better days. The stairs creak loudly, and the paint is so chipped that it's hard to tell what color the building is supposed to be. When I reach her door, I can hear the rumble of noise inside, and I take a deep breath.

There's every possibility that Kalli won't be happy seeing me here. I promise myself that this is it. I'll chase after her tonight, but if she doesn't give me some indication that she's as into this as I am, I'll let it be.

Not too long ago I was on the receiving end of an unwanted pursuit by Bridget. Or hell, maybe it's not fair to say unwanted. We dated for six months after all. And we were friends long before that.

I should have listened when Rook said not to get involved with her. We were good friends, and I knew she could be a little crazy when it came to guys, but she was never like that with me. She was cool and comfortable and a blast to be around. I thought maybe it would be different with us. We knew each other. We were familiar. And she was exactly what I wanted when the rest of my life was in upheaval and nothing felt familiar or comfortable or *right*.

She wouldn't go all clingy with me. There wouldn't be any need. We trusted each other. Or so I thought.

We had one good month, and then shit started to go sour. She couldn't get past all the time I now have to spend on work and class and homework. Most of the time, she seemed to think I was lying. We had two just okay months followed by three miserable ones. All because I didn't know how to end it. I kept thinking I could get the old Bridget back. That eventually she would settle down and realize she didn't have to spend every moment of the day with me, and she didn't have to hate every single girl I talked to, and she didn't have to be the center of my every waking thought.

Eight months ago, I finally pulled my head out of my ass and ended it. And every time I hung out with our group of friends since (Bridget included), I alternated between feeling guilty for how hurt she was and pissed that she'd had to be so different just because we were sleeping together. Then there was the annoyance at her continued bouts of clinginess and jealousy despite our break-up. And it all finally gave way to exhaustion because I couldn't even relax with my friends anymore.

These days it seemed like I couldn't relax anywhere. There were too many things to do, to take care of. Too many things to *be* that took work and perseverance and *effort*.

That night I'd seen Kalli down on Sixth Street, I'd been faking my way through a night out with friends that wasn't the least bit fun. That's why I thought Kalli was a hallucination. I'd been standing there on the street while my friends decided which bar to hit up next with Bridget inching closer to my side when Kalli had caught my eye after days of being on my mind. And then she wasn't just my mental sanctuary, but physical too.

She'd cleared my head of everything else with her mystery. She just wiped it all clean. And then she filled up all that empty space with thoughts of her, memories, possibilities.

Shit. I shake my head, realizing that I'm still standing on Lennox's porch, and I haven't even knocked yet. I rectify that, and then stand with my hands in my jacket pockets while I wait for someone to answer the door. It must be too loud because no one answers, and I have to knock again.

I'm trying to decide whether it's weird to just walk inside or if I should give up and leave when the door is ripped backward, revealing Lennox on the other side. Her hair has been dyed a vivid scarlet since I saw her, and she clings to the door like she might not be able to stay standing without it.

"You came!"

I smile in response, not only to be polite, but because she's obviously drunk. A happy drunk too, if the way she topples into me for a hug is any indication.

"I'm so glad," she continues. "Kalli is being all anti-social, and no matter how many times I threaten her, she won't loosen up."

She pulls me over the threshold as I ask, "So you want *me* to threaten her?"

"I want you to dazzle her into having a good time."

"Dazzle? How much have you had to drink?"

She waves a hand, gesturing toward my face. "Come on. You're a dazzler. With those eyes and that hair. You have distinct dazzability."

"I'm going to guess the answer to my question is 'too much.'"

"You say too much. I say just enough."

She leads me out of the entry way into the living room, and I barely keep my jaw from dropping. The outside of her apartment might be less than impressive, but the inside…it's incredible. Every inch of space is packed with interesting furniture and artwork and unusual decorations.

She has a mural painted along one wall that at first glance looks like a sort of abstract cityscape, but when I look again I can see that what appears as buildings are also people. Different shapes and sizes, shadowed so that they're more silhouettes than realistic portrayals. Even though they're mostly dark, there's a surprising amount of emotion painted into them. Their eyes are lit up like building windows, and through that single detail I can see that some figures are sad, some angry, some afraid. I stare at the painted wall for a long time, trying to figure out exactly how the artist accomplished so much with so little.

"You've got another fan, Avery," Lennox says.

I turn toward her, and she gestures to a girl sitting on the couch, a bottle of beer clutched between two small hands. She's got that same kind of hipster vibe as Lennox, only the wide-rimmed glasses feel more genuine on her. She sinks farther into the couch in response to my gaze. She's not who I would have pictured for the mural artist. She seems shy and unsure, and I can't understand why. She's clearly got talent. She's also very pretty. Her hair is short and straight, but it's this pale blonde that catches and reflects the light.

"It's incredible," I tell her, and I look back at the work. I could probably stand in front of it all day, and continue to notice new things, subtle brilliance. "Really, it's amazing."

She pushes at her glasses even though they've not slid down her nose and says quietly, "Thank you."

"Okay then," Lennox begins. "So you've met my roommate Avery. The hottie beside her is my boyfriend Mick." I try not to blink too much in surprise. I would expect a boyfriend of Lennox's to have the same kind of artistic vibe, but this guy looks straight country, right down to the worn out old boots. I try to keep up while she introduces the rest of the people in the room to me. Kim and Krista (sisters). Dan and Eric (preppy boy next door types). Jack (another hipster with prettier hair than most girls I've seen). Then she starts to move fast enough that I lose track of which name belongs with which person, but somewhere on right side of the room are an Olivia, a Morie, and a Jane. Some are direct friends of Lennox. Others she introduces as friends of friends that needed a place to chill on the holiday. And overall, the group is undeniably eclectic. But they're all at ease as they sit around the living room chatting. Though that could have something to do with the immense amounts of alcohol bottles and cans and glasses littered across the coffee table and bookshelves and every other flat surface.

After the official introductions, Lennox leans close to give me some more specifics, and that's when I realize what really connects them all. "Avery is a painter, obviously. Though some days, I swear I have to convince her to believe it. Jack too. I've known him since freshman year, and met Avery through him. Mick does wood and metal work. He's built a lot of the furniture in the room. Kim and Krista are in the fashion design program with me." By the time she's finished, it's evident that everyone in the room has some kind of artistic talent, and I understand now how all these different people could fit together.

"So how does Kalli fit?" I ask.

"Hmm?" Lennox tilts her head to the side, and her eyes are a little unfocused.

"Kalli. You guys are all artists of one kind or another, so what is she?"

Lennox frowns. "Kalli is…She's not an artist. Not really. But she's incredibly knowledgeable about it all, so she fits right in. She can talk building stuff with Mick and clothes with me and art with Jack. She's just one of those people who is an incredibly good sounding board, you know? She's only been hanging out with us for about a month and half, but everyone really loves her. Jack even painted her. Between you and me, I'm pretty sure he would give his left testicle to be with her, but she hasn't really showed much interest so far."

My eyes flick to Jack, and I try not to tense, but even drunk, Lennox picks up on my reaction. "Relax, Dazzler," she says, laughing. "I asked her about you after you left, you know. She *blushed*. It's the most reaction I've ever seen out of her with a guy. And believe me, she gets hit on…*a lot*."

I scowl. She's fucking gorgeous. So, it's not like I thought there wouldn't be any competition, but Jesus. Lennox laughs again. "Well, this is a fun game." I turn my glare on her. "She wouldn't answer any of my questions about you. She said it was nothing, but I'm pretty good at reading people. The look she had after you left? Totally not nothing."

My eyes skip back to Jack. He's good looking, especially with all that hair of his. "He really painted her?" I ask.

"Oh yeah. It's good, too."

Damn.

"She's in the kitchen," Lennox says. "If you want to get to dazzling."

She points the way, and I don't care how transparent I am as I move immediately in that direction. She grins and whispers, "Good luck," at my back.

And I need it. I need it so fucking bad.

Because as I step through the entry, I see Kalli leaning against a carved wooden island. Her eyes are closed, and she has an empty wine glass pressed against her full lips. For a moment, I just take her in. She wears dark jeans that hug the smooth shape of her thighs. A gray sweater clings to her waist and breasts, and she looks effortlessly beautiful. Stunning in a way that's hard to put into words, but I feel it like a punch to the gut. Her chest rises on an inhale, and I find myself breathing in tandem.

She exhales, and I take a step farther into the kitchen. The floor creaks, and her eyes pop open. They land on me, and as her expression morphs into shock, the glass slips right out of her hand and shatters at her feet.

Chapter Twelve

I notice she's barefoot a second after the glass breaks, and I move on instinct. I reach her in two long strides, wrap an arm around her waist, and lift her off the ground. I settle her on top of the island counter before glancing down to make sure she hasn't been cut.

The light reflects off a few tiny shards along the top of her foot, and near one is a tiny dot of blood.

"Stay there," I order, before crossing to the sink. I grab a paper towel, fold it into quarters, and then turn on the faucet just enough to dampen it. I cross back to her, and the glass crunches beneath my boots.

I cup my hand around her heel, and lift the foot up where I can see it better under the light. I don't want to drag the towel across it because if there are any little slivers of glass, they could still cut her. So I bend over and carefully blow along the top of her foot to remove any debris.

She sucks in a breath above me, and grabs my shoulder at the same time that I wipe at the tiny knick.

I look up, wondering how that possibly could have hurt her, but that thought flees as I take in her expression. She's gripping the edge of the counter hard, and her mouth is open, frozen on an inhale. And her eyes are on me, and…damn. *This* is what I had hoped to see when I ran into her in that shop. She's looking at me the way she had in my shower, moments before it stopped being playful and started being about how quickly I could get my hands on her skin.

My hand is still holding her foot, and I can't stop myself from sliding my fingers up, over her ankle to the smooth skin of her calf. Her chin tilts up, and she watches me through hooded eyes. She's tense, waiting to see what I'll do, and my mind is bursting with thoughts and ideas of how to touch her.

Lennox chooses that moment to barrel into the kitchen.

"What the hell is going on? I thought I heard—"

She trails off, and even though I can't bring myself to look at her, Kalli does, and she immediately shifts, pulling her leg away from my touch.

"Shit," Lennox says. "I'm an idiot. Don't mind me. Carry on. Pretend I was never here."

But there's no pretending that. Not anymore. Kalli won't meet my eyes, not even as she loosens her grip on my shoulder, and pushes me away instead.

"I'm so sorry about the glass, Len. Do you have a broom? I'll clean it up."

She moves as if to slide off the counter, and I drop my hand down to her hip. "Stay. I'll get it." She starts to complain, and I add, "You're barefoot. *I've got it.*"

Lennox opens a pantry door next to her, and I cross to pick up the broom and dustpan she offers.

"Since when did dazzling involve breaking things?" she asks, and I glower.

"Right. Right. As you were."

She slips out of the kitchen without another word, and I return to my spot in front of Kalli. I place the dustpan on the counter beside her, and then proceed to sweep up the glass. As I do, I allow myself one quick glance up at her.

"What is it with you and being barefoot?" I ask.

She crosses her arms over her chest in a defensive gesture, and it makes me smile.

Rather than answer, she turns it around on me. "What are you doing here?"

"Lennox invited me. She thinks I'm *dazzling*. Her words. Not mine."

"She just invited you? Out of the blue?"

"When you were avoiding me the other day, yeah."

"I wasn't avoiding you. I just—"

"Ran into the dressing room to get away? You seem to have a habit of doing that kind of thing." I finish sweeping the glass into a pile, and straighten up to grab the dustpan. It brings me close enough that her knees graze my abdomen, and we both freeze at the touch. Something that small shouldn't be so powerful, but I swear there's this pull between us, and every time I touch her, every time I even look at her, it gets stronger. Like she's an ocean tide, and I'm caught up in her current. And there's no point in fighting my way to the surface because I don't know which way is up or down. I don't know anything except that I want her.

Before I sweep up the last of the glass, I take hold of her other foot, checking it for shards. I don't see any, but I keep checking just because I'm reluctant to let her go. I'm too afraid she'll run from me again. But I do release her. And then I bend to sweep up my pile of glass.

"I'm sorry," she says, her voice so soft I almost can't make it out.

"Accidents happen. And Lennox didn't seem all that worried about the glass."

"I don't mean that."

I straighten, but she's looking down at her hands. She's got long, elegant fingers, and I watch her tangle them together for a moment. I cross to the pantry where Lennox had gotten the broom. There's a trashcan in there, so I empty the glass and stow the items away when I'm done.

I stay where I am and face Kalli. "What are you sorry about then?"

Maybe I'm a dick for making her say it. But I had to wake up to the empty bed. I had to lay there and curse myself for not touching her just a little longer, tasting just a little bit more. If I had to do that, she can sure as hell say it.

"We weren't supposed to see each other again."

"So, if we hadn't run into each other the other day, you wouldn't be sorry?"

"That's not what I'm saying."

"So you *are* sorry?"

She nods.

"Then just tell me straight. Why *did* you leave?"

She rubs her hands over her eyes, and then pushes her fingers into the hair at her temples. "I don't normally do that sort of thing. In fact, I never do that sort of thing. But I was dealing with some things, and I just needed…"

She trails off, and I move toward her. I don't go as close as I want to, leaning instead against the corner of the island.

"What did you need?"

My control is barely leashed, and if she gives me any indication at all that she *still* needs something…

Her head stays bowed, but her eyes lift to mine. Framed by dark lashes, the look she gives me isn't the heat I hoped for. It's vulnerable. Lost, maybe.

"I needed to not be alone. I needed someone to lean on just for a night."

The urge to take her in my arms is so strong I'm surprised I don't buckle under it. Her emotions are so clear, so open, and yet she's still a mystery. Her gaze might ask for help, but her body language is a clear roadblock.

"Did it help?"

"Yes." She gives me a small smile, but her hands are clenched tight in her lap.

"Liar."

"Excuse me?"

"It didn't help." A fleeting expression of panic crosses her face. "Or at least it didn't help for long."

She braces herself on the counter as if she's about to slide off, but I step in front of her. "Wait. Don't run again."

"I'm not…" Her protest dies as our eyes meet. I don't have to call her a liar again. I can see the admission in her face. She was sure as hell about to run.

"Let's just start over," I suggest. "That night was out of the ordinary for both of us. So let's turn the page. Do this the normal way."

She frowns. "I don't do normal very well either."

"Fine. Normal is overrated anyway. Let's just not put this in a box at all. We'll take it one moment at a time, starting with me telling you Merry Christmas." I brace a hand on the counter beside her, close enough to tease us both with the nearness. "Merry Christmas, Kalli. It's good to see you again. Do you want another glass of wine? I promise not to surprise you this time."

She glances toward the door, but she doesn't make any movement to leave. "I really should go."

I pause for a few seconds, waiting to see if she'll do just that. She doesn't.

"But you don't want to…do you?" Her pursed lips are the only answer I get. "So stay. One moment at a time. That's all it has to be," I tell her. "There goes one. And another. Look at that…nothing disastrous has happened yet."

She gives a reluctant smile, and when I pick up a new wineglass from the counter and hold it up, she nods. "Just a little."

I snag a bottle of already open red wine, and pour a little for her. When she reaches out to take it, I ask, "So you're pretty cautious, huh? *Normally.*"

I can't quite decipher her expression as she answers, "Not nearly as cautious as I should be."

"You and your mystery. If you're trying to run me off, you're doing it wrong. I enjoy a puzzle."

"I am not a puzzle you want to figure out, Wilder."

"Sorry, I forgot everything else you said once you used my name."

She sighs, but it's more playful than genuinely frustrated, and I think I might have finally cracked her. A little anyway.

"So tell me about your friends. They seem like an interesting group. How long have you known them?"

"Not long."

"One of these days, I'm going to figure out how to get real answers out of you."

"How's Gwen?"

"Changing the subject on me."

"No, you said to start fresh. This is me starting fresh."

Baby steps.

I shift and lean back against the counter next to her and try not to think about the scant inch between my hip and her thigh.

"She's good. I did Christmas stuff with her and my mother all day."

"How was that?" She seems genuinely interested, and I wonder about her family. She'd said that she had sisters, but they were estranged. How long has it been since she's seen them? Since she's spent a holiday with them?

"It was pretty good. A little too much tea party for my taste, but I survived."

She laughs, and I vow to hear that sound as much as possible tonight. "She played with all her new toys for about half an hour each before she lost interest. She ended the night playing with an old hand-me-down toy of mine. I'm not sure why we bother. We could probably just wrap up toys she already has, and she'd be just fine as long as she still got to open the presents."

"Maybe she liked the old toy because it was yours."

"Doubtful."

"Come on. She practically worships you."

I choke on a laugh. "If you'd seen the fit she threw the other day when I didn't let her have candy, I guarantee you would think differently."

"Kids throw fits. It doesn't matter who's with them."

"I'm willing to bet she wouldn't throw one with you."

"That's not fair."

"What? You don't count as a normal person? The rules of children throwing fits don't apply to you?"

Her smile falters just for a moment before she jumps right back into the conversation. " I just mean…I'm new and different. Once she got used to me, I'm sure she wouldn't treat me any differently."

"There's a way to test that theory, you know."

She shakes her head and raises her eyebrows in what's probably a reprimand. It doesn't do any good though because I like her eyes on me, whatever the reason.

She continues, "All I'm saying is that I've seen you two together. That day in the grocery store with the magazine—"

"Oh God. Don't bring that up. Not my favorite moment…having to explain to her in the car why that particular magazine wasn't for kids." I groan.

"She just wanted to be like you. You were reading a magazine, and she wanted one too."

"Yes, well, I've officially given up reading magazines."

She's still smiling when she lifts her wine glass to her mouth, and watching her lips part over the rim is definitely one of the sexiest things I've ever seen.

"So how did you meet Lennox?"

She tilts her head, as if considering her answer. "Well, I met Jack first."

Damn. I wish I could rewind and un-ask that question. But clearly I'm a masochist. "How did you meet him?"

"At an art exhibit on campus."

I can't resist the urge to pry for more details. "And when was that?"

Her forefinger taps at her wineglass, and she seems almost nervous. Maybe Lennox was wrong. Maybe Jack has a better shot than she thinks. "About six weeks ago, I think."

So right after her night with me. Fuck. *Fuck.*

"He introduced me to Lennox and Avery, and something just kind of clicked. I've never had a group of friends like them before, but...I think it's working."

"Working? What do you mean by that?"

"Um, well..."

She takes a larger gulp of wine, and after a prolonged swallow (that does nothing for my attempts to keep my eyes off her mouth), she shrugs. "I mean that it's good, I guess. I usually have just one...close friend. But they're this tight knit group with all these personalities and talents, and they welcomed me in without any hesitation, and it's...good."

I don't get how someone like her isn't surrounded by people all the time. She's vibrant and interesting, and surely it can't be only me that she has this effect on.

"Well, I'm glad you found them then."

Maybe I'm imagining it or seeing what I want to see, but her eyes track down to my mouth for just a moment.

"Me too."

Silence settles between us, but I'm still watching her, and she's watching me. And there goes that pull again. I shift a little closer so that her thigh touches my hip, and I feel the barest pressure as she returns the contact, accepts it.

"I have a confession to make."

She asks, "A confession?"

I nod, and then go all in. "I don't think I'm going to be very good at this whole fresh start thing." I try to gauge her response, but her expression doesn't change. Curious. Maybe a little wary. It's the curious part that I focus on. "I'm trying really hard to pretend that I don't know what it's like to kiss you, but I don't see myself forgetting that anytime soon."

Chapter Thirteen

She's warring with herself. I can tell. And I just wish I knew what has her keeping her walls so high. I'll take them down piece by piece if I have to.

"Wilder. I—"

"Tell me you remember how good it was. I'm not imagining that, am I? I get that you don't do hook-ups, and that seeing me again is a reminder of that, but you don't just throw a connection like that away because the timeline is wrong."

"It's not about that timeline."

"Then tell me what it is. I want you. You want me. I'm not giving that up without a fight."

"I'm not good for you."

"First of all, bullshit. And second, what about what's good for you? You're in here alone while your friends are out there talking and laughing and drinking. You find someone you have mind-blowing chemistry with, and rather than seeing where it goes, you cut it off before it even gets started. Something happens in your life that throws you so off-kilter that you seek out comfort from a stranger. I don't know what that is. I don't know why. But I know you deserve more than one night. I know you deserve to laugh with your friends, not stand on the sidelines." I brace one hand on the counter beside her and lift the other to curve around her cheek. At my touch, her eyes flutter closed, and she exhales so strongly that I wonder how long she's been holding her breath. "Stop telling yourself what you can't have or shouldn't have. You deserve more, Kalli."

I throw my patience out the window, and bend to touch my mouth to hers. It's just a light touch, but it causes a tug of desire at the base of my spine all the same. She doesn't quite kiss me back, but her lips part, and I can feel the puff of her breath against my mouth, sharp and uncontrolled. I remember how much she liked it when I told her what I wanted to do to her, so I take a chance and push things a little further. I grab hold of her knees, and gently pull her legs apart. She gasps, and her eyes pop open, but she doesn't move away. Our faces are an inch apart, eyes locked together as I settle between her thighs.

"*This*," I whisper against her mouth. "I remember how fucking good this was. To have your legs around me. The way we fit…it's like you were made for me. I remember how you taste. The sounds you made. If we were alone, I'd show you exactly what you deserve, sweet. You'd come apart on my fingers and my tongue and my cock." Damn, just imagining what it would feel like to be inside her is enough to make me ache. "Then we'd do it all again. I'd make up for all the days that have passed since I last touched you. Would you let me do that? Or will you try to run from me again?" Her only answer is to close her eyes and let her head fall back. I lower my lips to the hollow of her neck and kiss her pulse. It beats frantically beneath her skin, and my touch is gentle even though all I want to do is crush her against me. "Maybe I should tie you to my bed," I suggest. "You wouldn't run then."

Her right hand comes up to grip my bicep, and she squeezes hard.

"You like that?" *Interesting.* "You could let go with me, Kalli. I'd take care of you. If you'd let me."

I pull back from her neck, passing my lips over her jaw first, then the corner of her mouth. But I don't go any farther than that. I'm okay with being on the offensive, but I want her to be the one to drop the walls. If not, I'm only going to end up climbing them over and over again.

"I—" She swallows, and her eyes flick back and forth between mine. "I don't know if I can. If I can risk…" I brush my lips over hers, dragging my tongue over her bottom lip, and she moans. I swear to God, I can almost taste the sound on my tongue. So fucking sweet my head spins.

I want her to choose this, but clearly I'm not above playing a little dirty. All I can guess is that she's been burned before, and she doesn't want to chance it happening again.

"You've got to risk to get the reward," I tell her, sliding a hand around her waist and inching her just a little closer. "I won't hurt you, Kalli."

She exhales sharply, and makes a noise that's almost a laugh. Pressing her lips together, she looks as if she's steeling herself. Whether to push me away or pull me closer, I'm not sure. And I don't get the chance to find out.

Because at that moment, Lennox charges into the kitchen again. "Time for a drinking—damn it. I have the worst timing ever."

Yes. Yes, she does. Kalli's hand drops from my arm, but I don't release her or move away.

"Well, it appears you've done your job, Dazzler. Now both of you come celebrate Christmas with us by getting blackout drunk."

"Gotta say. I've never had a Christmas quite like this one."

Lennox crosses her arms over her chest and says, "You're welcome. Now come hang out with us." She refuses to leave the kitchen until we're with her. And even though I really want to keep Kalli to myself, I meant what I said about her being with her friends. She talks about them as if she's never really had friends before, at least not that many. And I get the feeling that it's all tied together with why she's keeping me at arm's length and why she was so upset the night we were together. I take her hand as she slides off the counter. She tiptoes across the floor, just in case I missed any glass, and the two of us follow Lennox into the living room. Avery has moved to a spot on the floor just below Jack, leaving half of the couch open for Kalli and me to sit beside Lennox and her boyfriend. I shed my leather jacket, and lay it over the couch arm. It's a tight squeeze with me on the outside, and Kalli ends up nearly on my lap. I lay one arm along the back of the couch to give us a little extra room. She only hesitates for a few seconds before pressing into my side.

"Alrighty," Lennox says. "For you newbies, first up is Merry Mustache. You don't get much simpler than this." She nods at Mick, and he strides over to the TV and tapes a construction paper mustache a little left and down from the center of the screen. "Thank you, Mick. Now, we put on a variety of Christmas movies that everyone is sick of. You can watch it or don't. But if during the movie, the fake mustache lines up correctly with someone's face on the screen, yell Merry Mustache. Everyone else besides the Merry-Mustache-wisher then has to drink. Dazzler, where is your drink?"

I shrug. "You ran me out of the kitchen before I had time."

"Mick, be your usual amazing self and get Wilder a drink."

Her boyfriend holds up his own beer in question, and I nod in approval.

"That's the first game," Lennox continues.

"First?" Kalli asks. "There's more than one?"

"Of course. It's Christmas. No way in hell I want to be sober. And you two," she points a finger in our direction, "have some catching up to do."

Mick returns then with my beer, and I nod in thanks. I'm starting to realize that he's a pretty silent dude. Again, the complete opposite of Lennox. He sits down at the other end of the couch, and Kalli is squeezed even tighter against me.

"Game number two involves the Secret Santa presents."

"I was supposed to bring a present?" I whisper to Kalli.

Lennox must have stellar hearing because she says, "Don't worry, Wilder. I've got you. I forgot to tell you, so I went ahead and got a second one. Unlike regular Secret Santa, every single one of these presents is alcohol. Because that's how we roll at Orphan Christmas. We'll pick numbers, and when it's your turn to pick a gift, you have to try and guess what type alcohol it is. If you're right, everyone else has to take a shot. If you're wrong, you have to."

"Someone is going to get alcohol poisoning," Kalli says.

"That's how we roll at Orphan Christmas," Jack replies sarcastically.

Kalli laughs, and irritation burns in my chest.

Lennox has us all choose numbers from a hat to determine the order in which we pick our presents. Jack is up first, and when he looks in Kalli's direction, I feel an irrational urge to keep her from looking at him. I lean in close to her. Playing with one of the curls on her shoulder, I say, "Tell me something about you that I don't know."

She tilts her chin toward me, enough that my lips could meet her cheek if she leaned just a little farther.

"There's a lot you don't know about me."

"Then we better get started. How about we play a little game of our own? Every time one of us has to drink, we also have to tell the other something about ourselves."

"Anything?"

"To start."

"Planning to make it more interesting?"

"With you, I think things can only get more interesting."

"Len is right about you being a dazzler."

"You know she's on my side, right?"

"There are sides?"

"Definitely. And I don't want to alarm you or anything, but I'm pretty sure your side is losing. Anytime you want to jump ship, just let me know."

She rolls her eyes and shakes her head, but she relaxes a little more against me, and I'm hyper aware of the way we're touching from chest to thigh. My blood pounds in my ear, amplified by adrenaline. This night feels important, like I'm coming up on a summit, and if I can just get there, it will open my eyes up to all the things I haven't been able to see before.

As expected, Jack fails to guess what type of alcohol is in his gift, and Lennox hands him a shot glass so he can get acquainted with his gift, a cheap looking bottle of gin. We're on gift number three (after another failed guess for gift number two) when Kalli says quietly, "Merry Mustache."

The room pauses, and our heads all swivel to the television, and sure enough the mustache has lined up perfectly with a woman's lip.

"Merry Mustache!" Lennox cries. "Everybody drinks but Kalli."

Kalli grins at me, and I hold her eyes as I tip back my beer and swallow. "Guess that means I'm up first. Anything in particular you want to know?"

She considers for a second, and then draws a finger over my forearm. The contact lasts for one, two, three seconds, and it makes my jeans feel impossibly tight.

"How many tattoos do you have?"

"In all?" I think for a moment. "Maybe fourteen? Fifteen? My friend Rook is a tattoo artist, and I let him practice on me when he was first starting out."

Her eyes linger on my forearm, and I'm about to lift it up to give her a better look when Avery guesses her alcohol correctly. A few people cheer and a few others groan when she reveals a bottle of vodka.

There's a group of shot glasses in the center of the coffee table, and each of us reaches out to take one. Avery twists open her bottle, and we pass it around the circle, each pouring a little out. I pour mine first, then Kalli's when she holds her glass out to me.

Lennox laughs and drums her hands against her thighs in anticipation.

"I don't know how she's coherent right now," Kalli whispers. "She's been drinking since I came over earlier this afternoon to help her cook."

I look at my own glass, not exactly eager to start mixing beer and liquor. But at least I'll get a little information out of Kalli for it.

"You like to cook?"

"I guess so. It's relaxing, I think." Maybe that's why she was in the kitchen when I came here. A sanctuary of sorts.

Once everyone has his or her vodka poured, Lennox holds hers up in a toast. "Merry freaking Christmas, friends!"

A few people clink their glasses together, and I touch mine to Kalli's. I keep eye contact for a long as I can, and then both of us throw it back. It's definitely not smooth, and I squint while the burn settles in my chest. Kalli doesn't even bat an eye.

"Damn. Somebody is a pro."

She shrugs. "I've had some practice."

"That doesn't count for your thing. I want to know something I can't figure out by watching you." Because God knows I'm going to be doing that all night.

She catches her bottom lip between her teeth and holds it there while she thinks. When she lets it go, it's a dark red. It reminds me of the inside of a plum, and shit…I should just not compare her mouth to fruit. The thought of kissing her is already on repeat in my head, and that's doing nothing to make it slow down. It's this steady thrum in my ears, a not-so-gentle urging to touch her, and I've never felt this dangerously close to losing control of my own impulses.

"I…I don't know what to tell you."

"What do you like to do for fun?"

She shrugs. "Come on. Give me something. You into reading? Movies? Dancing?"

"I told you I like cooking."

"Doesn't count. That was before I actually took the drink. Give me something else."

"I used to like poetry." Used to? How is it that I can never get a straight answer out of this girl? Over anything. Hell, I could probably ask her favorite color, and she wouldn't give me a real answer. "Your turn," she prompts before I have a chance to dig deeper. "That night in your bathroom…"

"I like where this is going. Does this mean you're officially jumping ship for the winning side?"

She doesn't even acknowledge my flirty tone. "You said…you said that everything changed. That you couldn't do what you wanted anymore. I want to know what changed."

Damn. Right for the kill shot. I'm saved from trying to figure out how to talk about my dad without ruining the whole night when Lennox asks, "Who's got number four? Number four?"

I look down at my slip at the same time that she says, "Wilder? Are you fourth?"

"Yeah. That's me."

I stand and shoot a quick look to Kalli. Her brows are pinched as she watches me, and I buy myself some time with a smile. I look over the remaining presents. They're all wrapped in paper, so there's no chance of peeking inside a gift bag. I pick one of the bigger ones, and return to my seat. Kalli shifts beside me, turning on her hip, and this time it's her arm across the couch behind us. I run my hands over the outside of the gift, feeling for the shape of the bottle beneath it. It's heavy, definitely glass not plastic. It's shaped like an old-fashioned decanter with rectangular cork style top. I smile. "What if I can guess the brand too? Will everyone else have to drink twice?"

Everyone looks wary but Lennox. "Oh come on, people. Have you ever been in a liquor store? Do you know how many different brands there are? He's not going to get it. And even if he does, it's two shots. You'll live."

"Not all of us can consume alcohol like it's water," Avery says.

"I'd like to keep my liver for a few more years at least," Jack quips. Avery laughs, and I'm way too pleased to not hear Kalli do the same.

"I'll do two shots if I'm wrong," I offer.

"Three," Kalli replies. "If you're so sure."

I laugh, and she gives me this challenging look that goes straight to my dick. She could have told me to climb one of the skyscrapers downtown, and I would have tried for that look. "Sure I'll do three."

One by one, the rest of the room agrees, and I say, "It's 1800 tequila."

One of the girls whose name I can't keep track of groans, and I'm guessing it was hers. I peel away the paper, and the familiar top of the bottle comes into view. One more tug and the rest of the paper gives way, revealing that I'm right. Someone drops the f-bomb right before Lennox gives a maniacal laugh.

"How did you know?" Kalli asks.

I shrug. "I've had a lot of tequila in my life?" Most of that I blame on Rook. "Plus, the cork on this one doubles as a shot glass. It's come in handy a few times."

I twist and pull the top until it comes loose. "Who's ready to do shots of tequila?"

Avery actually looks sick at the thought. "Do we have limes or something?"

"I don't think we have any," Lennox answers.

"Chaser break?" Mick offers. "Go raid the fridge if you need something to wash it down."

I place the bottle down on the coffee table and lean back into the couch. I can feel the pressure of Kalli's arm behind me, and she's still sitting on her hip, tilted toward me. For the first time all night, I'm able to resist looking at her as people evacuate to the kitchen, but that's just because I know what will happen after I look at her. I see Mick walk to the kitchen out the corner of my eye, and Lennox follows close behind. In a matter of moments, it's just Jack and us in the living room.

Kalli stays close by my side even though the rest of the couch is open. Jack glares at me for a moment before he, too, stands and goes into the kitchen. She slides away just an inch, and for just a moment, I think I feel her touch the collar of my shirt. But it's gone before I can be certain.

"What changed?" she asks.

I sigh. "This isn't exactly normal get-to-know you talk."

"I thought we ruled out normal."

I look at her, and for a moment I get lost in her face. The high arch of her cheekbones and impossibly long eyelashes and perfectly symmetrical features—she's stunning. Absolutely stunning, and I keep thinking I'll get used to it. That it will stop twisting my insides with want eventually, but I kind of hope it doesn't. I hope she always makes me feel this way. Because it makes me willing to do some crazy shit. Like come to a party full of strangers and put myself on the line and tell her about my dad. And I just don't talk about that shit. Not with Rook or Owen or Bridget. Not with anyone.

"About a year ago my father was convicted of fraud and embezzlement. He was sentenced to forty-five years in prison, and my mom lost her house, her car, any asset that had my dad's name on it, which was pretty much everything. We knew it was coming. The evidence against him was pretty damning. It was just a matter of how long and how much he'd owe in restitution. I came home a few months before the conviction. I applied to school, and a family friend helped get me into the business program last minute. I got a normal job in an office and started saving money for the inevitable. So yeah, everything changed. I had to step up. It was time for me to quit messing around and be a real, productive member of society and all that shit."

When I finish, the living room is silent, filled only with the echoing conversations happening in the kitchen. I rub the palm of my left hand over the knuckles on my right, and glance at the Atlas tattoo that she'd been fascinated with. Rook and I had been about halfway through with my sleeve when I changed my mind and told him I wanted that on my forearm instead of our original idea. He'd reworked the design to fit in the mythic figure.

I'd been regretting it for a while by the time Kalli had pointed it out that night. It was back when I'd first returned home, and I was wrestling with bitterness over what Dad had done and what I'd chosen to do because of it. Then I got more comfortable around Gwen. I saw the toll that it was taking on Mom. I got used to not being in the bars night after night. And I didn't miss it as much as I thought I would. I missed parts of it sure. My friends. The freedom. The fun. But worse than the thought of losing that was the feeling every time I looked at my arm and remembered that there had been a point when I'd considered my family a burden. A punishment. Gotta love feeling like a selfish bastard every time you catch sight of your own arm.

When Kalli had told me, all matter of fact, that it wasn't the world that Atlas held up, but the heavens…she'd changed the tattoo for me. When I'd woken up the next morning, the first thing I did after searching the house and coming up empty was to jump on the Internet and see if she was right.

She was.

Not that I'd expected anything different. By that point she was already taking on mythic proportions of her own in my head. Now, I could look at that tattoo and see not a burden, but a responsibility. The ink held strength instead of bitterness.

I lift my head and finally meet Kalli's gaze. She's as close as she can possibly be without touching me, and I wonder how that sliver of space between us can feel so small and so big at the same time.

"I'm sorry," she says.

I shake my head. "Don't. No one should feel sorry for me. I spent a lot of years being a spoiled prick. And I've still got it a lot better than most."

She toes off the ankle boots she's wearing and pulls her socked feet up underneath her on the couch. Then she leans on the arm she has perched on the back of the couch, her cheek resting in her hand. She's still not touching me, but she feels closer. If we both happened to breathe in at the same time, we'd make contact.

She says, "There's this funny thing about empathy. It's not actually in limited supply. Just because other people have it worse doesn't mean you don't deserve to be understood. To feel comfort."

"Says the girl who took only one night of comfort for herself."

"If you had any idea how big a step that was for me…"

"I don't have any idea. Why don't you explain it to me?"

She lifts her head from her hand, her fingers trailing down her cheek. But just as I start to hope, her expression goes blank, and she draws that hand in a fist to lean against. And I know…she's not going to tell me anything.

Still careful to keep our bodies separated, she bends toward me and places a chaste kiss against my cheek. It's light, so damn light, but I swear I can feel the exact texture of her lips. The bow at the top and the tiny grooves that form when her lips pucker. It should feel good to have her lips against me, but instead it's torture. Not just because I want more. But because everything about this kiss feels like an apology, the metaphorical 'but' before everything goes to hell. A goodbye.

Then she's pulling back and climbing to her feet.

"I'm going to go get my own chaser."

She walks to the kitchen without looking back, and the words come to me then, as fresh and easy as if I hadn't been quelling the urge for nearly a year. I picture the stroke of my pen on the page, the messy script as I always hurried to scrawl the words down before they left my head. The notes I occasionally drew in above, already imagining how it would sound against the strum of my guitar.

I need a chaser for you, babe.
Something to take the sting away
I'm trying not to chase you, babe.
But my heart wants its own say

No. That's not quite right. *Its own way?* Maybe…*But my heart just won't obey.*

I'm still thinking over options, cycling through rhymes in my head for a song I'll never let myself finish when the party returns to the living room. And in a gesture that no one misses, Kalli sits on the floor on the other side of the coffee table. She's in the open space between the girls with names I can't remember and Avery and Jack. Carefully alone, just like she prefers.

As everyone pours out their two shots, I pour two of my own even though I technically won. Because suddenly, I understand exactly why Lennox wants to be drunk on Christmas.

I need a chaser for you, babe.
Something to ease the sting I feel.
I wish I didn't have to chase you, babe.
But you're a burn that just won't heal.

Chapter Fourteen

"Merry Mustache!" Lennox and I scream at the same time. She jumps up from her spot on the couch, hands on her hips. I follow, and when she's left looking up at me, she climbs up onto her seat cushion so that she's higher.

"I said it first," she says.

"I'm pretty sure we said it at the same time."

"So what now?"

We look at each other, and I'm grateful when her eyes don't flick to Kalli. She'd given me one sympathetic look about four shots ago, but since then she's been my partner in crime, in complete lack of sobriety. Our eyes bore into each other, and somehow we come to a nonverbal agreement.

"Everybody drinks," I say.

"Yep." She ends the word with a particularly forceful *p*. I finished my beer a while ago, but rather than getting another and continuing to mix beer and liquor, I decided to embrace the inevitability of getting completely shit-faced.

I pour us both a shot of tequila, and we cheers before we tip them back.

We're not the only ones trashed. Mick was already quiet, so nobody noticed he had passed out until it was his turn to pick his Secret Santa gift. Lennox had tried to wake him, but the dude was gone. So, Lennox chose his gift for him. Then she got right in his face and said different types of alcohol until he finally groaned and tried to push her away after a particularly loud and drawn out, "Whiskey." We took that as indication of his guess, and miraculously, his present was indeed whiskey.

That shot was the last straw for one of the you-have-a-name-and-I'm-a-dick-for-not-remembering girls. She convinced one of her other friends to head home, but the third stayed to flirt with one of the preppy dudes. Whose names I have also forgotten. I'm apparently an equal opportunity name forgetter.

I've been avoiding looking at Kalli. Because the more I drink, the more likely I am to do something stupid at the sight of her. Like leap over the coffee table, throw her over my shoulder and drag her into the kitchen where I can pay her back for that kiss on the cheek. I could fight those walls of hers. Press my body to hers. Whisper the things I want to do in her ear. I could make her change her mind.

But just because I could do it, doesn't mean I should. For one, I'd feel like an asshole (though likely only up until the moment she gave in, then I'd just be thinking about her, how fast I could get her alone). And more than likely, it would end exactly the same way our first encounter had. Her gone, and me wanting to bang my head into the wall to relieve the ache of pent-up want.

Jack has gradually moved closer to her, inching his chair forward every once and a while in a ploy to get closer to the table, but I know it's about her. Because it's probably what I would do, too. I'm tapping my fingers against my knee to keep myself from tensing up in frustration, and eventually I find myself tapping out the same beat again and again. It's the rhythm to go with the words I'd thought of earlier.

This drunk, with my mind full of Kalli, I don't think about all the promises I'd made to myself to let go of the music. I'd made a choice when we I came back to Austin, cutting short the band's tour last summer. The gang had all been really cool about it. No one threw a fit that I'd ruined our summer plans. Rook went back to the tattoo parlor early. Owen took the opportunity to catch up on partying. And Bridget…well, that's when things had started with us. In the beginning, I tried to juggle it all. We played a few local gigs, bars where we'd gotten our start a few years prior. But there was a reason we had organized the summer tour. We were bored with playing the same old places, tired of feeling like we weren't going anywhere.

Then things got busy. I was jumping through hoops to get into the business program last minute. Mom needed help. There was all the shit with the lawyers and getting ready for Dad's trial. I had to skip a gig here and there, and though Owen and Bridget could both sing, they weren't used to singing lead, and neither of them really cared for it. Then they weren't so cool about it (not that I blame them). A few blow up fights later, and I decided that I had to cut myself off. It wasn't possible to keep the music and become the man I needed to be for Mom and Gwen. I'd come home. I'd made the decision to be here, and I had to see it through.

So, I quit the band completely. That was around the time that Bridget got particularly difficult, too, so I welcomed the break. But I learned fast that quitting the band in name only wasn't enough. When I wrote in my spare time or played the guitar for Gwen, I could feel the bitterness creeping in, whispering that I'd given up too much.

By the time Dad was convicted, I'd forced myself to make a clean break. I am no longer Wilder the musician. I'm the Wilder who goes to school and works part-time at an accounting firm. I'm the Wilder who's going to get a good, well-paying job and take care of his family. I'm the Wilder who's determined to prove that I have more integrity than my father.

I can't be the Wilder who writes music anymore, even if that music is about the most fascinating girl I've ever met.

But still, my finger taps on. And I let it.

Finally, it's Kalli's turn to pick her present, and I have an excuse to watch her, to drink her in. She bends to choose the last remaining gift, and her curves are burned into my brain. Lush and round, I know what it feels like to have my hands on her thighs, her ass, but that doesn't make the itch to touch her any less maddening.

She settles back onto floor, and just as she's about to tear away the wrapping paper, my phone starts ringing. The song is a familiar tune, heavy on the drums. The kind of alternative rock I used to enjoy playing myself. I drag my hands over my pockets, but I don't feel my cell. Confused, I stand, searching again as the song carries on.

"Try your jacket." It's Kalli who says it, and when I look over at her, the phone goes quiet. My phone had been in my jacket pocket that night downtown. She'd been wearing my jacket, and she'd looked so damn good in it.

My phone starts ringing again, snapping me into action, and I grab my jacket, fumbling clumsily through the pockets until I get lucky.

Vibrating in my hand, the phone reads *Mom*, and my stomach sinks. As I hit answer, I step over piles of used wrapping paper, weave drunkenly around the coffee table, and head for the kitchen. "Mom?"

I plug my other ear with my finger to block out the noise of the TV as I step out of the room. I can only pray I don't sound too drunk as I ask, "Mom, is everything okay?"

There's a beat of silence on the other end, and I start to panic.

"I'm sorry to do this, honey. I know I told you to go to the party and have fun with your friends, but…"

"What's the matter? Did something happen?"

"Everything is fine. But the hospital called. They had two nurses call in sick, and they asked me to come in. I would say no, but because it's the holiday, it's time and a half."

Shit. I nod for a few seconds before it occurs to me that she can't actually hear that. "Sure. Of course. You should do it. I'll —" What will I do? She can't go unless I can stay with Gwen, but I can't drive home. Not like this. I'll just have to call a cab. I'll figure out how to get my car back tomorrow. "I'll get there as soon as I can, okay?"

There's another extended silence before Mom answers, "I'm sorry, Wilder. I really am."

"Don't be. I was getting ready to call it a night anyway." Not entirely true. But I'm probably better off this way anyway. No sense torturing myself being so close to Kalli and being unable to actually have her. I've been enough of a masochist for one night. "See you in a bit."

I hang up the phone, and shake my head. I take a deep breath and try to gauge how drunk I am. The room seems to move slower than the shaking of my head, and *yep*. Definitely drunk.

I sigh and walk back into the living room.

"What's up, Dazzler?" Lennox asks.

I hold up my phone and say, "I've got to go actually." I glance at the time; it's just after midnight. I wonder how long it will take for a cab to get here once I call.

"What happened?" Kalli asks, and my stomach tightens at her interest. Our eyes meet, and I have to struggle to remember that she's the one who keeps pulling back.

"My mom got called into work and needs me to watch my little sister."

I cross to the couch and pick up my jacket, checking my pocket to make sure I've still got my keys.

"You can't drive," Kalli says. I bristle a little, annoyed that she gets to pick and choose when she's interested in me.

"I'm not planning on it. I'm calling a cab."

I pull up the Internet on my phone to search for a cab company when Kalli says, "I can take you."

I frown. I mean…don't get me wrong. I like the idea of leaving with her, but I just don't get why. This girl twists my head around so good, that I'm surprised it hasn't popped off yet.

"You've had nearly as much to drink as I have."

She shakes her head. "I'm fine. I'm not drunk."

I raise an eyebrow. "That again?" Unbidden, my eyes drop to her socked feet, and her lips quirk in a smile.

"It's just as true this time as it was last time." She climbs to her feet, and starts heading toward me. The closer she gets, the harder my heart beats, like it's trying to leap right out of my chest to get to her. She slips past me and bends down to get her boots. Right in front of me. Her perfect ass is just there, and I really don't have the willpower right now not to look.

"I don't think that's a good idea," Jack cuts in, standing from his chair. "Just let the guy take a cab."

"Really, Jack, I'm fine."

Still standing, she lifts a foot to slip on her boot. She teeters a little, and I grab hold of her elbow to steady her. As much as I hate to admit it…"Maybe Jack is right."

"That wasn't because I'm drunk. That was because I'm standing on one foot trying to put on a shoe. I promise that I am one hundred percent okay to drive. I don't feel the slightest bit drunk."

She does *seem* sober. She stands with her hands on her hips, looking up at me, and her eyes are clear, focused. I'd been determinedly not watching her for the last hour or so. Maybe she'd been cutting back, and I hadn't noticed.

"'Touch your finger to your nose," I say.

She rolls her eyes, but does it.

"Now switch and touch it with the other finger…now switch back and forth."

"Is this really a thing?" she asks between touches.

"Faster."

She scowls, but obliges, her eyes boring into mine as she alternates touching her nose with her right and then left hand again and again. She never misses a beat, her movements perfectly in control.

"Are you even human?" I ask. She stiffens and stops touching her nose. "You must have an incredibly high alcohol tolerance. Or lightning fast metabolism."

"Something like that."

I take in her face. There's no hesitation. She doesn't seem like she'd be doing this out of pity or for some other reason I can't pinpoint. "Sure. Okay. If you don't mind, a ride would be great."

She nods and turns toward the door. I give Lennox a quick nod, and then a silent wave for the rest of the room. "Thanks for inviting me, Len. I had fun."

"No problem, Dazzler. You're welcome back anytime."

I glance at Kalli to gauge her reaction to that, but her back is to me. I take a few steps toward the door, catching up with her, and rest a hand on her back. I'm about to murmur a thank you, but her steps falter and she sucks in a breath. "You okay?"

She steps sideways, sliding away from my touch, and adds, "Um…give me just one second before we leave."

I drop my hand to my side, and her gaze scans the room. She's looking for something, but I'm not sure she knows what it is. She skips past a sleeping Mick, and Lennox, and the other girls. Finally her eyes land on Jack, and he's staring right back at her, still standing from when he'd protested earlier.

She squares her shoulders, and moves toward him, and for a moment I'm entranced by the sway of her hips. I'd enjoy the sight a lot more if she weren't moving away from me and toward him. I can't hear what they're saying as they talk, but he's got his head bent low toward hers, and they're entirely too close for casual conversation. I watch them, and I swear my spine feels like steel and my skin actually starts to itch with impatience as their conversation stretches on. This isn't some simple goodbye or a quick word. They're having a full-fledged discussion, and when Kalli reaches out and lays a hand on his arm, I have to close my eyes to keep my cool.

Once again, she's driving me fucking crazy with her mixed signals. She volunteers out of nowhere to take me home, and I think…*maybe*…but damn it. She's still touching him, and I skip from impatient to furious in seconds. I *get* that she's got issues. I've not exactly been looking to date anyone since the disaster that was Hurricane Bridget. But I don't get the back and forth, and I don't have fucking time for these kinds of games. Not even for her.

She's still touching his arm, nodding as he talks, occasionally opening her mouth to reply. Then he smiles, slows down, and lifts a strand of hair from her shoulder. And that's the last straw for me. I grip the doorknob and haul the front door open.

"I'll be outside," I say to the room in general, and then I bolt. My feet pound against the creaky stairs on my way down, and I'm sure I'm waking up everyone who lives below Lennox.

You twist me up, twist me up so good
I should cut you loose, slip off the noose
But with you, it's a lot of should and would
And I'd sure as hell quit if I thought I could

Goddamn it. I can't get away from her, not even in my head. And even though I know it's wrong, that I'm going to regret letting myself think about the music later, I don't try to shut it off. Because I might not have had her back in that apartment, but in the music, I don't have to share her with anyone else.

"Wilder!"

Her voice carries from up above me, clear and almost crooning. I don't stop, continuing my way down the stairs until they give way to the sidewalk, and I can march out into the parking lot where it finally feels like I have a bit of distance.

I can hear her booted feet tapping against the stairs as she follows, and I swear to God, they almost match the rhythm I'd envisioned for the song. That's when I know I'm either a lot drunker than I thought or going crazy.

"Wilder, hold on."

I slump against the bumper of my SUV, and blow out a breath. The temperature has dipped since I went inside, and my breath frosts in front of my face.

"Hey." I don't look, but I can tell from the sound that she's down to the parking lot now, heading my way. "Sorry about that. I told Jack that we could talk about a project he's working on, and I didn't want to leave before we got to chat."

"You get that I'm kind of in a hurry, right?" There's an uneasiness in my gut from snapping at her, but I'm too riled up to pull myself back. "No one asked you to drive me home. If you want to stay and talk to Jack, go ahead. I said I can get a cab."

She frowns, and wraps her arms around her middle to fend off the cold. Or to fend off me, maybe.

"I don't want to stay and talk to Jack."

And here we go ahead. The Kalli merry-go-round.

"Fan-fucking-tastic. Let's go then."

Her eyebrows draw into a troubled line, and *damn it*, why can't I stop noticing this shit? I don't want to analyze every expression she makes or the silences between her words or what it means that she starts toward me, but then stops. I want to be as indifferent as she is.

She points a key to my right and says, "My car is this way."

I shove my fists into my pockets, and follow her. She stops at a small, dark sedan. It's nice, but not too nice either. A recent model, but nothing too expensive. It's carefully inconspicuous, and wouldn't stand out on campus or downtown or even in this rougher part of town. That reminds me of my earlier worries, and before I can remember that I'm angry, I ask, "How often do you come here to Lennox's?"

She shrugs. "I told you that I haven't known her long. So just a few times. Mostly, I meet her at the store when she's not busy or at the studio they have on campus for people in her department."

"Good. You shouldn't be in this neighborhood alone."

"You know, I'm not as vulnerable as you think I am."

"Well, if your alcohol tolerance is any indication, maybe you're right. How often do you drink to get to that point?"

"Now you're mad at me for drinking?"

No. Yes. Damn it.

She continues, "I'm not some naïve sorority girl. I've been through a lot on my own, and I've come out just fine."

"Yeah, I can tell how much you like being on your own."

I'm being a dick, and I hate myself for it, but I just can't shut my mouth off.

She tugs her car door open a little forcefully and climbs in without another word. I hesitate, wondering if this is a bad idea after all. But Mom is waiting, so I pull open my door and slide in, too.

I tell her where to go, but other than that the cab is quiet and stiff as she heads back to the highway. I tell her to head north and what exit to watch for, and then we settle into silence.

She's tapping her finger on the steering wheel, and again, it's almost the right beat. I don't know whether I want to yell at her to stop or show her how to beat out the actual rhythm. I lean my head back against the seat, and try to just shut everything out.

And almost like she knows it, she wedges open the door that I'm trying to close. "I'm sorry I stopped to talk to Jack. It didn't mean anything. I can't explain it, but it was important that I...*talk* to him. But I'm here now. Here with you."

With my eyes still closed, I mutter, "For now anyway."

PART THREE

"Love is composed of single soul inhabiting two bodies."
Aristotle

Chapter Fifteen
Kalli

His anger shouldn't sting so much. In fact, I should embrace it. Angry Wilder is much better than charming Wilder or sexy Wilder or sweet Wilder. Because all of those versions of him are incredibly hard to resist.

And I'm *supposed* to resist him, right? I have to.

Except that I'd gone to talk to Jack about his new project so that I could push a little inspiration into him to take the edge off in case *something* happened with Wilder. In case my impulsive decision to give him a ride home turned into something else impulsive. Though I doubt I can still call it that when I've planned ahead.

That now appears to be a non-issue. He's furious. And I don't blame him. I know I'm not being fair. Fair would have been me sticking to my original plan and never seeing him again after that night at his place. Or better yet, never going home with him in the first place. But then he'd shown up at the store, and then again tonight, and a little voice whispered in the back of my mind, "Why not?"

After everything with Van, I couldn't bring myself to just find another guy. I tried with Jack, but every time he showed the slightest romantic interest in me, I panicked. What if he ended up like Van? What if I broke him too?

So when he'd introduced me to Lennox, and she'd immediately begun to integrate me into their group of friends,

I'd decided to try something different. By spreading out my ability between Jack and Lennox and Mick and all the rest, I could stay longer. I could move slower. Usually, depending on the artist, I can go anywhere from three to nine months with someone one-on-one. But like this...the possibilities are greater than I'll ever let myself say out loud.

That doesn't stop me from getting my hopes up though.

Which is why I currently have a death grip on my steering wheel while I attempt to ignore the near painful pull toward the man sitting in the car beside me. Because the moment I realized what my friendship with this group meant, I thought of Wilder. I thought of what this kind of longevity could mean where he was concerned. Not only could I stay here in Austin longer, but with so many *friends*, I'd be unlikely to ever cut it as close as I did with Van. And since there wouldn't be any more break-ups like the past, there's even a possibility for expansion. There were two girls tonight from Lennox's program that I've not met before. Jack has a few painter friends. There's a welder that does metal work with Mick sometimes. If my circle became big enough...

There are tears in my eyes, and I'm struggling to breathe through the excitement and fear and anticipation when Wilder says, "You need to get over or you're going to miss the exit."

And just like that...I'm shot back down to Earth.

I turn my blinker on, and let him direct me through the next few turns until we end up in a residential neighborhood. The truth is...I don't know the first thing about being in a real relationship. Every guy I've ever dated (if you can even call it that) came with an expiration date. They were a job. That's how I had to think of them to keep from getting attached or feeling guilty or letting it all go to my head. Fact is...there are teenagers out there with more experience living and loving than me.

And that might be the most depressing thought I've had in ages (literally...*ages*).

I clear my throat. "So...what did you think of everyone?"

Wilder's eyes flick to me briefly, but he still doesn't turn to face me. "I like Lennox."

"Because she's on your side?"

He does look at me then, but it's a look so dark and filled with frustration that it cracks something in me. I'm not sure I've ever been given a look quite like that before. Even the artists who grew to hate me after I ended things had looked at me with a obsessive passion that didn't know whether it was hate or love and tended to hover somewhere in between.

Wilder doesn't look at me with *hate*, per say. But he very clearly wants to be done with me. There is anger and annoyance and possibly a little hurt in that look. But he isn't addicted to my energy the way men have been in my past. And perhaps without my ability, I'm not quite as desirable as I've always believed.

"Slow down. It's up here on the right."

I do as he says, even though I feel like I'm shedding layers of my long dormant heart every time I hear the flatness of his voice that used to be so warm and low.

The apartment complex he has me pull into is reminiscent of row houses, but these are boxier, plainer—the knock-off version designed only with cost in mind. He directs me to the third cluster of buildings, and I pull straight into an open parking space right in front of the curb. His seatbelt is undone before I even get the car in park. Then his door is open, and he's unfolding his long legs, and he's disappearing.

I've never allowed regret a foothold in my life. There's no point, not when you live as long as I do. If you miss out on something in one century, you'll catch it the next time history decides on a replay. Forever means unlimited opportunities to get things right.

But now I can taste the regret, clogging up my lungs and lining my throat. I'm very nearly choking on it because this, *Wilder*, is not something that history will ever repeat. It's now or it's *never*.

"Thanks for the ride, Kalli."

The whole car shudders with the thud of his door closing, and his strides up the sidewalk toward the house on the far right are quick, one step down from a jog.

Before I can think about it long enough to weigh the pros and cons, I turn off the car and bolt after him. I run. I've never in my existence ran after anything. There was never that kind of urgency. Generally, if I'm running, I'm running away. Maybe it's the invisible cord around me buzzing with approval, but it feels right that Wilder should be the one that changes that.

"Wait. Wilder, wait!"

He's ascending the small flight of stairs to the front porch by the time I catch up to him. He turns, and I slow as I climb those last few steps. Time gets away from me then, making a mockery of all my thoughts of it being my constant. The seconds skip like a scratched record, and my heart jerks just as unpredictably in my chest. I take the one final step to put me beside him on the porch. There's a lantern suspended to the left of the door, and the glow reflects off his face, catching on his blond curls and turning them a reddish gold.

His expression is wary, but it's not as dark as it had been in the car. His hand is outstretched, paused in the act of reaching for the door handle, and I'm so terrified that he'll finish the movement and escape inside before I can put my thoughts into words that I step in front of him, blocking the way.

I take a breath, try to ignore the thunderstorm of emotions in my chest and say, "I'm sorry." When in doubt, apologize, right? "I know that you're angry."

His brows knit together, and that darkness is creeping back into his expression and his stance. I rush on to add, "I don't know how to say this. I don't know how to *do* any of this. But I—" Oh gods. There's no turning back after I say this. I'm at the ledge, and I either back away or leap over. There's no in between. My feet say jump. My knees and my hips and my belly and my breasts—they're all dying to move forward, to close the distance and reclaim that spot in his arms. But my head holds out.

Because this...*experiment* isn't just about me. He should have a say in this. But I can't explain, and even if I could, he wouldn't understand. If I'm wrong, if I'm unable to keep the two halves of my life separate...he'll be the one to pay the price.

"I—" The words won't come. They just won't. I look at him, lost and sorry and wanting, and then he takes the choice from me.

One large hand presses into my stomach, pushing me back against the outer glass door. The glass is cold even through the layers of clothes, but his hand is warm as it slips from my abdomen to my side. His body crowds mine, and I love the way he towers over me. The thread between us is nearly electric now, and it winds tighter and tighter as he moves closer. He plants a hand next to me on the door, and dips down enough that his forehead rests against mine. This close, our noses touch and our gazes collide, and I can feel his exhale on my lips.

I feel the urge to beg. For what...I don't even know. For something. For *him*.

"Yes or no, Kalli. You don't get it one moment at a time. Not anymore. I can't fucking take that. You're in or you're out."

I think *YES* so forcefully that it hurts. But my mouth remains stubborn. "First, you have to know that I'm not like other girls you've been with."

"Don't I fucking know it." His fingers fist at the back of my sweater, pulling it tight against my belly and lifting it just enough that the cool winter air nips at my waist.

"I mean it. There are things you don't know. I wasn't lying when I said that I'm not good for you. I'm really not. But I think I might be selfish enough not to care."

The hand at my back slides down until it rests just shy of the curve of my behind, and his other hand takes hold of my jaw. Tipping my head up, he drags a heavy thumb over my bottom lip. It stretches and pulls under his attention, and he touches my teeth, followed by the soft, wet inside of my lip.

"And I'm selfish enough to want you all to myself. This mouth…I want to be really fucking selfish with your mouth, Kalli. I want to kiss and lick and bite it. I want to feel it on my skin. I want *to use* it *and worship* it, and I want to do it a lot. Every day. Who knows if anyone is good for anyone else? There might be someone out there better for you than me, but I'm selfish enough to hope you never meet him. All we ever know is who we want, and I think you want me just as badly as I want you."

I tilt my chin up, my whole body straining forward to meet his. My underwear grows damp and my nipples tight—my body begging for more since my mouth took too long. Against his lips, I whisper, "Yes."

"Don't say that unless it's your answer for the whole thing. We're talking all or nothing, baby."

My eyes catch on the Atlas tattoo on his arm. And maybe it's a sign that I'm doing something worthy of punishment. But

I choose to think of it as a suggestion. If he can hold up the heavens, keep the worlds separate and safe, then I can keep the same distance between Kalliope the muse and Kalliope the woman.

"All," I answer. "I want it all."

Then his tongue is in my mouth, and he tastes like alcohol and heat and everything I never let myself want. His lean, hard arms wind around my middle, pulling me so far into him that I have to bow my back to keep our mouths connected. His legs are braced wide, and my own press tight between them so that I can feel him hard and heavy beneath the confines of his jeans. The contact sends a shudder through me, leaving me *honest to gods* weak in the knees.

I slide my hand over the nape of his neck, and up into his hair, and he groans into my mouth. I soak up the sound, overwhelmed with a frantic energy that can only be joy. Supreme, complete, life-altering joy. Every part of me is humming with it—my body as it remembers the shape of his, my mind as he eclipses every other thought, and the indefinable connection as it jumps and pulses between us like it carries a heartbeat of its own.

Fate. Destiny. Whatever it's called…I've never been so grateful for mine. And as I allow myself to admit that Wilder is part of that destiny, I feel a tear coast over my cheek.

"God," he murmurs against my mouth. "Kissing you is even better than I remember."

I laugh, positively giddy at his words. "Could be the alcohol."

"No, it's you. There's something about you. About us together…" he groans. "I don't have the words, and I hate that. I hate that I can't tell you exactly how beautiful you are or how good you feel because everything feels pale in comparison to the reality. If there are words that do it justice, I don't know them. But I swear I'll learn them, invent them if I have to."

I breathe in, and he pulls me closer. "Maybe we don't need the words. Maybe it's enough that we both know."

"Do we? You feel it, too?" His voice is ragged and raw, and the intensity in his eyes makes me shiver.

"I feel it."

With a growl, he claims my mouth again, pulling me in so tight that he lifts me up onto my toes. I bury my other hand in his hair, too, holding tight to him and this moment and a future that I'm suddenly terrified to lose. Wanting to be closer, needing to feel more of him, I wrap my legs around his waist. He slides one arm down from my waist to my bottom to brace me, and just as he leans me back into the front door, a brighter light washes over us from behind. A creaking noise tells me that the regular door behind the outer glass one has just opened. We're both reluctant to break the kiss, to end this moment, but when we do, I glance over my shoulder to see a middle-aged woman in scrubs. She's pretty and has Wilder's light hair and expressive eyes. With one hand on her hip, her eyes skim me briefly before settling on Wilder with a frown.

My head is still wrapped up in the chaotic excitement of giving in to our attraction, so it takes me a few seconds to remember than my legs are wrapped around his waist, and I immediately let them fall. He keeps his arm bracketed around my waist until my feet are back on the ground, and then he pulls away. His hand goes to the nape of his neck, and he gives a tentative smile.

"Hey Mom. I was just about to come inside." She makes a noise that sounds distinctly disbelieving and raises her eyebrows in response.

This can't be happening. I cannot meet his mother like this.

"This is Kalli. I'd had a few drinks so she gave me a ride home."

My eyes get stuck on a smudged handprint Wilder left on the glass, and I see her eyes track there too. Oh gods. It just keeps getting worse.

"Well." I clear my throat. "I should probably get going. It's nice to meet you, ma'am."

She smiles, and though it looks a little stiff, it seems genuine. "Nice to meet you, too."

Wilder grabs my hand, lacing our fingers together. "Don't leave yet. Stay."

My eyes widen, and my cheeks flush. He can't possibly think it's a good idea to bring me inside after *that*. Before I can devise an answer that will please him and prevent his mother from hating me, a high-pitched squeal distracts us all.

Gwen appears at her mother's side, two small hands pressing onto the glass door a few feet below the mark that Wilder and I left.

"Kalli! You're here. I asked Santa for you to come to Christmas, and you're here!"

"Well," Wilder's mother says, her expression unreadable. "It seems I'm the last to meet you, Kalli. Come on inside before I have a mutiny on my hands."

"Really, I don't want to intrude."

"Nonsense, Wilder could probably use some help getting Gwen settled down and back to sleep once I'm gone. She can be a handful." She says this with an almost vindictively sweet smile, and I can imagine that she thinks a few hours with a five-year-old will act as a deterrent to what she saw when she opened the door.

But all I can think about is that first day in the grocery store, how jealous I'd been of Wilder and his relationship with

Gwen. And I know I'm not just in danger of falling for him, but falling for all of it.

Him. His family. His life.

This is what it's like to crave something. To get addicted from one tiny taste.

Chapter Sixteen
Wilder

Probably not the brightest move, asking Kalli to stay after Mom caught me practically dry humping her against the front door. Okay, so there was no *practically* about it. But then again, I hadn't made a lot of bright moves tonight period.

Funny, though, how I don't regret any of them.

I open the door, and Gwen tumbles forward in her eagerness. I barely manage to throw out a hand and catch her before she falls over the threshold and onto the concrete porch.

"Easy, girl. Why don't you just step back so Kalli and I can come inside?"

She does, bouncing on her toes like it's broad daylight instead of the middle of the night. I wonder if she's just woken up or if she's been awake for a while. I start to ask Mom as I usher Kalli inside with a hand at her back, but the look she's wearing silences me.

I expected the awkwardness. It doesn't matter how old you get, it's still weird to make out with someone anywhere near your parents, let alone with them watching. I'm surprised by how upset she seems, angry even. She's quick to hide it when Kalli looks back at me over her shoulder.

"I really need to get going," Mom says. "But can I speak to you first? In the kitchen?"

Shit. That can't be good.

"Uh, sure. Kalli, you mind watching Gwen?"

She gives me a smile so sweet, so *brilliant* that I actually lose my train of thought. It just snaps and flies away into the void, and I'm left staring until my mother says, "Wilder? Kitchen."

"Right." I look back once more because I can't help it and say, "Gwen, don't maul Kalli too much. Or she might not come back."

"What's maul?" Gwen asks.

Mom mumbles, "Something your brother is a little too familiar with this evening."

Kalli blushes, and I steer Mom toward the kitchen before this situation can spiral any more out of control. There's a swinging door that separates the kitchen from the living room, and it's still swaying when Mom spins and focuses on me.

"God, Wilder, I can smell the alcohol on you from here."

And just like that, the high I'd been on since Kalli caught me outside on those steps vanishes, and all the alcohol in my stomach starts to feel like cement.

"I didn't think you were going to need me tonight."

Mom sighs, and digs her fingers into the hair at her temples, messing up her smooth ponytail. "I know. I'm sorry. You're right. It's just…your sister woke up when the hospital called. And I'm stressed. And I guess I've gotten used to the way things have been lately. It's been a while since you've gone out and done…" She trails off and makes a sweeping gesture that encompasses me and then flicks off in the direction of the living room. Kalli's direction, presumably.

I don't like how disappointed she sounds. The alcohol, I can live with. But I want her to like Kalli, because I plan on making this one stick around for a while.

Then maybe don't feel a girl up on your porch like a horny high school kid if you want to impress your mom, asshole.

I sigh and run a hand over my face. With my eyes closed, it hits me just how heavy and tired I feel.

"It's not what you think it is, Mom," I finally say. "This wasn't like the days with the band. I was at a friend's house. Everything was under control. And Kalli—"

"Yes, please explain who this girl is and how my daughter knows her. Tell me you're not taking Gwen around random women. I thought you knew better than that."

"Don't, Mom."

"The key word in that sentence is *Mom*. And because I'm your mother, you can't tell me not to be concerned with how your behavior affects your sister."

"You're acting like she's some girl I picked up off the street. She's not. I like her."

"Well, I'm certainly glad you at least like the girl you molested on my porch."

God. I'd forgotten how exhausting it could be to have a parent around. I'd moved out right after high school, started doing the music thing. It's been a while since I had to answer to anyone else for my actions, and it fucking chafes.

I take a deep breath, trying to order my thoughts. Because with this much alcohol in my system, saying the first thing that comes to my mind is *not* a good idea.

"Gwen and I ran into Kalli one day at the grocery store. Gwen was throwing one of her fits, and Kalli talked her down. Then we ran into her again when I took Gwen dress shopping. One of her friends works at the second hand shop. That's whose house I was at tonight actually. I know what it looked like out on the porch, but I swear…this is a good thing. You'll like her. Or I hope you will anyway, because I'm thinking she's going to be around a lot more."

Mom looks only slightly appeased by my explanation. "Fine. I trust you. And you're obviously old enough to make your own decisions. I shouldn't pry. But please...think about your sister before you do things like this. She's clearly already attached to this girl, and she's had enough upheaval in her life lately without you bringing people in and out of her life."

"I'm not doing that. I swear. This is..." I trail off because my gut wants me to protest and say how serious this is. But then I remind myself that I've probably not even spent twenty-four hours with Kalli when you add up all our time together. There's no way it should feel as serious as it does, especially considering I've never been the type to jump into a relationship, and even an hour ago I was convinced I needed to cut myself off from her completely.

"Well, like I said," Mom continues, "I trust you. Or I'm attempting to anyway. I need to head to the hospital. I don't mind if she stays for a while, but Wilder...your sister is in the house. And she's a light sleeper. I hope you'll be considerate and smart in my absence."

I'd be lying if I said that I wasn't dying to get my hands on Kalli again, but Mom is right. My mother's house isn't the best place for that. Because I have every intention of making my first time with Kalli so fucking memorable that she won't even think about running.

"Of course, Mom. I promise."

She purses her lips, and I can tell she's worried about leaving. I lean down and press a kiss to her forehead. She gives an exaggerated cough and waves a hand in front of her face, reminding me that I reek of alcohol. When our eyes meet again, we both laugh, and I say, "Any chance you already made some coffee?"

She lifts her chin in the direction of the countertop across the room and says, "In the pot."

I sigh and head that way. I hear the kitchen door swing open, so I assume she has left as I pour myself a mug. I turn to go ask Kalli if she wants one, only to find my mother standing in the open doorway, still staring at me.

"What's up, Mom?"

She shakes her head, blinking her eyes, as if she wasn't even aware that she'd been staring. "Nothing. Just…it's strange how life can change so very drastically, but somehow, underneath, it feels the same."

I'm still a little too drunk to parse out the meaning behind her words, so I just say, "Love you, Mom. Have a good shift."

"Sure. Thanks. And let's have dinner sometime soon. *All of us.*" She tilts her head back in the direction of the living room, where I can hear Gwen talking a mile a minute through the open door.

That's a lot. Dinner with the family. Kalli might have said she was in this out on the porch, but that doesn't mean I should throw her straight into the lion's den. I nod to appease Mom, and so that she can be on her way. I'll just postpone until things are more…stable.

I grab my mug, and follow her out. She stops to hug Gwen, but I don't even think my sister notices. Or at least she doesn't stop talking. Kalli smiles patiently as she talks, lifting her eyes momentarily to my mother, and I can read the unease in her expression.

Mom grabs her things, says her goodbyes, and heads out the door. Gwen pauses momentarily after the door thuds shut, and in the silent moment, my eyes meet Kalli's. There's a softness there that I think is a good sign, but other than that I can't tell what she's feeling.

"You want some coffee?" I ask.

She shakes her head. "No, I'm good. Thanks."

"Water? Soda? Food?"

"No, Wilder. I'm fine. I promise."

Okay then. I focus my attention on Gwen, who has pressed herself a little closer to Kalli's side. In a moment, she'll likely be sprawled across her lap if I don't do something.

"Okay squirt. Time for you to go back to bed. It's way too late for you."

Immediately, she starts to whine. "Can I stay up just a little while with you and Kalli? Please, please, please?" When I don't answer, she rises up on her knees on the couch and continues, "Please, please, please?"

"Gwen." I sigh. God, I'm so bad at saying no to her. I glance at Kalli, and she's holding in a laugh. " Do you mind?"

She shakes her head quickly. "Not at all."

"Okay. You can stay up a little while longer. But you have to sit on the couch and be calm. If you don't settle down, you'll never get back to sleep. How about I put on a movie and you can watch a little of that before bed?"

And that's how I end up watching Frozen, drunk, in the middle of the night with my little sister and the girl I'm infatuated with. Because once again…I don't know how to tell her no.

I start the Disney movie, and then flip the living room lights off. The hallway light keeps it from being too dark. I hit play on the DVD remote, and while the movie begins, I pop into the kitchen and empty the last of the coffee into my mug. I'm rinsing the pot out in the sink when I feel a hand low on my back. I turn, expecting it to be Gwen, but it's Kalli. Her hand lingers, and the visceral attraction I feel for her comes back with a vengeance. She says something, but my eyes are stuck on the movement of her lips, the way they curve and purse, the tiny peek of her tongue when she enunciates something.

And I have to kiss her. The urge comes on so strong that I don't have any time to stifle it. I curve my hand around her neck, and pull her forward, stopping her mouth mid-sentence. She laughs against my mouth, but when I coax her lips open with my tongue, she moans. Her fingers grapple against my chest, pulling the fabric into her fists.

The lightness in my head that came from the alcohol amplifies into something so buoyant, so electric that it doesn't feel real. It occurs to me then that I could be dreaming. Maybe Christmas hasn't even happened yet. Or maybe I passed out at Lennox's place, and this is my brain reacting to my own subconscious desires. My hesitation gives her the chance to break away.

With her hands still fisted in my shirt, she turns her head to the side, and laughs softly under her breath. Those few short chuckles give way to a long sigh, and she leans in until her forehead rests against my chest. I wonder if she can feel the way my heart is booming beneath her.

"Sorry," I murmur, my voice a low rumble. She loosens her grip, and then smoothes down the parts of my shirt she'd pulled on. Her hands run over my chest, and it sends a shock of need through my system. I know if I don't get us back into the living room with my sister, I'm going to lift her up on the kitchen counter, and get the taste I'm dying for. "What were you saying? I got a little distracted by your mouth."

She pulls back, tilting her head up to look at me through long lashes. "Your sister is cold. I was asking where I could find a blanket."

I graze my knuckles over her cheek, marveling at how soft her skin is. "I'll grab a couple. You go get comfortable." Before I let things get *too comfortable* in here.

She steps back, and I let my hand fall. She begins to turn, but then pauses. "I meant what I said outside. I am in this. But…" She swallows, and nerves knot in my throat, making it hard to swallow. "This is all new to me. And I want to do it right."

My hands itch to reach for her, but I think the distance she put between us is purposeful.

"I want to do it right, too."

She swallows, and stares down at the floor for a few moments before her gaze flicks back up to mine. She squares her shoulders like she's about to face off against an enemy and tilts her chin up bravely.

"I think we should take things slowly. It's not smart for me to just jump in head first. I know you said we couldn't do this one moment at a time, but I need us to take small steps, to do this at a more normal speed."

I do close the distance then, cupping her cheeks, and tilting her face up to mine. "That's not what I meant when I said that. I just needed to know where you stood, that was all. I needed to know you were willing to give this a shot. But there's no pressure here beyond that, I promise." Shit. Maybe I'd gone too far in the kitchen at Lennox's apartment. She was there, her skin under my hands, and I got carried away. Was it my own damn fault that she was so indecisive? She said she wasn't the kind of girl to do a one-nighter, but maybe that night was even farther out of her wheelhouse than I imagined. "You set the pace," I tell her. "As long as you're here, that's all I care about."

Her eyes flutter closed, lashes casting shadows on her cheeks, and she presses her face a little harder into my palm. We head back into the living room together, and Gwen has already zoned in on the movie, shutting out the rest of the world. I lay my coffee on the end table, and grab two blankets out of the hallway closet.

Back at the couch, I squeeze into the space between Kalli and the armrest, then start unfolding one of the blankets.

Before I even get it open, Gwen crawls over Kalli's lap, and shoves herself between us, so that she's resting partly on each of our laps. But that's not good enough. Wordlessly, she continues wiggling until Kalli laughs and inches over enough that my little sister plops down between us.

Gwen grabs my unfolded blanket, pulling it up and over her, and my eyes connect with Kalli's above her head. She's not laughing anymore, but I can still see it on her face. Her eyes are bright in the dim room, and I lay my arm across the back of the couch. Gwen is small enough that I can still wrap my arm around Kalli, even with her between us. And while my sister focuses back on the cartoon, we stay staring at each other.

And something happens in me. Bigger than the night we spent together, or our talk in the kitchen, or even than our moment on the porch. I don't know how to describe it except to say that it feels…simple. Like finally finding the right fit for a puzzle piece after spending too long trying to cram it into a space that wasn't quite right.

With the movie playing in the background, Gwen's cold feet tucked under my thigh, and my hand brushing through Kalli's silky soft hair, more music filters through my mind, underscoring the moment.

Is this how it feels to fall?
Not so complicated after all.

Chapter Seventeen
Kalli

Forty-five minutes into the movie, both brother and sister have fallen asleep. Gwen is slumped over into my lap, her feet stretched out over Wilder's thighs, and he's leaning into the armrest, his head dropped back against the cushions. I give in to the strange impulse to cry when I look at them, and in seconds my cheeks and neck are damp from flowing, silent tears.

I want to scold myself for being ridiculous. Or laugh at my absurd mind, but I can't. Not here. Not when it's dark and quiet, and I can feel Gwen breathe against me, and Wilder's hand still lays warm and heavy against the back of my neck, even in sleep.

I can't stop my tears because this…this simple moment is something I never would have let myself even dream of, and it's opening doors that have long been closed, and it aches in the best possible way to feel the dust being blown away.

This is what it's like to just be. To exist at the very pinnacle of the present. To exist not for another person or a purpose or because of some bigger plan by fate, but for my own fulfillment. When I held onto the inspiration, when I let it take me over, I'd thought *that* freeing. I remember thinking that I felt truly alive for the very first time. I was wrong. This. Here. On this lumpy couch, I know better than I ever have what it means to live.

I let them both sleep a little while longer, alternating between watching the movie and watching the siblings. Gwen's hair is lighter, finer, but it curls the same way Wilder's does. His other hand, the one not resting against my neck is strewn over one of Gwen's ankles. They've got the same skin color, only his is marked and decorated with black and colored ink.

Finally, I decide that Gwen is completely out, and that she'd be better off in her bed. Besides...I can't stay all night. Even if I want to, even if could spend days just soaking up what it feels like to be with them. I don't want his mother to come home and find me here. And if I'm honest, I don't know how safe it is. The energy in me is at low, definitely manageable levels. But it should be nearly non-existent after my last connection with Jack only hours ago. I don't know what it is, but something about Wilder calls not just to my heart and my spirit, but to my ability too. It rises faster when he's around. And before I know what that means, I shouldn't spend prolonged, unnecessary time with him.

Carefully, I slide an arm beneath Gwen's legs, and another around her shoulders. I maneuver her as gently as I can into my arms. She doesn't stir, and it takes all my core body strength to stand up smoothly. I kick off the blanket that clings to my feet, and walk her back through the hallway in the direction of where I think her room is. Luckily the first door I nudge open with my toe is definitely hers. Small pink twin bed in the middle. Toys and stuffed animals strewn about. Messy, slept-in sheets.

I lay her down as gently as I can, but it's hard to control the limp weight of her body, and I end up having to adjust her into a comfortable position. She must be exhausted because she stays sleeping through the entire thing. A lamp is on near her bed that I assume is her night light, and I leave it on just in case. Tucking the blankets up to her chin, I push a few blonde curls back from her face.

She's such a pretty little girl. Vibrant and enthusiastic, and I think I might love her already. Somewhere in the back of my mind, warning bells go off.

It's not smart to love mortals.

They're vulnerable and breakable, and they age and die. All things I knew going into this, but I hadn't expected my reaction to Wilder and his world would be this potent. If this is how I feel after one night, how will I feel in a week? A month?

Unease prickles along my spine, but when I make my way back into the living room and lay eyes on a sleeping Wilder, it's replaced by the shivering excitement he always seems to induce in me.

Even though I had planned to go, I find myself sitting down beside him again. The need to feel close to him is stifling, but I meant what I said to him in the kitchen. I can't just dive into something serious with him. The pull toward him is serious enough, to add in sex on top of that, especially when I'm still not sure how all of this is going to work…not a good idea. But it won't hurt to just lay beside him for a while, right? He's asleep. And I made my stand in the kitchen even though I was terrified of what he'd say.

Most of my relationships with artists have been about sex. It's the only truthful kind of intimacy I could ever have with them. And I've spent my entire existence knowing the worth of my beauty and my gift. I had been afraid that without my ability and without sex…I might not hold as much interest for Wilder.

Now I feel stupid for that niggling fear. When he'd held my face in his hands, and pinned me with his eyes…gods, he made me feel like the world revolved around me. Like I was the sun, and everything else existed in relation to me, depended on me.

Carefully, I slide a little closer, and without putting too much of my weight on him, I lean into the crook of his arm and rest my head between his heart and his shoulder. His scent and heat surrounds me, and I let myself fall a little deeper into him. His arm drops from the back of the couch, draping along my side and curling around my hip. I tense, and look up, but other than a slight shifting of his body, sinking farther into the cushions, he doesn't appear to be awake.

I stay for another hour, flirting with the edge of sleep in his arms, but when I find myself beginning to replay the night in my head again, I decide I've lingered long enough.

But he apparently isn't quite as out of it as his sister. He groans and shifts when I climb out from under his arm. While I slip my shoes back on, he blinks sleepily at me, looking almost confused.

"I have to go," I whisper. "Gwen is in bed. I'm sorry. I didn't mean to wake you."

The fog in his eyes clears, and he wipes a large hand over his face before standing. He wobbles slightly, so I assume he's still a little drunk. I would be too if my body didn't reset at midnight.

"You were just going to sneak out again?"

"I was going to leave you a note."

He crosses the gap between us, and his hand slides around my neck, pausing to rub a circle around my nape before tangling his fingers in my hair. His grip is claiming, possessive, but his nose nudging against mine is sweet and playful. "New rule. We never leave without a proper goodbye."

A smile sprawls unbidden across my mouth.

"And what does a proper goodbye involve?"

His nose rubs against mine again. "It involves me thanking you for spending time with me, and reminding you of why we should do it again soon."

He kisses me then, slow and still a little sleepy. His mouth moves against mine with a laziness that feels easy and gentle, and like an introduction to a new part of us. This is what it's like to touch with no endgame, no destination. This is a kiss that doesn't ask for anything, it just *is*. This kiss is closeness and comfort, and when it's over, I'm battling the same urge to cry that had gripped me when I watched him sleep.

Who would have thought that at my age, I could still experience a new kind of intimacy from a mere kiss? Something altogether different from everything I've ever experienced.

"Thank you," I whisper when he pulls away.

One corner of his mouth lifts in a devilish smile.

"I think you're confused. That kiss was *me* thanking *you*."

"I know. But still."

"Well, now I have to say you're welcome."

But instead of saying it, he kisses me again, his tongue sliding against mine with a little more force, a little more urgency. I have that falling sensation I sometimes get in dreams when he pulls away, and I stare at him for a few long moments before I remember that I'm supposed to be leaving.

"When can I see you again?" he asks as I shuffle toward the door.

My immediate response is to say tomorrow, but I stop myself. I should wait and see how I'm feeling tomorrow, where my energy levels are at.

"I'm not sure. How about you call me, and we'll figure something out."

I have to give him my number because he doesn't have it, and when I'm done rattling it off, I'm tempted to make another excuse to stay. But he yawns again, and I know I should let him get some sleep. I say a final goodbye and head out the door. He stays on the porch, arms crossed over his chest to fight off the cold, waiting until I get in my car and pull away.

You've got time, I tell myself, and resist looking back through the rearview mirror. Time to see him, time to figure out how this will work, time to explore the happy hum of the connection I feel between us. But in the back of my mind, I can't help but think that time is relative here. Wilder is human. Which means I've never been lower on time than I am right now.

∞

He calls the next day, and I make an excuse as to why I can't see him. It hurts, because all I want to do is find out where he is and run straight there. But I was right…my energy levels are higher than they should be. I should have been good for at least another day before needing to expend some of my influence, but there's a restless churning in my chest that tells me otherwise. Normally, I would probably be fine to go a little while longer, even with my energies this high. But what if I saw him again like this? What if the level spiked, and there was no one else around, no other option? What if I lost control again like I did in that club? What if Gwen was there when it happened?

I feel physically ill at the thought. No. I need to be smart. Safe.

I start a journal to chronicle my experience, trying to make sense of it. I can't very well write the truth of what I'm feeling where someone else could find it, so I settle on a number system.

Today is about a five on a scale from one to ten. It's manageable, but worse than I'm comfortable with. I wonder if it could be connected to time? I spent, let's see, about four hours yesterday, two to three of which contained a high level of exposure. But I...relieved some pressure...about halfway through that time. What number would I be at if I hadn't done that?

For now, I think I should cap myself at five hours. And go in as calm and close to zero as possible. That should keep me at a comfortable level.

He calls again the next day, but I haven't been able to get any time alone with anyone in Lennox's friend group. My friend group. Most of them work a day job on top of their craft or schoolwork, and they're working pretty heavily now since there's no school and the holidays are busy.

"I'm sorry," I murmur into the phone. More sorry than he could possibly know. "But I can't today either."

"Do you have to work?" he asks.

I consider telling him the truth, that I don't, but it would be nice to have a ready-made excuse for situations just like this one. Not because I want to lie to him, but I don't see any other way around it. A job would definitely be convenient, though I've not had much use for a real one in centuries. That's one benefit of immortality. It's easy to build up wealth when you've got centuries to do it, and when knick-knacks and other objects from your past are old enough to be worth millions to the right collector or museum. Every few decades, I start over as a new version of my self, new birth certificate and identity and all that jazz. And that new me is always the sole beneficiary of my wealth when the old me "dies."

"Yes, I have to work," I lie.

"Oh. Okay. Where do you work?"

Damn. *Damn.* Where can I say? It has to be somewhere that he can't actually drop by to see me. Or…where he can drop by and see me, but it's under my control.

"I work from home."

"Really? Doing what?"

"Uh, just some online stuff. Nothing all that interesting. But I'm pretty backed up because of the holidays, and I need to get it all done before the end of the calendar year."

"Online stuff? So you're some kind of tech genius?"

"Hardly."

"So, since you work from home, does that mean I can swing by sometime? Maybe distract you with a lunch break? Or a foot rub? Or maybe you get carpel tunnel?"

I laugh. He sounds so cute and eager on the line, and I wish I could see his face right now. I wonder if he's shaved yet, or if his facial hair would be even thicker than the last time I saw him. I wonder if he's wearing his glasses or if he's giving responsible Wilder a break.

"Not this time," I tell him, but I soften my tone and hope he can hear the smile in my voice. "I've got too much to do. But maybe soon. I'll see what I can do."

He sighs on the other end, and rather than letting him go like I should (especially considering how much *work* I supposedly have), I keep talking. "How are Gwen and your mother?"

"They're good. They've both asked about you actually."

"Really?" I'm a little frightened to know what his mother asked.

"Yeah. They'd both like to see you again, but I told them they'd have to wait. I want some time with just us before we have to watch another Disney movie with my sister."

"I don't mind Disney."

"Of course you don't. You're like a real life version of one of those princesses."

I scoff a laugh. "I'm not a princess."

"You look like one."

"I have eyes too large for my face and a waist disproportionate to the rest of my body?"

He chuckles, the sound low and deep on the other end.

"No, your eyes are the perfect size for your face, and I happen to *really like* your proportions."

I lean back against the pillows on my bed, and laugh. A little too loud. A little too eager to hear him keep talking.

"So I'm *not* a Disney princess."

"Maybe not. But you're definitely beautiful enough. And Gwen is just as obsessed with you as she is with *letting it go*."

"I like her too."

"I'm glad." He suddenly sounds serious. "I told you that she's a big part of my life now. She and my mom both. When classes start back up again, I won't have much free time left between those, work, and my family."

"Are you saying I might have to help babysit if I want to spend time with you?"

"Not always."

"I wouldn't mind. I like your family, Wilder. I like your life."

A beat of silence stretches between us and then he asks, "I know you said you're estranged from your sisters. But do you have any other family? Parents? Cousins? Aunts? Uncles?"

I've got a tremendous amount of family, really. I mean my sister muses are the closest ties by far, but all the gods are connected to each other in some way. But it's been a long time since I've seen any of them. The only ones who still walk the Earth are my sisters, the furies (who are also dependent on humanity to satisfy their need for justice and punishment), and the watchers, the sons of Argus.

I suppose the fates might still be here too, but they've never been the type to mingle with humanity. They were always isolated…from everyone and everything. There are descendents, too. But the bloodlines are so watered down now that there are unlikely to be any mortals out there with significant ties to deity. Oracles, perhaps, might be the rare exception. I've never met one myself, but I heard rumors of them long after the greater gods withdrew from the world.

"Kalli? Are you still there? I'm sorry. I didn't mean to pry."

"No…no, it's fine. I'm sorry. I got a little lost in my thoughts. And to answer your question…it's just me. I don't see any of my family anymore."

He's silent for a long time on the other end. Maybe waiting for me to say more. Or perhaps unsure of how to reply. Other people never are. They usually apologize or offer sympathies or attempt to pry. When Wilder does reply he only says, "I wish you were in my arms right now."

"Me too," I answer without thinking.

We stay on the line a little longer, not really saying anything. But I can hear him breathing on the other end, and it somehow helps with the emptiness I always feel when I think about my sisters. A part of me knows that we would have had to split up eventually, even if things with Mel hadn't gone so wrong. We couldn't have all lived and gone unnoticed together in the modern world. But that doesn't mean I don't miss them, that I don't feel the barely there tug of our intertwined fates behind the larger more vibrant thread that I'm currently feeling with Wilder.

"I should go," I finally say.

"Okay."

"Can I call you tonight? Before I go to bed?"

He pauses for a moment, and I imagine him smiling.

"I'd like that."

After we hang up, I text a few people in the group again, trying to see if anyone has any free time or is working on anything interesting. No one is available. I didn't text Jack yesterday since he was the last person I had contact with as a muse and I'm trying to space them out, but I'm desperate enough to see Wilder, that I text him anyway.

He replies almost immediately. He has tomorrow evening off. And he wants to know if I'd pose for him again.

I waver, knowing that Wilder probably wouldn't like the idea if his reaction to Jack on Christmas is any indication. But I don't have much of a choice. And besides…that was before we talked, before I made my decision. He knows now how I feel. And really, Jack isn't even remotely a threat to him. No one is.

I text him back, *yes*. And we make plans to meet the following evening at his apartment.

Chapter Eighteen
Wilder

Kalli calls late that night while I'm going through some files for work. I smile when I see her name on the caller ID, and I start packing up my work as I lift the phone to my ear.

"Hey you," I answer.

There's a long silence, enough that I pull the phone back to make sure I didn't accidentally hang up or lose the call.

"Kalli? Are you there?"

"I'm here. Sorry."

Her voice is soft. Warm. It reminds me of caramel for some unfathomable reason. Christ, this girl turns me into a total idiot.

"How did your work go?"

"Um. Okay. I've got some more that I need to do tomorrow, but I think I could take some time off the next day."

I run through my schedule in my head. That's a Monday, and I'm working through most of the day. And I think Mom has a night shift, so I'd have to be at her place that night to keep Gwen, but I could swing something in between.

"How about dinner?" I ask. "I could pick you up around six-thirty?"

"You got your car back okay?"

"Yeah. Mom took me by to grab it. So, six-thirty? We good?"

She hesitates again, and I wonder if she's trying to keep me away from her place. I don't have the slightest clue where she lives. "We could meet somewhere if that's easier?"

"Yeah. Yeah, that would be great."

"Any requests on where or what we eat?"

I can almost hear her shake her head on the other end. "How about you take me to one of your favorite places."

I rack my brain for a moment, but come up empty.

"I'm not sure any of the places I frequent are good first date material."

"I don't care. This hardly counts as a first date anyway. And I'd rather go somewhere that will teach me about you than a first-date-appropriate restaurant."

"Are you sure?"

"I'm sure. I don't want either of us to feel like we have to impress each other or be something we're not. I'd rather skip over all that posturing and just get straight to what matters."

God, this girl. I can tell already that I'm going to fall so damn hard for her. It's not a certainty I've ever felt before, and it freaks me out. But that doesn't change how inevitable it all feels. And I like the idea of us just getting to know each other for real. Normally, the first few weeks of dating someone are filled with dinners I can no longer afford and small talk carefully balanced so as to be interesting, but not tipping into dangerous zones. It's like walking a damn tight wire, trying to get to the other side where you figure out whether this is a person you'll actually want to be with when real life sets in.

I already know that I want her for more than a first date and a second and a tenth.

"I like you Kalli…" I trail off, realizing I don't even know her full name. "What's your last name?"

She hesitates again, and I have to fight a sigh. It's the only thing I don't like about her...that inability to open up without thinking about it first, weighing her options.

"Thomas," she finally says. "My name is Kalli Thomas."

It's not what I would have guessed for her. It seems too plain and ordinary for this girl that is anything but that.

"Well, Kalli Thomas. Tell me something I don't know about you."

She laughs. "That game again?"

"It's a good game."

"You start."

I sigh. One day, we'll get past that. "Fine. I'll reveal one of my biggest secrets to you."

"Oooh. A secret?"

"No one outside my family and my best friend Rook know this."

She perks up on the other end, her voice raising an octave as she says, "Tell me. *Tell me now.*"

"You promise not to judge me?"

"I am *so good* at being non-judgmental."

I leave the living room for my bedroom, and settle down on my mattress with a smile. "Okay. The secret is...I don't really like chocolate."

"*You don't like chocolate?* Who are you?"

I chuckle, and she continues, "No, seriously. *Who are you?* We've discussed my massive sweet tooth before. I'm not sure I can trust a person who doesn't like chocolate."

"I mean, I can eat it. It's not like it's awful. But I could take it or leave it."

She makes a noise on the other end somewhere between shock and horror.

"Is this our first fight as a couple?" I joke. "Over the merits of chocolate?"

A pause.

"*Are* we a couple?"

My smile stiffens and then drops completely. "We did say we were in this. Is that still the case?"

"No. It is. I just...wasn't sure what exactly that entailed."

I sit up in my bed, dragging a hand through my hair. "Then let me be as clear as possible. I like you, Kalli. I want to be with you and no one else. I want you to be with me and no one else. By my definition, that's a couple."

"Then I guess we're a couple because I want that, too."

The ache I always seem to feel around her flairs up again, and I wish she was here or I was there. Either way, I just want to touch her, to run my fingers over her cheek and her neck, and make her say those words again. To taste them on her lips.

"Your turn," I say, a new rasp of want in my voice. "Tell me a secret about you."

I count the seconds before her reply. Five. Five seconds. The longest pause so far.

"I don't have any good secrets." The lie is obvious in her voice: the flat tone, the carefully clipped words.

"So then tell me a bad one."

"Wilder, I—"

"I'm not asking for your deepest and darkest here, Kalli." Though I had told her about my dad already, and that's not something I ever care to talk about.

"Okay. Let me think. Um...my name, my full name is actually Kalliope."

"Kalliope." I say it a few more times, liking the way the complicated name rolls off my tongue. It fits her exotic, striking appearance. Then it occurs to me, "That's why you don't like Greek mythology, right? I think I remember a goddess named that."

She makes a barely audible noise of affirmation on the other end.

"So were your parents historians or something?"

"My parents were…" She drifts for a moment before finishing, "Complicated."

And we're back to dodging the questions.

"Okay. No more secrets. How about you just tell me something that makes you happy."

She considers for a moment and then answers, "I like simple things."

"Like?"

"I don't know. Sunrise. Warm weather. Ice cream." We both laugh. "Watching a movie on a couch with you and Gwen."

My chest tightens. "That makes you happy?"

"It does. Like I said, I've had a whole lot of complicated in my life, and not nearly enough moments like that."

"I think I can give you more of those moments."

"I think you can, too."

∞

I can barely concentrate the next day through my work shift because I'm so damn eager to see her again. I spend the day clenching my teeth, trying to stop myself from glancing at the clock every couple of minutes. And as luck would have it, something big comes up right before end of day, and I end up having to stay over.

By the time I'm done, there's not enough time to run home and change before meeting her, not unless I push back our date. And there's no way I'm doing that. I head toward the restaurant where we made plans to meet. I'll be there a little early, but what the hell.

Caught at a red light, I take a moment to unbutton the cuffs on my gray work shirt, and roll the sleeves up a few times. I lose-the tie too, popping the first couple buttons so I feel a little more like myself.

About twenty minutes later, I pull into the small parking lot next to Chords. The restaurant is in an old brick building, one of those places that looks vintage not because someone designed it to look that way, but because it's been around forever. This was the first place I ever played my guitar and sang in front of people. The café serves home cooked country food, and instead of playing some radio station over the loudspeaker, Cordell, the owner, used to play his guitar from open until close. First time Rook and I came here was in high school because we'd heard they were a little lax about checking IDs. Both of us ended up spending more time watching Cordell pick away at his guitar than drinking beer we were too young to buy. The guy was so absorbed in the music, like no one else was even there. It wasn't until we came back again and again that we realized he was like that *every night*. Playing wasn't about attracting customers for him. It was love, plain as day. And it made it so fucking easy to fall in love with the place, peeling paint, creaking floors, and all.

Cordell was diagnosed with cancer about a year after it became our regular haunt. The chemo wore him out so much that he couldn't play all day like he used to. Hell, some days he was lucky to play at all. That's when Rook and I made a deal with Lori, his wife. We'd play shifts whenever we could in exchange for free food. Cordell passed about two years ago, but Lori still has the place going strong.

I've been avoiding Chords for a while now, since I quit music. It was just too hard to think about being here when I couldn't play. But when Kalli said to take her some place that I loved…well, I couldn't think of anywhere else but here. I want her to like it for reasons I can't even parse out in my head, considering me and music are no more. But it feels important all the same.

I park my car and jump out, intending to run in and say a quick hello to Lori if she's here before Kalli arrives. But there parked in the row right behind me is Kalli's sedan.

Her head droops down onto the steering wheel, and she's huddled into a little ball like she's cold. I blow out a breath, the air just barely fogging in front of my face. I wonder if maybe her heater is broken, and the stab of pain I feel at the idea of her sitting in that cold car shocks me. I take a few steps toward her, and rap my knuckles lightly against her window.

She snaps up quickly, her head whirling around toward me, and I smile at the look of shock in her eyes. For a moment, she just sits there, frozen, before fumbling for the door handle.

She pushes it open harder than I expect, and it whacks into my knees. I step back, wincing, and hear her call out, "Oh crap. I'm sorry."

"It's fine." I move aside, and she opens the door all the way, and a wave of heat pours out. I frown. So she definitely wasn't cold.

"You're early," I say.

She starts to get out of the car, then remembers that she's still got it turned on, and she wrestles with the keys for a moment before pulling them free, grabbing her purse, and rising to stand in front of me.

"Yeah. I wasn't sure exactly where I was going, and I didn't want to be late."

I bite my tongue against the suggestion that she should have let me pick her up, and instead gently close her door for her. We stand there for a moment looking at each other awkwardly. I feel so connected to her, but at the same time, we've only seen each other on a handful of occasions, and none of those have been purposeful. This is entirely new territory for us. I lift my hands to touch her arms, running them up and down over the sweater she's wearing, and say, "Come on. Let's get you out of the cold."

She nods, her lips pressed tightly together, and while I'm deciding whether or not it's presuming to drape my arm around her, she begins walking off toward the restaurant entrance. I jog to catch up, but I've missed my moment to hold her. She's walking too fast now for me to coolly slide my arm over her shoulders. I do get far enough ahead to open the door for her, and she gives me a brief smile before ducking inside.

Chords is a small place. Seats maybe thirty people in all. There are about ten customers now, but the limited seating makes it look more crowded than it is.

"So this is one of your favorite places?" she asks.

I try to see it through her eyes. Mismatched chairs and tables. Mason jars for glasses, but not the kind that are made with handles. Real, actual mason jars. Just like always, there's a guy playing guitar off in the corner, but he's not anyone I recognize. There are old instruments, knick knacks, and photos on the walls. Stuff from Cordell and Lori's life together. I know that it's not much. Definitely not the kind of place I've ever taken any other girl on a first date, and my stomach twists and twists with worry.

"It is," I answer moments before I hear my name being called and Lori descends on me. She looks the same as the last time I saw her, white hair set in perfect curls.

"Wilder Bell, as I live and breathe."

I leave Kalli's side to accept the hug Lori offers. She feels smaller and more vulnerable in my arms, but her grip on me is as tight as ever.

"It's been too long, son."

I want to say something, offer up an excuse or an apology, but the words get stuck. Lori doesn't notice. She releases me in favor of Kalli and says, "And who is this lovely creature?"

Kalli starts to answer, but she gets folded into a hug, shocking her into silence. I shove my hands in my pockets, and her wide eyes meet mine over Lori's shoulder. Then after a moment, she returns my smile and softens in the woman's hold, hugging her back.

"Kalli, this is Lori. She owns the restaurant. And Lori, this is Kalli. We're here for a first date."

Lori glances at me over her shoulder, lifting an eyebrow, but she doesn't comment.

"It's nice to meet you," Kalli says, and Lori returns the sentiment. "Do you have a bathroom I could use before we sit down?"

Lori directs her toward the hallway back by the kitchens, and I watch her weave between the tables. When she's gone, Lori whistles.

"That's quite a look you're giving her for a first date, Wilder Bell."

She's only ever called me by my full name. Ever since the first time I sat on that stool in the corner and said it over the microphone before playing my first set.

"It's not a normal first date," I tell her.

One side of her mouth lifts high in a crooked smile, and her eyes crinkle as she looks at me. Shaking her head, she says, "No, I don't think it is. Did Cordell ever tell you about our first date?" I shake my head. "That fool took me bowling. On a first date. He very nearly didn't get a second, but he was just so damn charming."

"Are you making fun of me for my date choice?"

"You know I love this place with everything under my skin, but when you look at a girl like you look at her, I'd think you'd try a little harder."

I smile. "I thought about that. But she's different. She wanted me to take her some place that meant something to me. You don't get much more meaning than this."

I'm alarmed when Lori blinks, and then stubbornly wipes away a few tears that track down her cheeks.

"I'm sorry," I say.

She shushes me. "I just see a lot of my Cord in you." She nods, fighting off a few more lingering tears, and says, "You could get away with taking a girl bowling, too."

I laugh and hug her again.

She says, "Well, tell me how I can help. I'll make sure the cook is on the ball, of course. You wanna play for her? I'm sure Jimmy would welcome the break."

"No," I say, too fast, then sigh. "No, I'd rather not. I don't—I'm taking a step away from that at the moment. Going a different direction."

She looks troubled by that, but she doesn't give me any grief. I'm grateful because God knows just being in here is giving me enough grief already. Out of the corner of my eye, I see Kalli making her way back to us and I add, "We just want to eat and enjoy this place. That's all."

"Eat and enjoy, I can do. She's stunning, by the way."

"I know."

Kalli steps in front of us with a smile. Her eyes flick back and forth between us, and I'm sure it's obvious we've been talking about her. But for all the charm Lori thinks I have (and I used to think I had), I've got nothing to say. "Well, come on," Lori says. "Let's get you two seated."

I lay a hand on Kalli's lower back as we move to follow, and the touch sparks heat all the way through me. Lori leads us to a booth in the corner, far enough away from the kitchens and all the other patrons that we won't be interrupted, but still close enough to the music that we've got a prime spot.

Kalli takes a seat first, and I hesitate, unsure whether I'd rather be sitting beside her where I can touch her or across from her where I can see her better. Thinking of her request that we take things slow and do this the normal way, I settle for across.

Lori lays menus in front of us, and with a final wink at Kalli, leaves us alone.

I don't need to look at the menu. I know it like the back of my hand, but she picks up hers, and I watch her eyes scan over the words.

Lori wasn't quite right. Kalli is something more than stunning. She's otherworldly. I'd told her that there wasn't any need to dress fancy for this, and she's not. She's wearing jeans and a black sweater over a plain gray shirt with a colorful scarf tied around her neck. The scarf is really the only special item she's wearing, but she still somehow manages to look like she's stepped off the pages of a magazine or a movie screen.

She drags her dark, silky hair around so that it all sits over her left shoulder, and she sucks her bottom lip into her mouth as her eyes dart wildly across the menu. After another minute, she finally slaps it down on the table and says plainly, "I'm nervous. I'm sorry. I know I shouldn't be, but—"

"I am too."

"You are?"

"Hell yeah." I start to open my mouth to tell her all the reasons, but I decide better on that. It's not just bringing her here that has me tied up in knots. It's the fact that I missed her so much after only days apart. Even though we barely know each other. That fucking tears me up, and as badly as I want to say something and find out if it's the same for her, I'm more concerned with not scaring her off.

She blows out a breath. "Well, that helps. I guess."

"Why are you nervous?" I ask, which I know is unfair considering I'd just held back my own reasons, but I can't help myself.

She shrugs, her big brown eyes catching, ensnaring mine. "Lots of reasons."

"Give me one," I plead.

She runs a hand over her hair like she wants to pull it over her shoulder again, but it's already there.

"I don't know how to describe it, but this just feels different than dates I've been on in the past. Those were easy, and this…"

She trails off, and I try to ignore the way my stomach clenches over the thought of other dates she's been on. And the fact that she doesn't feel at ease with me. "Is it something I'm doing?" I ask. "To make things harder?"

"No." She reaches across the table, and lays her hand over mine. "I didn't mean that this was hard. Not like that. I mean that being here with you feels…bigger than those dates felt. More important."

I flip my hand over beneath hers and wrap my fingers around her delicate wrist. She does the same to mine, her fingers not quite long enough to reach.

"It feels that way for me, too. So maybe we should stop feeling so much pressure. We both want this to work. So I don't see why it shouldn't."

Her fingers tighten around my wrist, and an unreadable expression, almost like pain, crosses her face before she lets go and picks up her menu again.

"So what should I order here?"

I struggle to make sense of the change of pace and say, "Well, eighty-five percent of the menu is fried. Hopefully that's okay. I think they might have a salad on here somewhere."

"No salads for me," she says. "My only response to fried food is 'yes please.'"

I laugh. "Thank God. Well, in that case, you can't go wrong with the chicken fried steak. The barbecue is great too, especially the brisket. The meat loaf is always popular."

"What are you getting?"

"Chicken fried steak."

"Then that's what I want."

"You sure?"

"Yep. I want to know everything you love about this place. Starting with how you know Lori."

"This was one of my old haunts in high school. Rook and I came a lot."

"Rook. He's the guy who called you that night downtown?"

"Yeah. We've been friends for a long time, and Cordell, Lori's husband, sort of took us under his wing. We both had corporate parents who were gone a lot. We could have gotten into way more trouble than we did without this place."

"You still got into *some* trouble?" she asks with a smile.

"Any teenage boys with limited parental supervision are going to do that."

A waitress comes up then to take our orders, and we go ahead and put in our drinks and food all at once. When she's gone, the silence settles again, easier than before, but still with a touch of pressure.

She brings back the drinks pretty quickly, and then leaves again.

"So do I get to hear stories about this trouble you got into?" she asks.

"Oh, I'm sure when you meet Rook, I won't be able to stop him from telling you."

"Tell me about him."

I do, describing how we were with each other growing up. I tell her about his job as a tattoo artist now. "He's the one who did all this." I gesture to the section of my sleeve that shows from where I've rolled up the fabric of my shirt.

Her eyebrows lift. "He's talented."

"Yeah, he is." In more ways than just that. I bite down on the urge to tell her about the band. About how Rook can play damn near any instrument, but he's the best on the drums, and how he always seems to be able to invent the right music to go with my lyrics. I want to tell her about it because it's such a huge part of my life, but I don't trust myself to talk about it. Not with her. Certainly not here.

When Lori suggested I play for her, the idea latched onto my heart, and now I can't get it out of my head. From the moment I met her, it's been harder to fight the urge to write. And there are all these little pieces of songs and melodies that make me think of her. I want to share those things with her, and a little part of me is aware of how girls have always reacted to my music. Maybe it will impress her and make up for the fact that I've brought her to a grungy cafe instead of a nice restaurant for our first date.

But I know if I do that, if I open that door, I won't be able to shut it again.

And it has to stay shut. Music isn't the way to build a life and support a family. Maybe someday down the road, when Mom and Gwen are settled again, but not now.

So I tell her about my life and my friends without telling her about the music, even as the intricate guitar-playing coming from the corner underscores our conversation. After we talk about me for a while, I turn the tables and say, "How did all your work go yesterday? Did you get it done?"

She fiddles with the straw in her drink as she answers, "Oh, I took care of a pretty big chunk yesterday. Enough that I can take it easy today."

"So computer stuff, huh? Is that what you think you'll major in, too? You said you were undecided, right?"

"I did. But no, I don't plan on majoring in anything like that. It's just something to bring in money."

"So then what? You can't go too much longer without picking a focus, can you? You're what…a junior? Will you even be able to graduate on time if you don't pick soon?"

She lifts her cup to her mouth, wrapping her lips around the straw for a long pull. "I might have to go a little longer, yeah. I've been thinking about maybe arts management. I don't really do much in the way of fine arts myself, but I like that world. Arts management would give me an opportunity to be around it still, but with a more business focus."

"Yeah, Lennox mentioned something about how you fit in with all the artistic people in your group."

She stiffens a little. "What do you mean?"

"I just noticed that everyone in your friends group is an artist of some sort, and you are the only one who doesn't fit into that mold. She said you kind of work as a sounding board for all of them. It makes sense now. Arts management sounds right up your alley."

"I don't know. Like I said, it's just something I've been thinking about."

"You should do it. Who knows, maybe we'd even get in some business classes together."

"That's right." She gestures at my office clothes. "You're the business guy."

"I don't know about that, but I do take classes for it. We should look at your options if you go into arts management. It's not too late to adjust your schedule for next semester. I think it would be cool to have a class together."

Rather than answering that, she asks, "So the glasses. Do you always wear those to work?"

I reach up, pushing at the frames that I'd forgotten were there. If I'd had time to go home, I would have switched into my contacts.

"Usually," I answer. "I spend all day looking at a computer or small print on paper, and it irritates my eyes less when I wear them."

Our food arrives then, and I'd almost forgotten how huge the chicken fried steak is here. It takes up so much of the plate that they bring the sides out in extra little bowls. The conversation slows then in favor of food, and I swear I nearly lose it when she lifts her first bite to her mouth and moans in response.

No longer is the edge between us at the table awkward and nervous. Now, it's filled with a greedy desire that I'm just barely holding back. It's incredibly erotic watching the fork slip past her lips, and I've never in my life had to fight off an erection just from watching a girl eat. The effort makes me even more quiet as dinner continues, and before I know it, we're done and she's declining desert, and it's time to leave.

We say our goodbyes to Lori, who raises an eyebrow at me on our way out, and I can almost hear her whispering *bowling* in my ear. That's why when we're halfway across the parking lot, I grab hold of Kalli's wrist and pull her to a stop.

"Wilder?" she asks. "Did you forget something?"

I can still hear the guitar music inside as it filters out through the back door that opens up to a patio that's closed for the winter months. It's a slower tune, soft and a little longing.

"Dance with me."

Kalli blinks a few times. Then laughs.

"What?"

I pull her closer, the gravel shifting beneath her feet, and use a finger to lift her chin. "Dance with me, please."

"Right here?" she asks, skeptical. But despite her tone, she leans into me, and I slide my free arm around her waist, dragging her tighter against me.

"Why not? We've got you, me, and music. We don't need anything else."

"We're outside. It's December."

I drop my touch from her jaw to take her hand before leaning close and sliding my cheek against hers. With my mouth near her ear, I promise, "I'll keep you warm."

Chapter Nineteen
Kalli

I can feel Wilder's breath against my lips. More than that, I can *see* it. The sun has set and the temperature has dropped, and air fogs between us. There's something about actually seeing it, like our lips are touching, *we are touching*, despite the distance between. And as we sway from side to side, my heart gradually begins to pick up speed.

The strains of guitar music flowing out from the restaurant are nearly indecipherable over the heavy heartbeat in my ears. But Wilder must hear it. His hands are strong on my body, guiding my movements, and I'm practically clay in his palms.

We dance, eyes on eyes, lips nearly on lips, and there is lightning beneath my skin each time his body brushes against mine in a new way. His touch is firm, but gentle, never pushing or pressuring, though I can tell from the dark look in his eyes that he's just as affected as I am. The music shifts, building to a crescendo, and he spins us. My chest pushes tight against his, and I bite back a gasp. I don't know if it's the cold or him or some combination of both, but the tips of my breasts are painfully tight. Just the pressure of my bra is enough to rub them raw.

I remember the night at his apartment, the way he'd taken his time learning my body. I think of the heat of his mouth on my skin, and the memory alone is enough to make me shiver and clench.

He's back to being business, grown-up Wilder tonight in his button down and glasses. Only now that I know him, it doesn't seem like such a stark difference. He is neither the straight-laced man nor the tattooed bad boy. Or perhaps he's both. Regardless of what he's wearing, Wilder is caring and loyal and strong and so sexy that I'm having trouble remembering why I shouldn't push him into the backseat of his SUV and crawl on top of him.

It doesn't help matters when he leans in to place a feather light kiss on my jaw. He pauses there for long enough that I wonder if the kiss might have just been an accident, but then he shifts a little lower, kissing the spot just below my ear. My fingers tighten on his shoulder, and when he plants his next kiss farther down my neck just above my scarf, it's no longer light, but hot and wet with just an edge of teeth.

"Wilder," I breathe, unable to stay silent any longer.

He spins me again, continuing to dance even when I feel like my legs have turned liquid below me. Then softly, slowly he gives the same treatment to the other side of my neck. And when he reaches that final, sucking kiss he continues down, nudging my scarf aside as far as it will go. I'm trying to stay quiet, but little noises keep escaping with each breath anyway.

"I think I neglected to tell you how beautiful you look tonight. I'm sorry. It should have been the very first thing that left my mouth."

"I'm glad it wasn't."

He pulls back, and I groan at the loss of his mouth. Resting his forehead against mine, he stares in my eyes and asks, "Why?"

I break our gaze, even as I tell myself not to. I don't know why I'm shy with him, or even if that's what it is. I've never had any issues with confidence, but being with Wilder is different. I never wanted the other men to see anything beneath the surface. Beauty and magic were all I gave them, and I knew the worth of both of those things.

But it's been a long time since I offered anyone the rest of me, and that's not a worth I know, especially when it has to be balanced with all the dangers and drawbacks of who I am.

"Kalli," he whispers, tipping my chin up and forcing me to meet his eyes.

"I like the idea that you might like more about me than the way I look."

He kisses me then, and even though my nose and my fingers and my limbs are cold, heat flashes through me, quick and potent. I release his hand to wrap mine around his neck and pull him closer. He's tall enough that I have to be on my tiptoes and he has to bend, but the need to be close to him is so strong that I don't even notice the burn in my calves. His tongue sweeps against mine, hot and just shy of frenzied.

He breaks the kiss, and I desperately try to follow, but his cheek presses against mine. Against my ear, he rasps, "I do like the way you look. I like it way too much considering we're in public. But I also like the easy way you smile. The way you listen. I like that you're a mystery I can't wait to unravel. I like how good you are with my sister, and that you're the kind of girl who doesn't blink an eye when I bring her somewhere like this for a first date or ask her to dance in a cold parking lot. I like the sound of your voice and your dedication to chocolate and your skill in a water fight."

I descend into laughter, and even as I'm struggling to catch my breath, a part of me notices the way he watches me. The way his eyes light up because of me. It's my turn to kiss him then. His lips move hard and fast against mine, not quite pushing over that line that would lead to more, but it's *close*. His whole body is tense with tight control, holding us both away from that edge.

And on the other side, heat beckons. Heat and relief and the memory of all the other talented things he can do with his mouth.

When I find myself rooting for that control to snap, I know it's time to pull back. My lips are wet and swollen as I bury my face in the crook of his neck. I place a small kiss there, so he knows that my stopping wasn't a rejection, and his chest rumbles with a groan against me. I wrap my arms around him, tunneling under his jacket for warmth, and his arms twine around my back, pinning us together.

We're no longer dancing. Not really. There's a slight sway to his body that I follow, but our feet don't move, nor do we make any attempt to leave the cold and get in our vehicles.

I don't think either of us wants the night to end. I've never been this greedy for someone's time and attention, and I'm baffled at how I waited a few days for this. It won't be that easy next time. Now that I know what it's like to be with him, I start imagining the way his presence could alter every other moment in my life. I think of us in class like he said, and going to the grocery store, and the movies, and studying. I imagine all the mundane human tasks that I do to fill the time or keep up appearances, and they're no longer a hassle in my head, but a new opportunity to spend time with him. A new way to see this world.

I lift my head to look him in the eye and ask, "You need some company while you babysit?"

His smile tightens the thread binding us, reeling us closer together, and I wonder if there will come a point when it's more than not wanting to leave his side. What if there comes a time when I can't?

∞

"You just can't sit still today, can you?"

Jack gives me a laughing look from over the top of his canvas when I shift for what is probably the thousandth time.

"What has you so restless?" he asks.

The fact that I'm having Wilder withdrawals after only a few days without him. That I lied and told him I had work to do this afternoon before I could go out with him and meet his friends tonight for New Year's Eve. That I'm here with Jack at all.

The whole thing feels wrong.

But this is what I have to do to make it work, so I need to find a way to be okay with it. It's either this or do without Wilder completely.

As if he can feel me thinking about him, my phone rings and when I shift to answer it, Wilder's name is on the screen. Feeling queasy, I send the call to voicemail and say, "Sorry Jack."

I put the phone on silent, and try to be the good little muse, but it's not easy. I sit for another half hour, my eyes directed off to the wall in an attempt to ignore Jack's gaze on me. It's not as if I'm doing anything risqué. I'm fully clothed. I'm in a dress, but it's not overtly sexual. But still…we're alone. And there's a reason why my typical artist/muse relationship has always been romantic in nature. Art is already an intimate thing, and staring at someone long enough to capture her likeness amplifies that. I concentrate on allowing the inspiration to escape my system in small, gradual waves. When I'm nearly empty and have started thinking about ways to extricate myself from Jack's apartment, his phone rings.

He starts to ignore it, but then he glances over at me where I'm fidgeting once again and answers it with a sigh. "Yep."

It has always bothered me that he answers his phone that way. No hello, nothing.

"I don't have much of anything planned. I was hoping to just stay in and get some work done." He glances at me again. "Let me ask Kalli, she's here."

He rests the phone against his shoulder and says, "Lennox traded shifts and is now free tonight. She wants to go out for New Years. You in?"

I give him a half-hearted smile. "I've got plans actually."

I don't miss the way he stiffens, setting down the paintbrush he'd been using.

Lennox talks for a moment on the other line, and then he wordlessly holds out the phone to me. I hop off the chair he has me seated in and cross to take it.

"Hello?"

"Who do you have plans with, and why do I not know about them?" Lennox demands. I turn my back to Jack, wishing I could leave the room, but considering I'm talking on his phone that would be incredibly rude.

"I'm going out with Wilder. Meeting some of his friends."

She whistles and says in a sing-song tone, "Meeting the friends. That sounds promising."

I have the urge to tell her that it's more than promising. It's lovely and exhilarating and beyond my wildest dreams. Wilder is everything I could possibly want, if I can just find a way to make it work.

But the careful silence of the room reminds me that Jack is listening.

"Yeah."

"Are you excited? Nervous?"

"Both. A lot of both."

"We should combine groups. That way you'll have back-up."

"I don't know."

"Oh, come on. I'll be the perfect wing woman, I swear."

"It's not really my decision to make, Lennox. It's his friends."

"Great. I'll call him then."

"Wait, Len—"

The phone clicks off. I squeeze my eyes closed for a few moments before turning and offering Jack back his phone.

"What's she up to?" he asks.

I shrug and say, "I think she's calling Wilder. Wants to combine plans."

He starts cleaning up his supplies, so I guess we're done for the day. I relax, glad for that.

"So, you're seeing him?"

I lick my lips nervously and nod. One of the main benefits to this new *style* of inspiration is that as friends, I can stay with everyone longer. And I can continue to add new people to my circle. But if Jack makes a big deal out of this, it might not be possible. It could ruin everything.

"Since when?"

"Christmas officially. But we met a little over a month before that."

He frowns and then moves off to the kitchen in his studio apartment to wash his brushes. Unsure of what else to do, I start gathering my things. When I'm done, I think about just calling out a goodbye and leaving, but I know that's not the right way to handle it. So, I take a seat back in my chair and wait.

He finishes washing his brushes, and then turns. "Thanks for sitting for me."

"Of course. You know I love your work."

He nods.

Oh gods. Could this be any more awkward?

"Well, I'm sure I'll see you soon. How many more sessions do you think you'll need before we're finished?"

He shrugs. "I don't know. Two maybe. I didn't get as much done today with all your wiggling." He gives me a half smile, and I relax a little at the friendly gesture. Jack is a nice guy. We'll get past this weird patch, and it will all be fine.

"Who knows, maybe I'll see you tonight if Lennox has her way."

My stomach twists uncomfortably at the thought. I don't really want to see Wilder and Jack together again. It will kill me to have this secret between us.

"Maybe."

I grab my things and head for the door, but at the last second I pause, the twisting in my gut nearly painful.

"Listen," I say. "If you do come tonight, can you not mention to Wilder that I was here? I haven't told him yet because you and I are friends, and I didn't want anything to come between that."

"You think he'll be jealous?"

Yes. And I don't like the slightly eager tone to his question.

"I don't know. But if you could just…not mention it until I find a way to ease him into the idea, that would be great."

His eyes linger on mine for a second longer than is comfortable. "Sure, Kalli. You know I'm good for whatever you need."

My smile is brittle because that offer felt a little *too* honest.

"Bye Jack."

"See you later, Kalli."

∞

Wilder is picking me up in half an hour, and my levels are in a good place. Very close to zero. It makes me a little nervous to have him picking me up, but when he asked he said something about me keeping my place a secret from him, which wasn't really my intention. It was more about having my own vehicle, my own means of escape should I need some time to breathe and…reevaluate. But I don't want him to think I'm hiding things from him. Or…at least not little things that don't matter, like my apartment. So I gave him my address, and now I just have to hope that one night will keep me within acceptable levels. And if I do need to leave early, I know that Wilder won't hesitate to take me. I just have to hope that's enough.

I slip my journal underneath my mattress for safekeeping, and check myself over in the mirror once more. I'm wearing slim fitting jeans, boots, a simple shirt and a black leather jacket that I'd chosen specifically because I know Wilder will most likely be wearing his. Not that I want to be all matchy-matchy, but I like the idea of feeling like we belong together. I tie a turquoise scarf around my neck, and am pulling my hair out from under it when my doorbell rings.

I glance at the clock.

He's ten minutes early.

I wipe my palms against my jeans and head for the front door. When I pull it open, he looks even better than I remember. He's leaning against the railing just outside my door in that familiar leather jacket. No glasses tonight. Just sinful blue eyes and tousled hair and enough scruff to make him look absolutely irresistible.

"You're early."

Millennia of experience, and I'm still stating the obvious.

"Correction," he says, crossing to stand in front of me. He bends to say in my ear, "I'm eager."

"I don't think you're supposed to admit that."

"Why not?"

"I don't know. Aren't you supposed to keep your cards close to your vest or something? Not give up your power?"

His fingers graze my stomach before he flattens his palm there and pushes me back enough that he can step inside. He closes the door behind us, and then presses me into it.

"I'm not trying to keep any power here, sweet. If it's not entirely clear that I'm powerless when it comes to you, then you haven't been paying attention." The tip of his nose grazes my jaw, tickling as he slides close to my ear. "And I don't care if you know that I'm eager to see you. In fact, I've been dying for it."

His words calm all the restlessness that's been building in me the last few days, and I decide to go for honesty, too.

"Is it strange that I missed you? I know it has only been a few days, and I talked to you on the phone last night, but—"

"But it wasn't enough? Yeah. I know the feeling."

I face facts then. I've seen it often enough in others to recognize that I am utterly addicted to him. It won't matter how often I see him or speak to him, I'll always want more.

"So this is your apartment?"

When he turns to take it in, I'm tempted to pull him back and use the few extra minutes we have to get reacquainted with his lips, but I know he's curious.

"This is it."

He looks around, and I can't see the place through his eyes. It's a relatively new building, and I got it already furnished since I tend to move semi-frequently. The furniture is all sleek and modern. It looks barely lived in at all, unlike his apartment. I have very few personal items, and all of them are hidden away in my bedroom.

He stops in the middle of the living room, and I can't help but notice that his foot falls directly on the section of the carpet that covers the only remnant of the destruction I caused after Van and that whole mess. If he were to step aside and peel back the rug, he'd see where I wrote *Inspired* so many times that I scratched it into the floorboard.

"I could give you a tour of my bedroom," I offer.

He shoots me a sly smile. "Always so tempting. How about we save that for later? If I got you in your bedroom, I'm not sure we'd leave it before the year ends."

"I see what you did there, funny guy."

"You don't think I'm funny?"

"I think you're hilarious. And sweet. And sexy. Are you sure you don't want to skip tonight and celebrate the New Year with just the two of us?"

He walks back to where I'm standing by the door and smoothes both his large hands up my arms before sinking them into my hair. His fingers tease at my scalp, sending shivers down my spine. "I'm starting to think you like trying to tempt me past control."

His grip on me is firm, restrained, and I have to fight the inclination to arch up into him and surrender completely.

No sex, Kalli. Not yet.

I smile and say, "I don't hate it."

He chuckles, but his laughs turn into a groan a moment later when he thumps his forehead against the door beside me. "We should go. Rook has been giving me shit all week because I haven't introduced you. And I've skipped every hangout since Owen got back into town."

I frown. "Because of me?"

"Sometimes because of you. Sometimes for Gwen. Don't worry about it. It's been like this for the last year. They're used to it."

He has so little free time as it is, and here I am, wanting more of it.

"Stop," he says. "Whatever you're thinking, stop it."

"You're a mind reader now?"

"I can just tell when you're thinking about pushing me away or shutting me out. The look you get. It's not one I'm fond of."

I smile guiltily knowing I can't promise that will change. "Let's head out then. I wouldn't want to deprive your friends of your coveted company."

I grab my purse, and after locking up, he takes my hand to lead me to his car. He keeps that hold the entire time we drive, only pulling away for brief moments when he needs both of his hands on the wheel. We end up downtown, and I try to fight back the sense of déjà vu as he pulls into a parking garage. The place is packed, as was all of the street parking we saw as we drove. I guess that's to be expected downtown on New Year's Eve.

The streets are congested, and every bar we pass is already overflowing with people even though we've still got two hours until midnight. We eventually stop at a place a few blocks off of Sixth Street, where the streets are less crammed. But the bar he leads me into is plenty busy. There are booths on our left, and a bar to the right, and most of the open space is filled with bodies. I can hear live music, but I don't see a band, so I'm guessing they're up the stairs I spot in the back. It's definitely an eclectic place. There are pictures on the walls of various guys with mustaches. Some historical like Einstein. Others are celebrities. The two bartenders I spot behind the bar also have mustaches, and I can't help but laugh. There are other odd little statement pieces around the room. A few of those twenty-five cent kiddie rides that you find outside of grocery stores. Some strange taxidermy. But as another facial-hair-inclined waiter passes us, I can't help my laugh.

"What?" Wilder asks over the music.

I pantomime twirling up the ends of a mustache, and he smiles. "Rook likes this place. Good drinks. Good music. In the warmer months, they've got a great rooftop patio, too."

I loop my arm around his elbow, pulling myself close to his side in the crowd. Honestly, I could care less about where we are as long as I'm with him. It only takes the amount of time for us to head for the back and climb the stairs before I rethink that statement. There is indeed a band upstairs, and the place is standing room only. Bodies are pressed tight together, dancing to the rhythm of the rock beat that's playing, and the déjà vu comes back full force. And not any good memories. The last time I was in sea of dancing bodies, it didn't work out so well for me. Or for the people dancing.

"Come on," Wilder says, close to my ear. "Rook texted that they've got a table up front."

He pulls me into the crowd, and I hold my breath against the panic that rises up in me. What if the energy gets too high in here? What if the same thing happens all over again? I could hurt all these people, hurt Wilder. Not to mention bringing the Argus down on me once and for all.

Each time I squeeze through another set of bodies, my pulse thrums a little faster. The sound of it in my ears mixes with the heavy drums of the band, and my head feels like it's being battered from the inside and out. I suck in a breath when we get past the standing crowd to the few tables up front, but even those are overflowing with people.

Wilder leads me over to the very first table on the left, crammed close to the wall. There are two guys and a girl already seated, and just one open chair. The guy on the left catches sight of us first, and stands to wave. He's immensely tall. Enough that he stands with his shoulders hunched and his head bent as if he's always having to duck under things and just got stuck that way. And the first thing that comes to my mind when I look at his face is *dark*. Dark hair sticking up every which way. A dark beard. Eyes so dark they look all pupil. Covered in ink. Not just his arms like Wilder, but his hands and his neck, and nearly every piece of visible skin except his face. Who knows, maybe the beard is hiding some ink, too. He calls out something to Wilder that I can't hear over the music, and I see the glint of a silver piercing in his tongue before the two of them collide for a back-slapping, manly hug.

Then his eyes meet mine over Wilder's shoulder, and I suck in a breath. The darkness lurks there too. Not anger really. Or sadness either. But some mixture of both, wrapped in a threatening aura of strength. This is not a man to be messed with. If I'd been looking for an artist, he might fit in several of the categories. His appearance and feel are definitely along the lines of a guy I might approach, but he's the type I would have thrown back after an up-close look. He's on an edge, this one. The kind whose reaction to my ability would definitely be…unpredictable. And the kind Mel would have gone for in a heartbeat. She would have seen the edge and wanted to find a way to get him off it. That's probably one of the many reasons Mel is no longer with us, her willingness to dive into darkness better left untouched.

Wilder holds out a hand to me, and I take it, allowing myself to be pulled close to his side.

"Kalli," he practically shouts. "This is my best friend, Ellis Rook."

"Fuck, Wild." He looks at me, and up close I can see that his irises are a deep brown. "It's Rook. No one calls me Ellis." He looks back at Wilder. "No one better call me Ellis," he warns.

I can't fathom how these two fit together. I've seen hurt and pain in Wilder, but he reacts to it constructively, normally. Most of the time anyway. He tends toward guilt a little too often. But at his core, he's sweet and giving and steady. Ellis Rook is the very antithesis of steady.

"It's nice to meet you, Rook."

"Nice to finally meet the girl that has this one wrapped around her finger. You know, normally this idiot talks my ear off about girls he's with. But with you, all is quiet on the Wilder front."

I want to smile at his joke. Maybe he's not all darkness after all, but I'm too pre-occupied by his words. He doesn't talk about me? Is that a bad thing? It has to be, right? Wilder must see the dilemma written across my face because he leans down, pressing his lips to my ear and says, "He means I complained when things didn't go right. I don't have anything to complain about where you're concerned, Kalli. And God knows, I'd tell him the good things if I knew how to put into words the way you make me feel."

I can't help it. I kiss him then, right in front of his friends. I mean it to be quick, just a better thank you than the shouted one I would have had to give him over the music. But as soon as our lips touch, his arm tightens around my waist, fingers digging in to my hip. His mouth opens, sweeping his tongue over the seam of my lips, and I immediately open to him, eager to taste and twine together. His kiss makes me forget about the noises and the bodies and my worries—he just blocks it all out. Always does. And the only thing I know is the crush of his mouth on mine, the plunge of his tongue, the heat building between my thighs. I won't be able to hold out much longer without letting our relationship turn physical again. I want him too much. I need to feel *connected* with him more than I've needed anything else in my life.

A trickle of energy unwinds in my chest, tickling at my lungs, wanting me to breathe it out.

Immediately, I pull back, panting.

Wilder's eyes are hooded as he looks at me, and I can see how badly he wishes he'd taken me up on my offer to stay in tonight.

"Don't stop on my account," Rook says. "I like a little voyeurism as much as the next guy."

A blush detonates across my cheek, and when Wilder pulls me under his arm, I keep going until I bury my face in his chest.

"Don't be a dick, Rook."

"Easier said than done, man."

My face is still heated when Wilder introduces me to the other guy at the table, Owen. He has long brown hair, tucked underneath a gray beanie. And unlike Rook, he's all smiles.

"Don't listen to anything Rook says. He's a bitter old man trapped in a punk dude's body." Rook scowls, and Owen amends, "I think there might be multiple bitter old dudes in him actually. Like he's some soul-eating demon that feeds on wasted lives."

"Yes, thank you, Owen. Please tell my girlfriend that my best friend is a soul-eating demon. That's always the best way to start."

All of the guys laugh, and I smile so wide I feel as if my cheeks might separate from my face. *His girlfriend.*

"He's a lovable soul-eating demon," Owen tries.

The glow fades just a smidge when I realize that if anyone is a soul-eating demon here, I'm the closest in nature. But I shake that off, too happy with Wilder's arm around me to let anything bring me down.

Then I meet the final friend in the group.

Bridget.

She's stunningly blonde, stick thin, and she *really* doesn't like me.

I offer a quick wave. "I'm Kalli." And she barely smiles in response, and then retakes her seat. "Will you guys sit down already before some vultures swoop in and steal our table?"

Wilder tenses beside me, but doesn't comment. And my stomach sinks when Rook and Owen take a seat, only to leave the one for Wilder and me. I glance around, looking for another chair, but as expected, there are none available. Before I can think beyond that issue, Wilder's hands are on my hips, and he's pulling me over and down to sit in his lap. He grips my thighs, turning me sideways and pulling me in tight to his hips. I feel the beginning of a bulge against my leg, and my gaze meets his knowing eyes. I wrap an arm around his neck to steady myself, and it brings the side of my chest against the front of his.

"This worked out rather well for me," he says with a smile.

I laugh and roll my eyes. And then a wicked idea occurs to me. Ever so slightly, I shift so that my thigh rubs against his groin, over and then back again. He drops down to rest his forehead against my temple and groans. "I don't know," I say. "Are you really going to hold me like this *all night long*?"

That earns me a quick nip on my earlobe, and it's my turn to stifle a reaction.

"We're out of here right after midnight," he growls. "I'm talking one minute after. Mom doesn't work tonight, and I don't want to share you with anyone else longer than I have to."

Wilder gets a text then, and he shifts me on his lap to fish out his phone. It's Lennox. He sends her a quick message to explain where we are in the bar, and a few minutes later, I see her pushing through the crowd with Mick, Jack, and Avery in her wake. Jack's eyes immediately find mine, and I stiffen.

"So you told them to come?" I ask.

"Yeah. Lennox called this afternoon. I figured the more the merrier." He takes a strand of my hair between his finger and thumb and adds, "Plus, I thought if our friends became friends, we could all hangout together. That will mean more time for us together."

I smile because he's just so sweet. But I'm not sure I can ever envision his friends and him spending time with Jack. The rest maybe, but not him. Wilder makes quick introductions when they arrive at the table, but with no seats, the four of them end up squeezed between our table and the wall.

"You want a drink?" Wilder asks in my ear.

I shake my head, and then I glance around the table again where a few people are having individual conversations because it's too loud for any kind of group discussion. I think better of it and say, "Actually, yeah. That would be great."

"What do you want?"

"Any kind of cocktail is fine. Surprise me."

Wilder leaves, and I immediately wish I had convinced him to stay or gone with him. Rook is on my left, in conversation with Lennox. Jack is directly across from me, and I look away fast before he thinks I want him to come talk to me. By avoiding him, I end up turning to Bridget on my right. Her eyes are narrowed on me, the slightest wrinkle of distaste on her nose as she takes me in.

"How long have you known Wilder?" she asks.

"Uh, we met a couple months back. You?"

"Six years."

Damn, she had that answer ready fast.

I nod, uncomfortable under her intense focus. Is she just a protective friend? Who maybe wishes she was more than a friend? God knows, I've seen plenty of those. She shifts her chair a little closer to mine, and then opens her mouth to ask me something else. But before she can, a hand closes around my wrist, and I'm pulled to my feet.

It's Rook.

"Dance with me."

I splutter for a moment, unsure how to respond.

"Wilder won't mind. Trust me. Besides, I'm a *great* dancer."

He gestures for Lennox and Mick to fill our spots at the table, and then pulls me away and into the crowd of moving bodies. It's a faster song, not something that's easy to dance to, but I try. I keep getting hit by elbows and flailing extremities though, so I end up close to Rook, just barely shifting from side to side. I can feel the bodies pressing around me, and I have to concentrate on breathing.

"Sorry about Bridget. She can be kind of a bitch."

I frown. Why hang out with her then? Why say something like that about your friend?

"She can be really cool. I swear. But there's history there between her and Wilder."

I flinch, blindsided. I hadn't even considered the idea that she might be his ex. I don't know why. But the thought that he brought me here with her, that they're still friends, is enough to make my stomach churn with nausea.

"It's over between them. They were shit together, and Wilder ended it a while ago. You've got nothing to worry about there."

Then why am I worrying?

"How long is a while ago?"

He shrugs. "Eight, nine months. Something like that."

Shit. I was hoping more for something in the years range. I take a deep breath, knowing it's not fair to expect him not to have exes. I sure as hell have a lot more than he does. But I never see mine again. She's his *friend*.

"Damn," Rook says. "I shouldn't have said anything. I know fuck all about relationships, but this is a new low, screwing up other people's. Listen, don't be mad at him."

"I'm not mad."

I'm terrified. I can't lose him. I just can't. We've only known each other a month, and have been seeing each other officially for a little over a week, but he's already imprinted on my heart. No, deeper than that. He's wrapped up in my essence, my soul. I thought it was the same for him. I need it to be the same for him.

"You're sure? I feel like this is usually the part where girls go storming off or start yelling."

"I'm not going to yell. Or storm off."

I might walk away though. Just to get out of the crowd of people and catch my breath.

"He's serious about you. Really fucking serious. Please don't let my shitty mouth ruin that. I just didn't want her talking shit, trying to poison things between you. He doesn't want her, and she's just got to get over her obsession."

The word rings darkly between us. Obsession. I think of Van. Of all the guys I've ever left behind that kept showing up, kept trying to win me back until finally I had to change my number or move or get a new life completely. I know a thing or two about obsession.

I also know that if things don't turn out how I want them to, I could end up doing that same thing to Wilder. I think of that ribbon of energy that had unfurled while he kissed me earlier, and I do a mental evaluation of my levels.

A three.

I started the night at a zero, and already I'm at a three.

"I need to run to the bathroom. Do you know where it is?"

"I don't think you want to go to the bathroom here."

"I just need a second away from the noise and all the people. Please, tell me where it is."

"You said you weren't going to storm off."

"I'm not. *Please*. Rook, you don't know me. But trust me when I tell you that I just need a break. Please."

He points behind me. "It's downstairs. Take a right as soon as you hit the first floor, behind the kiddie rides."

"Thank you."

I fight my way through the bodies, hyper aware every time someone's skin comes into contact with mine. It would be easy, just to let a tiny sliver of energy go with each of those touches. I could get back to zero quickly.

No. I can't do that. *Can't.*

I suck in a lungful of air as soon as I'm on the stairs. I take them fast, eager to have a moment just to shut down and process. Downstairs, there's a photo of a bearded lady hanging outside the women's restroom, and it swings a little as I push my way inside. There's a girl washing her hands at the sink, but other than that, the place appears to be empty. I push my way into a stall, lock the door, and then lean back against it, glad for the barrier between me and the rest of the world.

So he's friends with his ex. Can I really complain about that with all the *peculiarities* on my side of the relationship? I'll have to spend time with Jack. And Mick. And probably other guys. Besides…I know what we have is something extraordinary. Not just because of the way he makes me feel, but because of the fate thread I feel between us. I don't know if that means we're meant to be. If we're soul mates. But I know it means we're connected in a way that no one and nothing else can compete with. There are enough obstacles to our relationship without me allowing jealousy and fear to create more.

Already feeling better, I take a calming breath and concentrate on settling the energy inside me. My own anxiety antagonized it, and it's dangerous for me to let that kind of restlessness take over. I close my eyes, focus on breathing, and let everything else slip away but my body and the power. When it's settled, I'm relieved to feel that my levels are not quite as high as I'd thought out on the dance floor. Still above a zero for sure, but more like a two than a three. Much more manageable.

Ready to return to Wilder and the others, I push open the bathroom stall only to come to a halt when I see Bridget leaning against the bathroom sink. My steps falter, and my eyebrows raise. "Hi."

"Sorry if I came off rude out there."

Hesitantly, I take a step forward. Part of me just wants to bolt, but I decide to play it cool and wash my hands instead.

"Don't worry about it."

"It's just that Wilder means a lot to me. To all of us. And he's going through a rough time right now—"

"I know."

Her nostrils flare, and she stands up straight from where she's been leaning on the sink.

"He *told* you."

I nod. She's silent as I finish rinsing the soap off my hands, and when I reach for a paper towel. I can feel the tension rolling off her beside me, but she remains quiet. I'm not about to stick around until she decides what she wants to say, so I move toward the door.

"Hang on." She reaches out as I pass, lightly touching my elbow. But when we make contact, she gasps, and her fingers latch on like a vice around my arm. The energy I'd just cooled flairs to life, licking like flames at the inside of my lungs. Her body is shaking next to mine, and when I look up, her eyes have frosted over, pupils and irises covered by an icy white.

"Long have you kept your secrets, moúsa."

My body jerks to attention at the name. The Greek term for muse. I yank my arm, trying to free it from her grasp, but her hold is like stone. "Through centuries," she continues, "all your secrets and shame. The shroud of loneliness will be doffed. A reunion calls."

An oracle. Wilder's friend and ex-girlfriend is a *godsdamned oracle*.

"To be made whole, all must first be lost. Daughter of Zeus. Queen of the grove song. Oh, clearest voice among the crowd. You will lose him to your secrets. Daughter of Zeus, maiden muse, bringer of madness. Erebus waits for your move. First shall meet last on death's breath."

I yank again, and this time I manage to break her hold. We both gasp at the loss of contact, and I don't wait to watch her eyes clear and for the human half of Bridget to take hold. Oracles don't typically remember their visions and prophecies. She probably doesn't even know what she is. In fact, this could easily be her first episode. Coming into contact with me, someone with so much deity blood, could have called forth the dormant part of her nature.

I spin, storming for the door, and throw it open. Wilder is rushing toward me as I step out, and her words prick at my soul when I see him.

You will lose him to your secrets.

Chapter Twenty
Wilder

"I'm sorry what?"

I stand against the busy bar, waiting for the drinks I just ordered, talking with Lennox while she attempts to flag down a bartender of her own.

"I said I'm glad I called Jack today. Your friends seem cool. I'm totally going to have to check out Rook's tattoos online."

"Yeah. He's crazy talented. I'm sorry. What does Jack have to do with it?"

"I called him, and he was…" She trails off, and I catch the way her eyes widen just slightly. "Never mind. Don't listen to me. I did some pre-gaming before we came, so I'm already a little loopy."

"Was Jack the one who told you we were going out tonight?"

She hedges, turning to call out for the bartender again rather than answer me.

"I'll take that as a yes." If Jack knew our plans, that means Kalli talked to him. I don't like the guy, but I'm not about to tell Kalli who she can and can't be friends with. I do wonder when she talked to him, though. She's been busy working through the holidays. I'm about to dig for a little more information from Lennox, when Owen appears.

"Problem," he mutters next to me.

I sigh. Generally, when Owen is coming to me with a problem, Rook has stuck his foot in somewhere it doesn't belong. I love the dude, but I swear to God I spent more time putting out his fires than actually making music when the band was still going strong. Inevitably, he was pissing off some bar manager or taking the wrong girl home or talking shit to the worst possible person.

"What did Rook do?"

"Nothing much. He danced with your girl."

I frown. He's my best friend, but he also spends eighty percent of his life thinking with his dick, and I swear to God if he came on to Kalli, I won't be responsible for what I do to him.

"Then she went to the bathroom. Couple minutes passed, and I noticed Bridge was nowhere to be seen. Thought maybe she was on the dance floor, but I can't find her. Thought you might want to know."

Shit. Surely she wouldn't say something to Kalli. I expected her to pout and be a bit cold, but we're still friends goddamn it. She wouldn't sabotage my relationship just because ours didn't work out. I catch Owen's worried expression, and I know we're both doubting just what our friend would and wouldn't do right now.

"Fuck."

"Yeah," Owen replies.

"Bathroom, you said?"

He nods. "That's what she told Rook anyway. Maybe she just wanted to get away from his hairy mug though. Could have been an excuse."

I hand him a couple of bills and say, "Can you pay for the drinks I have coming? I'll be back."

"Sure thing."

I slip through the openings between people crowding the bar, trying to get a drink, and when I hit the stairs, I jog down. I head back to the half-hidden hallway that I know leads to the bathroom, and I'm a few steps away from the door when it flies open, and Kalli comes rushing out.

Her hair is a bit wild, and her pupils are dilated. Sweat dots her forehead, and when our gazes clash she slams to a halt. An expression passes across her face, fear I think, and when I reach out to touch her, she flinches away before I make contact.

"Kalliope," I say. I don't know why I use her full name. It just comes out, but her expression closes off and her jaw clenches.

"Don't call me that."

"I'm sorry. *Kalli*, I'm sorry." I take a step forward, reaching out a hand, but I don't make contact. Not yet. I don't know if I can handle seeing her flinch back from me again. "What's wrong?"

The bathroom door swings open again, and Bridget is framed in the opening.

"Goddamn it, Bridge. What did you say to her?"

Her brows furrow, and she looks between us in confusion. "I didn't say anything."

"We were supposed to be friends first. I've been patient with your bullshit because we've known each other a long time, but this is too much."

"Hey Asshat, I don't know what you're talking about—"

I bite back the slew of curse words I want to fling at her, and fist my hands in my hair to try to cool down. Then Kalli ducks under my arm and steps between us.

"Wilder, relax. She didn't say anything."

Kalli rests a hand on my chest lightly, but she winces when she does it, and when I try to move closer, that hand becomes more of a barrier than a comfort. "Kalli, what the hell is going on? What's wrong?"

She snatches her hand back, and moves to put more space between us. "Nothing is wrong. I just got a little overwhelmed and needed a break."

She flew out of that bathroom like she was being chased.

Or like she was getting ready to run.

I look over at Bridget. "You weren't rude?"

She rolls her eyes. "Oh, please Wild. Maybe I'm a little bit bitchy, but I wasn't mean to your precious girlfriend."

She steps forward and lets the heavy bathroom door swing shut with a thud. Then she maneuvers around us and leaves without making eye contact with either of us again. I return my focus to Kalli. She's leaning into the wall a few feet away, and her shoulders are rising and falling slowly with her deep, slow inhales.

"You didn't look like you'd just been taking a breather when you came out of that bathroom. You looked terrified. Tell me what happened."

She smiles, but it's weak. "Nothing. I swear. I just don't do well in crowds like this."

I frown, remembering the last time I'd seen her downtown. She'd been stumbling out of a club probably as busy as this one. And she'd been pale and panicked.

Damn.

"Why didn't you tell me? I never would have brought you here if I'd known that."

I move toward her, but she dodges my touch at the last moment.

"I'm sorry. Just give me a moment, please. Let me calm down for a second, and then…then I'll be fine."

I frown, grinding my teeth together.

"Was there anyone else in the bathroom besides you two?"

She shakes her head.

I don't touch her again, but I push open the door and gesture for her to come inside. When she does, I close the door and lock it. Then I wet a paper towel in the sink and hand it to her. I pace a few feet away and try not to brood too much as I watch her dab at her face with the towel. I have a thousand questions I want to ask, but I stay silent while she breathes and breathes and breathes for so long that I find myself doing it with her. The doorknob shakes, and someone bangs hard on the outside.

"You okay?" I ask.

After a moment, she nods. I unlock the door, and the two girls waiting outside narrow their eyes when they see me. I hold open the door for Kalli and apologize. "Sorry. My girlfriend got sick." I hesitate, but then place a hand at her lower back, relieved when she doesn't flinch.

"Let's leave. I'll text the guys and tell them we had to go."

She grips my arm over my jacket. "No, don't. I don't want to ruin our plans."

I cup her face in my hands and pull her as close as I dare. "The only thing that could ruin this night is seeing you uncomfortable or unhappy. We're leaving."

After a moment, she nods. I wrap an arm around her and pull her close to my side, and this time she reciprocates the gesture. Both her arms go around my middle, and she squeezes so tight that it's almost hard for the two of us to walk. It becomes especially difficult as we try to make our way through the crowd to the exit, but neither of us make any move to let go of the other. We wait it out until there's an opening or people move out of our way.

It's cold out, so we walk quickly through the busy streets until we get to our parking garage and can escape into my SUV. I turn the ignition on, and power up the heater as fast as I can.

It has heated seats, so I flip those on also. I stop then to retrieve my phone and send a quick text to Rook explaining.

In return I get:

I'm sorry, man. I wasn't thinking.

Shit. What did that mean?

Rather than hound him for the answer, I face Kalli. I swear, all I want to do is pull her over the center console into my lap, and hold her tight until my heart stops beating so hard.

"Can you explain to me what happened back there?"

She keeps her gaze trained on her folded hands in her lap and shakes her head.

"You're sure Bridget didn't say something to you? What about Rook?"

She looks up, tilting her head sideways to peer at me. "Why didn't you tell me she was your ex?"

I sigh. So someone did say something. Probably Rook.

"I should have. I just…things have been going so well, and I didn't want to screw that up."

Good job, Bell. You fucked yourself over with that one.

I continue, "I swear there's absolutely nothing there. It was when I first came back to town with all the stuff going on with my dad. We'd been friends for a while, and she was there when I needed someone. But we weren't good together. Not at all. She knows we're not together. She knows we're not *getting* back together. But the four of us…we've been friends for a long time. I can't just cut her out. Or ask Rook and Owen to cut her out. She's their friend, too."

She nods, looking down again. And damn it, I can't tell if she's pissed or sad or if she cares at all.

"Talk to me. Are you mad? I'm sorry. So fucking sorry."

"I'm not mad."

I slump back in my seat, only slightly relieved because there's still something I can't identify in her tone. Weariness, maybe? Is she just worn out from the crowd?

"Tell me what else is going on in your head. You're killing me."

Her eyes flash to mine then, a flare of something in those dark depths.

She purses her lips like she might cry and shakes her head.

"Everything is just so hard."

"What is?"

I don't like how this moment feels so outside my control.

"I don't want to lose you."

Screw being cautious. I reach over and unbuckle the seatbelt she'd already fastened, scoot back my own chair, and then pull her over into my lap. She gasps, wiggling in my arms.

"Wilder!"

I capture her face in my hands, and wait for her to still. "You're not losing me."

She releases a shaky breath and squeezes her eyes shut.

"You can't promise that."

"Bullshit. I am promising that."

"Wilder, I—"

I kiss her, unwilling to hear the words and doubts she has to offer. Her lips are taut and tense beneath mine, but when I graze my teeth over her bottom lip, she trembles in my arms, softening.

She opens her mouth to me, and I swear her taste is a drug. An aphrodisiac. Nothing and no one in my entire life has ever turned me on as much as she does. Just that small taste sweeps through me, lighting up my every nerve ending, and I feel it all over. In my muscles. In my bones. Every single part of me reacts to her.

"I love you," I tell her, too overwhelmed with it to even give a shit that I just blurted it out like an idiot. Her hands grip my shoulders tightly, and she drags her mouth away, pushing back to gape at me. "I know it's way too fucking soon. I know we haven't known each other that long, and there's still so much we have to learn about each other. I get that. I keep telling myself that it's not possible this fast, that I'm crazy for thinking it, but everything in me, every fiber of my being tells me that's wrong. Tells me that I love you so damn much it hurts."

"Wilder—"

"I'm not asking you to say it back. And I really hope this won't scare you off. But I can't pretend that every time I touch you or see you, I'm not thinking it. Every second we spend apart, my body is practically shouting it. I love you, Kalli. And that's why you're not going to lose me."

A tear slips over her cheek, trailing fast over her skin. I blink, thinking maybe I'm seeing things. But then there's a second and a third.

"Sweet, why are you crying? Damn it. Just tell me how to fix whatever this is."

She shakes her head, and her hands leave my shoulders to flatten against my chest.

"I love you, too."

The heater suddenly sounds like a roar in my ears, and I shake my head, trying to be certain I heard her correctly.

"You do?"

She nods, tears still streaking steadily over her face.

I exhale, almost laughing. "Then why are you crying?"

"Because…because I don't *how* to love you. I've never done that, and I don't know how to do it without ruining something."

I gather her close to me, winding one arm around her middle and slipping the other up her back to palm the nape of her neck.

"There are no rules for how to love someone. We'll both make mistakes. We'll say or do the wrong thing. We won't always have the answers. But you keep loving anyway."

She doesn't look appeased by that. I kiss the corner of her mouth, then the other side.

"It's the easiest thing I've ever done. Loving you. Stop worrying about how this is going to play out down the road. It's this moment that matters. Love me right now. Love me tomorrow. And the next day. The future isn't written in stone. We decide it. Choose to love me every second. We'll choose that together. The rest will all fall into place."

Her eyes flick back and forth around my face, and I know she wants to agree with me. So I give her another reason. Yanking her mouth closer to mine, I crush our lips together, feeding every bit of passion and longing and things too big to name into our connection. She sighs against me, chasing my tongue back in my mouth, and my body clenches at the feel.

The need to feel her skin, to touch more of her, crashes over me, and I start with her scarf. Tugging at the complicated twists and knots, I try to keep kissing her, but my fingers can't figure out how to undo the damn fabric. Laughing against my mouth, Kalli reaches up to help, loosening and removing the thing in a matter of pulls. She tosses it into her empty seat, and I'm transfixed by the skin she's uncovered. Her long, smooth neck gives way to the plateau of her collarbone. The shirt she's wearing is a plain v-neck, but it dips low enough to reveal the luscious curves of her breasts. And from my vantage point above her, I can see the center of a black and white bra and a tiny bow that lies in the valley of her chest. I was already hard against her hip, but now the last of the blood still circulating in my body seems to rush south to my cock. I'm so turned on, I can barely think straight.

I drop my mouth to her neck, licking and sucking and biting the sensitive skin there. She arches her back, and I use my hands to encourage her further, leaning into her until her shoulders rest against the door. She's cradled sideways in my lap, and God knows I'd love to have her straddling me so I could feel the heat of her rocking against me. But this position has its merits too. She's completely opened up like this, her body laid out over me in a way that enables me to touch her anywhere. I start at her waist, slipping a hand beneath her shirt to touch the warm skin of her stomach. Her skin jumps a little at my touch, and I wonder if my hands are cold. I kiss her again in apology, and with our tongues still tangled, slide my hand up. I dance over her ribcage, tracing the delicate architecture of her bones. She wiggles in my lap, shying away from my hand as though it tickles, but then pushing back against me for more.

I drag my fingers just below the bottom of her bra, and she kisses me harder, one hand clutched at my neck, and the other braced tight against the steering wheel. She's so fucking responsive. I've barely even touched her, and she's moving against me like she's on the edge of coming already. When her teeth catch on my bottom lip and pull, I groan and give in to the need to touch her further. I cover the cup of her bra, lifting and squeezing the flesh encased beneath. She cries out, releasing her grip on my bottom lip, but it's not enough for me. I reach up a little farther, tugging the strap off her shoulder enough that I can fold the cup down to reveal bare skin.

I can't see her tits beneath her shirt, but I know from memory how fucking perfect they are. Full and heavy with dark tight nipples, one of which is currently pebbled against my palm. Her skin is blisteringly hot, and I know my fingers are still cold as I pull at the peak. She whimpers against my mouth, her kiss going slack as I tighten the pressure. I drop my head lower, dragging my tongue over the cleavage I can reach above her shirt, and then use my nose to push the fabric aside so I can replace my fingers with my mouth.

She bucks in my lap, her hips lifting up and then slamming back down as I suck that tight little bud into my mouth. I drag my hand out from her shirt and cup between her thighs instead. She arches up into me at the same time that her fingers tangle and pull tightly at my hair.

"Wilder, oh yes." She breathes hard and fast above me, and I don't slow down my touches. Instead, I draw more of her sensitive flesh into my mouth and press harder against the juncture of her thighs. She squeezes her legs tight around my wrist, keeping me from doing much beyond rubbing the heel of my hand against her clit through the fabric of her jeans.

Nearby, a car honks, its lights flashing, and I force my head up long enough to see a group of people moving toward their car, having just unlocked it remotely. Damn. They'll end up too close to us not to notice. I'm painfully hard, and judging by the fact that Kalli didn't even notice the honk, I know she's close. But there's no time. I pull on her bra strap, jerking it back into place and dragging her shirt up too.

She whines in disapproval, and I pull her up to a sitting position, kissing her quickly on the mouth.

"Sorry, sweet. There are people coming."

Kalli blinks at me, her eyes hooded and dark. She bites her lip, and I can see her considering kissing me again anyway. If she does, I'll go with it. People or not. I can't resist her. Then her eyes flick off to the side in the direction of the car, and her shoulders slump. She starts to shift off my lap, but not before placing her mouth at my ear. Her hot breath fans against the sensitive shell, and she whispers, "Take me home. Fast. Please. I need you."

I groan, and my vision actually goes a little dark around the edges when she places a final sucking kiss just below my ear. She crawls over into the other seat, and as soon as she's got the seatbelt clicked in, I've got us in reverse.

"My place or yours?"

"Mine is closer."

Fuck yes. She lives up by campus, only a couple miles away. But it's New Year's and the traffic downtown is out of control. There are so many cars driving around the garage looking for a spot that it takes us five minutes to get out onto the road. I tighten my fists on the wheel, glancing over at her as we get stopped at our second stoplight.

I reach over and grab her hand, pulling it up to my mouth because I need to be touching her. I kiss the back, and one by one nip at her fingers before soothing them with a kiss.

"Wilder," she whispers, and I smother a groan against her hand.

"We're not far."

She shifts restlessly in her seat, squeezing her thighs together.

"God, I wish I were touching you right now," I breathe.

She smiles dazedly. "You are."

"No, Sweet. I wish I were really touching you. If I could drive and have my fingers buried inside you at the same time, I would."

Her whole body tightens in response to my words. Her hand squeezes around mine, her lips purse tightly together, and her legs and her chest draw closer to each other for a moment.

"Please drive faster."

"You could touch you *for* me."

"Wilder."

I'm really starting to like that exasperated, greedy way she says my name.

"Just until I get you home. You could tell me how it feels."

She slumps a little lower in her seat and looks up at me from beneath her lashes. Her fingers clench into a fist around the seatbelt. "Do you want me to do that?"

Her voice is breathy. Soft. But I feel it like a hurricane. And I'm immensely proud when I manage to say evenly, "Only if you want to."

We finally get past the bulk of the downtown traffic at the same time that she lets go of my hand to undo the top button on her jeans. The speed limit is thankfully only thirty miles per hour, so I have an excuse to go slow enough that I can glance over at her every few seconds. I hear the metallic whine of her zipper, and sweat is already beading on my skin. That could have something to do with the fact that the heater is still on full blast, but I can't wrap my head around the simple act of reaching over and turning it off. The only thing in my head right now is *watch Kalli, check the road, check your speed, watch Kalli, turn here, go straight, watch Kalli.*

Her jeans prohibit me from actually seeing anything as she slips her hand beneath the fabric, but I can hear her intake of breath as she makes contact with her skin. That alone is enough to make me feel strangled inside my jeans.

"You there, baby?"

She nods shakily.

"Tell me what you feel."

She bites her lip.

"You know I'm going to have my mouth there soon, so no need to be shy."

She exhales. "Hot. damp."

"Damp or wet?"

"Wet. Really wet."

I nearly miss the turn onto Kalli's street, and the wheels squeal as I push on the brakes and veer to the left. Kalli grabs onto my forearm with her free hand, her eyes still squeezed shut.

"Almost there," I say.

"Me too."

Shit.

I take her hand from my forearm, lifting it up to my mouth to swirl my tongue against her sensitive palm. She moans. "Get there, sweet. Press a little harder." Her movements quicken, and I slow my speed as we approach her apartment complex. I kiss her pulse point and then drag my teeth against her wrist. She arches her back away from the seat gasping, and I know she's right there.

"You are so beautiful," I breathe, turning slowly into her parking lot. "We're so close. I might die before we get inside your apartment because you are so damn incredible. Come on, Kalli. I love you. Let go for me."

Her hips roll, lifting up to meet her touch, her movements frantic now, and then she goes completely still, her legs drawing up and together, her back arched. The only thing moving is her mouth as she struggles to breathe through her orgasm. She settles back into the seat, eyes still closed as I pull into a parking spot.

I swear I get almost as much pleasure from watching her as I would if I'd been right there with her. Almost. As fast as I can with a near-painful hard on, I turn off the SUV and jump out of the door. When I make it to Kalli's side, she's half-heartedly fumbling with the door handle.

I pull it open for her, and reminiscent of the first night we spent together, I lift her straight into my arms and move as quickly as I can for her door. She loops an arm around my neck and laughs quietly, and I can't even be embarrassed by my impatience.

"Put me down."

I grunt my answer.

"Wilder, I need to get my keys out of my purse."

Begrudgingly, I lower her to her feet a little ways from her front door. She has a small purse dangling from her free hand, and she lets go of me to unzip it and begin searching. I move behind her, placing my hands on her perfect hips and kissing her neck while she looks. She leans back into me, sighing.

"You're distracting me."

"Not sorry," I mumble into her skin.

Finally, a jingle lets me know she found her keys, and she steps forward out of my embrace to unlock the door. I follow her into the dark room, tugging her back against my chest again as her purse thumps to the floor. I reach for her jacket, helping her out of it and dropping it on the floor too. I shed my own just as quickly, and grab for her again. I miss, and she flips on the light next to the door. I stalk forward to press her against the wall, but she thrusts a hand against my chest and our eyes meet.

"Wait."

She looks too much like she did outside that bathroom at the bar. Her eyes too wild. Her body too stiff. And just like then, her hand pushes hard at my chest, holding me off.

"What is it?" God, it actually hurts not knowing what's going on in her head.

"I need to ask a favor of you."

Not what I expected to hear. "A favor?"

Her touch lightens against my chest, allowing me just a tiny bit closer.

"Well, favor might not be the right word. It's more of a request."

"Anything."

She takes a deep breath, and her dark eyes search my face for a moment before she adds, "I need you not to touch me."

My spine turns to steel, and my eyes narrow. *Not touch her?* That was the exact opposite of everything I wanted to do.

"What I mean is…if we're going to do this, I need you to let me be in control."

Her expression is guarded, careful. I blink a few times, trying to wrap my head around this. We'd been in bed together before. We might not have had sex, but she hadn't shown any inclination then that she wanted or needed to be dominant. If anything, it was the opposite. I could still remember joking about tying her to my bed so she wouldn't run away. Her reaction had been instantaneous. She'd liked the idea. So then why now did she seem to be asking for the opposite?

"I don't understand. You want to…" I wasn't even sure how to put it into words.

"Just this first time."

Clenching my teeth, I can't make any sense of what she's thinking.

I push forward against her hand, and she lets me. She doesn't drop the barrier completely, but I get almost close enough to kiss her.

"Tell me what you're thinking. I hate not understanding you."

She tilts her chin up to better look me in the eye, and our mouths are an inch apart.

"I have—there's something…" She trails off, shaking her head and then trying again, "I can't explain it. But for this first time, for my sake, I need to always feel like I can pull away. Like I can stop it."

I stiffen, and on gut reaction alone, I wrap my arms around her waist and pull her tight against me.

"Kalli, I would never force you. Never make you do anything you didn't want to do."

She lifts a hand to my face, running her fingers along my forehead and then my cheek, making a quiet shushing noise. "I know. I don't think that."

"Then why…" Oh Christ. My heart clenches. "Did something happen to you?"

"It's not that either. I need you to trust me. I'm okay. I just need it to be this way the first time."

I don't like it. Not one bit. And it has nothing to do with who's dominant and who's not. I don't like that there's a piece of her, something this big, that I don't know. I can feel the absence of it in my chest, of all the things she hasn't told me, and they burn like bullets stuck underneath the skin.

"You know I'll give you anything you want, *do* anything you want. But can't you tell me why?"

She lifts up onto her tiptoes, kissing me lightly on the mouth. "I love you."

I wait for her to say something else, but it appears that's the only answer I'm getting. I sigh and drop my forehead against hers. She plucks one of my arms from around her waist and laces our fingers together.

"Come with me."

I follow. But the frantic need I felt to have her is buried under worry. There's something wrong. I know there is. She's afraid, and it's shredding me inside that she won't let me do anything about it.

She nudges the door to her bedroom with her foot, but doesn't turn the light on. There's just enough residual light coming in through the window from the street light outside to make her bed visible. It's neatly made, a deep plum color, the headboard a design of curved and curled metal. She pulls me closer to it, and then nudges me to sit down.

"I'll be right back, okay?"

I don't say anything, and she leans down to crush her mouth against mine. Her lips are hard, almost desperate, and a few seconds later I get pulled into the kiss, unable to resist. Her hands thread through my hair, yanking slightly as she steps between my legs. I grip her thighs, needing to feel grounded in her after the confusing request she'd made in the living room. Her mouth moves faster, exhaling a few tiny moans against me when I drag my hands up to cup her ass.

She pulls away, breathing heavy, and says, "I *will* be right back."

She leaves the room and I hear another door open and close before running water follows. The bathroom. I suck in a breath, trying to shake off the anxiety still clinging to me. Needing something to do, I bend to untie my boots, kicking them off when they're loose enough.

Well, damn. That took all of fifteen seconds.

I shuck off my socks too, tucking them inside my boots and throwing them close to the foot of the bed. I drum my fingers against my knee for the moment, and then decide to go ahead and pull off my shirt, tossing it on the floor too. It's not like I don't know where this is heading. But I still feel…hesitant. What if she doesn't really want to do this? What if she's just doing it because she knows I want to, and that's the reason for…everything? I sigh, scrubbing my palms over my face in frustration.

The door creaks open, and the beam of brightness on the floor from the hallway light blinks out.

I look up. My eyes have adjusted a little more to the dark, but only enough to tell that Kalli is standing back in the doorway. The door clicks shut behind her, and her soft footfalls move closer. When she's about three feet away, I get my first good look at her. And my mouth goes dry.

She's naked. No clothes. No underwear. Nothing. Completely bare.

She walks toward me, arms by her sides, not the least bit shy or unsure. My heartbeat picks up, and lust swallows up my earlier worry in a giant wave. Her dark hair is loose around her shoulders, a few long strands trailing down to curl against her breasts. My eyes get stuck there for a long moment, watching the way they move as she walks. The skin of her stomach looks silky smooth, and I know from memory how soft she is. Her hips curve outward, and she's a foot away from me being able to feel my fingers dig into the flesh there. I love the way her body looks. Not too thin or bony, her curves flow smoothly into the next part of her form, proportioned as if she were designed to be perfection.

I reach out for her as soon as she gets close, but her steps stall, just out of my reach.

"Wilder," she whispers.

Something between a groan and a growl sounds low in my throat.

"I can't touch you *at all?*"

"I'll touch *you.*"

I do growl then. "Not fucking good enough."

The smile she gives me is dark and sexy enough that my cock pulses within the tight confines of my jeans.

"I'll make it good enough."

Oh fuck.

"Lay back on the bed," she says.

I hesitate, but when she takes a step farther away from me in response, I comply quickly, scooting back and throwing myself against the pillows. I fold my hands behind my head to keep from reacting instinctively to touch her, but when she crawls up the foot of the bed on her hands and knees, I know that's not going to be enough. She moves between my splayed thighs, her tits dangling in her bent position. I groan, and she hasn't even touched me yet. She advances until her knees are a few inches below my groin, and her palms are planted on the mattress on each side of my abdomen. She smiles sexily at me before her gaze dips down, traveling over my body slowly enough to make my muscles tense in anticipation. The first time she touches me is a light graze just above the button on my jeans.

"I should have made you take these off first," she murmurs.

Sitting back on her knees, she bends over me to start unfastening my pants. Her hair falls around her, brushing lightly over my thighs and stomach, and I hiss at the barely there touch.

"Tease," I groan under my breath.

She laughs. "I'm not trying to tease you. I have every intention of following through."

She finishes lowering my zipper and peels back both sides of the fabric. Bending a little more, she presses a kiss against my erection through the stretched material of my boxer briefs.

My hands are out from under my head before I realize it, and I barely reign myself in before I touch her.

"Fuck."

Instead, I push at my clothes, trying to help her along. She's still leaning over me when my jeans and underwear get past my hips and down to my thighs. Her hair trails over my dick as she shifts backward to keep tugging, and it's all I can do to keep from bucking up toward her. In fact, I can't even help her anymore with my jeans. I have to direct my eyes to the ceiling and away from her, so close to where I want her. I close my eyes and breathe, trying to ignore the jerk and slide of fabric over my legs as she undresses me.

I don't know if I can do this without touching her. It's the closest thing to torture I've ever felt.

Her breath hits me first just above the base of my cock. Heat and just a hint of moisture. Then her lips graze my shaft, and I can't stop myself from looking.

I was wrong before.

This is torture.

Her eyes lock onto mine as her lips smooth up toward the tip, pulling away just before she gets there. I fist my hands in the comforter in an attempt to stay still and breathe, "What happened to not teasing?"

I let out a shout when she grips the shaft and pulls it away from my stomach to take the head in her mouth. I slam a fist into the bed when heat engulfs me, followed by hard suction.

I don't realize that the string of four letter words going through my head is actually escaping my mouth until Kalli laughs around me, the vibrations drawing a ragged moan instead of another curse. She shifts, placing her hands on my hips instead of bracing them on the bed beside me, and pulls back to swirl her tongue around the tip.

There's something about seeing her lips there, feeling the contrast between cool air and hot mouth…hot enough to burn. Her lips caress the sensitive underside, and my hips instinctively edge upward. But with her hands braced against me, she leans a little more weight into me, pinning my hips to the mattress.

When she takes me back in her mouth, going deep enough that I bump the back of her throat, I lose control. My hands are off the blanket and in her hair in seconds. She keeps me there, my tip against the tightness for another couple seconds, but then she starts to pull away.

"Fuck. I'm sorry." *Fuck. Fuck. Fuck.*

I disentangle my fingers, and this time I reach above me, curling my fists around the metal headboard. Instead of removing her mouth completely, Kalli bobs her head again, returning me to that spot that has me squeezing my fists tighter to maintain control. The metal on the headboard isn't round, so when I squeeze hard enough, the edges pinch at my skin, helping my head stay clear.

That's how I survive the exquisite torture of not being able to touch the woman I love as she blows my mind. Again and again, her mouth moves over me, and her eyes never leave mine except for the rare moment when her lids fall and she hums softly as if she's getting as much out of this as I am.

Instead of spitting out cuss words, I babble nonsense and appreciation as she works me. After a few minutes, she seems to think I've got control over myself, so she loosens her grip on my hips, sliding her hands down over my sensitive inner thighs before moving back up to circle the base of my erection with one and the cup the heavy sac beneath with the other.

I'm so overwhelmed with pleasure and lust and perfection that I don't even feel like a complete person. I've fallen to pieces over want for her, and my legs and arms and body aren't connected anymore. They're vessels of sensation. Nothing more.

But my heart…it's still slamming against my chest, and I think she might be on the verge of killing me.

"Enough," I beg. "I want inside you. Please, Kalli. I feel like I've waited a fucking lifetime to be there."

"Not yet," she whispers before starting again, her movements faster this time, a little rougher, too. I tense, straining hard enough that the bed creaks from my pulling on the headboard.

"Now," I growl.

She laughs again in response, and the unexpected sensation jerks me right to the edge. I hold my breath and tear my eyes away from her, scared just the sight of her will make me lose it.

"Kalli, stop. I'm going to—"

She takes me deeper than she ever has before. So damn hot and tight and *fuck*.

I reach down to pull her off me, but it's too late. Her questing fingers hit a sensitive spot, and that combined with the wet clasp of her mouth around me are too much. My orgasm slams into me, my hips lifting off the bed involuntarily. She sticks with me, continuing to touch and suck and lick as my cock jerks and I come in her mouth.

I sink my fingers into her hair again, not caring about the consequences this time. All I know as I lay there groaning and dying beneath her is that I need to see her face. I push strands back out of the way, smoothing my fingers over her cheeks and forehead, whispering that I love her again and again until she slowly slides her mouth off of me.

Struggling to catch my breath, I say, "You didn't have to. I tried to tell you."

"It was your turn."

I shake my head. "That in the car didn't count. You did that on your own."

She leans forward, planning a kiss low on my stomach before continuing up. "I meant from our first night together. You took care of me, and I didn't return the favor."

She places another kiss against the left side of my ribs, and I frown. "That's not how this works, Kalli. You didn't owe me anything."

Her lips land on my chest, just above where my heart is still thundering, trying to play catch up. She lowers her body against mine. Her hips are cradled in the V of my thighs, her chest rests just below mine. She props her chin up on my chest and smiles at me.

"I know. But you did something wonderful for me that night. Beyond the physical. You made me feel important and special and wanted not for what I could give you, but just for being me. You reminded me of things that I'd forgotten a long time ago. And you held me together when I felt sure that my only option was to fall apart. You changed everything that night. More than you will ever know. And I wanted to give you a little taste of what that felt like for me. To have someone solely concentrated on you and giving you what you need."

It's the most insight she's ever given me into her emotions, and that somehow means even more than hearing her say she loves me. My throat feels tight when I answer. Maybe from fighting the pleasure she just gave me. Or from hearing her words. Either way, my voice is raspy when I say, "You. If you want to give me what I need, the answer will always be you."

Chapter Twenty-One
Kalli

I know I should still be monitoring my energy levels and being cautious about how much we touch. It's the only way I can be certain that he's safe as we have sex.

Fact: Being with him causes the energy to build at an unnatural speed.

Fact: Prolonged touch amplifies that already advanced speed.

Fact: I want him to touch me anyway.

His eyes are hooded as he looks at me, almost lazy after the force of his orgasm. And it does something to my soul to hear him say he needs me. Makes it a little lighter, closer to the surface, as if my soul wants to get as near to his as possible.

So, I give my being and mind and heart what they want and press my body into his. I lay my head over his heart so I can hear the way it beats underneath his skin. Steady. Strong. I inch my fingers up his side, over his chest, and around his neck, hooking them together in a gesture of possession.

I want him to touch me despite the consequences because I want to feel like I'm his as much as he is mine.

And there's not an inch of me that doesn't believe he is that.

His chest rumbles beneath me when he asks, "Can I touch you now?"

I smile and nod against him. I'll probably need to instigate the no touching rule again when we're actually joined, just to make certain that the greater intimacy doesn't cause an even more drastic reaction in me. But for now? Feeling his relaxed body underneath mine? There's nothing I want more than his arms around me.

Half a second later, I get exactly that. One arm bands around my ribs, curling until his fingertips brush the side of my breast. The other drapes low across my waist, ending with a tight grip on my hip. I sigh in contentment, feeling like his arms are a heated brand on my skin.

His.

We lay like that for a while, and I enjoy the way my body moves with his every breath. Up and down. Up and down. I snuggle up his body a little more so I can press my face into the warm hollow of his neck instead.

He makes another rumbling noise beneath me, and my grin spreads wide.

"You're not falling asleep on me again are you?"

I laugh. "No." Then I open my mouth against his neck to prove it. The steady rhythm of his breathing falters a little.

"Good." The hand on my hip loosens and his palm smoothes down, rising with the curve of my bottom. "Because I'm not done with you yet." His hand squeezes once and then continues down, dipping lower to the heated juncture below. He grazes my inner thighs first, and I know without his groan that I'm damp there.

I've never in my life gotten that much pleasure out of going down on a guy. I've pretended I have, sure. That's sort of part of the routine. But every time his body had reacted instinctively—tightening or thrusting or squirming—my own body had clenched in response. It was just another part of feeling like he belonged to me. His pleasure belonged to me, too.

His fingers continue upward until they hit sensitive, swollen flesh. And I'm more than damp there.

"Kalli," he murmurs, placing a kiss on my forehead.

His touch is soft at first, exploring through my wetness. Then his arm stretches, reaching farther, touching the bundle of nerves at the top. I tighten my grip on his neck and tilt my hips into his. The movement takes me away from his hand though, so I press backward, rising ever so slightly on my knees.

He groans.

"Did I mention that the sight of you on all fours was the hottest thing I've ever seen? I think I'd like to see it from a different angle too though."

I lift up enough to throw him a sly smile.

"It would be awfully hard for me to be in control from that position."

He groans. Not from pleasure this time.

"Again?"

I nod. "The first time, yes."

I can tell he's not happy about it, but I can't take any chances. The thought of being under him, surrounded and pressed into the mattress by his body...gods, it makes me so hot. But I think about all the skin that would be touching. More exposure. And he has a way of making me lose my head. I just imagine me getting so caught up in him that I don't notice the rising tides of the inspiration. And then what? Risk hurting him? Or push him off and run away again, this time right in the middle of sex instead of the morning after?

No. Better to take it slow. To be sure. If it's manageable, there will be time later for him to be in charge. Hell, if it's safe, I'll let Wilder Bell do whatever he wants to me. I turn my head, kissing the center of his chest before pushing myself up. With a little wiggling, I end up kneeling between his legs again. His hands fall beside him on the bed once I'm out of his reach, and I meet his wary eyes before dropping my gaze. He's hard. Again. Or maybe still.

I rest a hand on his thigh and let it run up to his hip. I'm a touch unsure now that it's about more than just pleasing him. I don't want to just jump him. Well, I mean...I *do* want to just jump him. But I'm not sure if that's what I should do. This is our first time. The only first time that has ever really mattered or ever will matter. I want it to be perfect. I don't want him to remember it as that time I wouldn't let him touch me, and it was crap because of it.

Wilder must see my hesitation, and he seems to instinctively know what I need.

"I won't touch you unless you ask," he says, lifting his arms again to grip the headboard above him. "But that doesn't mean I'm just going to lay here either. I've been thinking about this night for too damn long to be a passive participant."

I grin. "I would never want you to be passive."

"Good. Then straddle me."

His expression is deadly serious, his eyes no longer lazy, but alert and watching my every tiny movement. I sit up, bracing my arms on each side of him, on all fours again since he mentioned he liked it. His eyes darken, and he licks his lips. I shift, placing my legs on the outside of his hips. He pulls his legs in, giving me more room, and I lower myself down on him. He groans, lifting his hips up to press into mine. I place my hands on his chest, one directly over his heart.

"Like this?" I ask, wiggling a little. He curses, and I smile. "Any other requests?"

He swallows, and his gaze dips down my body, lingering on my chest, and where we're pressed together, and then back to my breasts again.

"Touch yourself for me again."

My heart thrums, too fast to even really be called a beat. More like a vibration, the plucked string of a harp. I lift my hands, watching him watch me, and cup the weight of my breasts in my palms. He flexes beneath me, and I bear down on his hips. He grits his teeth, blowing out a breath between them.

I rock into him, stroking softly over my skin at first, and then gradually increasing the pressure of my touch and my hips. Wilder's fists clench and unclench on the metalwork above him.

"I can feel you," he growls. "How wet you are. All I can think about is flipping you over and driving inside you."

I slide over the length of him, slowly, torturing us both. Maybe a small part of me wants him to break, wants him to ignore my request and do it anyway. But I know he won't. Not Wilder. Not until I say so.

I love him for that.

I lean over and kiss him, the tips of my breasts touching the warm skin of his chest. His lifts up into the kiss and pushes his tongue into my mouth, hard and demanding. I let him keep control, following and accepting everything he gives me. I keep rubbing against him, addicted to the way it feels to be completely bare against him. The energy is pushing at my chest, and even though it doesn't make sense, I know it wants him. It's almost like the muse part of me is a separate entity all together, and she wants him to belong to her just like I do.

But I want him more. Enough that I will the energy down. I push and push until it's as deep as it will go, and then I break our kiss and slide forward so that his tip presses against my clit, and my chest hovers close to his face.

When I look down, his eyes are level with my breasts and his jaw is clenched tight.

"Condom, Kalli. I need you to get one *now*."

I bend my elbows a little, and he groans, taking a nipple into his mouth. He holds it between his teeth, sucking hard at the same time, and I gasp at the sensation. He pulls back, slamming his head against a pillow.

"Kalli, now please. I'm going to go crazy if I'm not inside you soon. There should be one in my wallet if you don't have any."

I lift up on my knees enough to reach down between us and take him in my hand.

"We don't need one," I whisper, stroking up the length.

He squeezes his eyes shut and jerks hard on my headboard, as if I'd tied him to it instead of just letting him hold on.

"You're sure? Please God, tell me you're sure," he says, eyes still closed.

I can't get pregnant. Or rather, I can't stay that way. Same goes for STD's. Even if I contracted one, I'd be perfectly healthy at the next midnight.

Rather than answering, I drag the head of his cock down the center of me until he's positioned outside my entrance. He inhales sharply, and his eyes finally open to meet mine. Then I sink down onto him. We moan together, gaze locked as I stretch around him. A little more. A little deeper.

"Oh baby. Fuck, you're so tight."

I raise myself up a few inches, and my legs shake at the feel of him dragging through me. Then I drop again, going farther this time, taking more of him inside.

"You feel," he says, breathing heavy. "Shit, nothing has ever felt this good."

I repeat the action, finally able to press all the way down the length of him. He fills me up completely, and I stare down at him, overwhelmed by the feeling and the thought that he's finally inside me. It takes all my concentration not to start crying again.

"This is real," I whisper, almost unbelieving.

"It's real, sweet. As real as it gets."

I know I should move, but I feel so full. In every way. I'm not new to sex. Not by a long shot. I've been with gods and mortals both, but it's never felt like this. I can already feel myself clenching around him, and nothing has even happened yet.

"Kalli, I need you to move."

"I can't," I whisper.

"Why? Are you hurting?"

I shake my head, and then I laugh because I know what I'm about to say will sound crazy. "I don't...I don't want to let you go. I don't want you not inside me."

Wilder goes still beneath me, his muscles pulled taut. Our eyes meet, and he swallows slowly.

"Let me touch you. Please, Kalli. You can still be in control. You can stop whenever you want. But just let me touch you."

I mentally evaluate the power in me. I'm somewhere between a four and a five. Not safe. But not drastic either. As long as I'm away from him by the time I'm up to an eight, everything should be fine. The build-up will slow once we're apart, and then I should be able to last another day or two before things get dire.

"Hands only," I concede. "And I stay on top."

He immediately releases the headboard. Taking hold of my shoulders, he yanks me closer until my stomach presses against his, changing the angle of him inside me. One hand slides up to my neck, pulling me down for a hard kiss. I melt into him, but keep myself propped up just enough that we don't touch completely. He nips my bottom lip, and my hips buck involuntarily. His touch drifts to my cheek, soft, but firmly holding me in place. Slowly, he tilts his hips into mine, sliding his other hand down to my ass to pull me tighter against him. Without putting any distance between us, I circle my hips.

"Say it again," he whispers.

"Say what again?" I swivel my hips a little faster, arching up into the hand he has curved around my backside.

"Why you didn't want to move."

Oh. That.

"I want you inside me. Always inside me."

The look he gives me…gods, I don't even have words for what it does to me.

"I love that. Fucking love that you don't want me to leave, and if I could stay here forever, I would. But right now, I've got to move."

I nod. Knowing that my desire is irrational, impossible even. The hand on my face slips down to join the other. He doesn't lift me off him, but he does rock me forward and up, tilting his own hips down at the same time. He slides out of me halfway, and I give up trying to keep the rest of our upper bodies separated. I drape myself over him, loving the glide of skin against skin. He pushes down on my hips, thrusting up at the same time, filling me completely again. He repeats the action, and this time I take a little more control over my movements, meeting him halfway. His thrusts are slow, but hard, and I gasp each time he fills me, hitting a tender spot inside.

Sweat beads up where our skin touches, making my skin slick enough that I slide over him in response to each powerful drive. I don't know whether I want to beg him to move faster or to continue his slow, even thrusts so that we can stretch this out as long as possible. We stick with slow for a while, managing a long, languid kiss as our bodies slip and roll in tandem. But eventually, slow is not enough. Wilder shortens his thrusts, using his grip on my ass to match my speed to his. When we're moving too fast to keep up our kiss, I end up hovering over him, eyes locked on his as he strokes into me again and again.

When I'm used to the new rhythm, he slides a hand up to cup one of my breasts.

"I want my mouth here," he growls. "Can you lean up and over me?"

I lift up, planting my hands next to his head. The new angle, draws my hips farther away, and it causes his erection to nearly slip out of me completely.

I moan at the change, and push myself backward to keep him, slamming my hips down on his. Both of us freeze and groan at the sensation.

"Again," he orders.

I do as he says, leaning far enough forward that he flicks a tongue out to tease my nipple, and then I crash back down onto him. This time, he thrusts up at the same time, and it rips a scream from my throat.

I don't wait for him to tell me again, repeating the motion. It feels so good that my head actually goes a little fuzzy, leaving me dazed and grasping for a release that's just out of my reach.

Eventually, I shorten my stride, not leaning all the way up to Wilder's mouth, but I continue to bounce my body back hard against his. There's no controlling the noises coming out of my mouth. There's no controlling anything. All I can do is dig my fingers into his chest for leverage and meet him thrust for thrust.

It had felt magnificent to have Wilder so full and perfect inside me. I didn't think anything could feel better. But each time he reenters me, it feels better than the time before. And my channel pulls tighter and tighter, as if it doesn't want to let him go.

My orgasm takes me by surprise. When Wilder begins to withdraw, my body catches just the right friction on his, and with only the head of his cock inside me, my muscles clench tight. The force of the pleasure makes me arch my back, pressing back down onto Wilder, but he feels bigger now. Harder.

"Kalli. Ah, *fuck* Kalli."

I get to see his face as he comes apart this time. Cheeks flushed, hair wild, mouth open. He is all chaos and beauty beneath me, his eyes lit with fire and love. He presses up into me as the moment stretches on and on.

I thank time. For making the best moments in life always feel longer than they are.

I thank the gods. For the gift that allowed me to live long enough to feel this.

I thank fate. For bringing him to me, and me to him.

I slump against his chest, feeling the comforting pull of the thread that binds us. This is meant to be, Wilder and me. I can't lose him. *I won't.*

The words of an oracle are not law, nor fate. They're a glance at the future as it stood at that very moment.

But I know in the very marrow of my bones that the future must be different now.

Because loving Wilder, being with Wilder, *changed me* after a millennia of staying the same.

"Happy New Year," he murmurs into my skin.

I glance up at the clock, and sure enough, he's right. 12:04 A.M. Hope fills my soul to the very brim. I gave up marking the passage of years a long time ago. There wasn't any point to it. Not then. Smiling, I tug, rolling at the same time so that my back hits the mattress and his body covers mine.

He looks down at me, his eyebrows lifted in question. I wrap my legs around his hips and smile.

"Wish me a Happy New Year again," I say.

His eyes blaze with what I can only call hunger. Leaning down, he presses my body into the mattress with the weight of his own, and together we celebrate a new beginning.

∞

"It's not a problem. I swear."

Classes have started back up, and the one marketing class Wilder and I managed to get together is the highlight of my week. Or rather, I know it will be. This is only our second week back, but I can already tell that this class is going to be perfect. We can't exactly have a lot of physical contact in a lecture hall, so it allows me to see him, to spend time with him in a safe setting.

"Are you sure, Kalli? If it's too much of a pain—"

I cut him off with a hand over his mouth. He stands in the hallway, looking incredibly handsome as he rubs at the back of his neck. I've really started to adore that nervous habit of his. I remove my hand from his mouth and lay my hand over the top of his, stopping the anxious movement.

"Baby, I've told you before. I love your sister. I can absolutely watch her until you get off work. We'll have fun."

"Mom might get off before me. I don't know how long it's going to take to fix the account I screwed up."

Lines form around his frowning mouth, and I take over rubbing the back of his neck, knowing how stressed he is, trying to once again juggle school and work with me added on top of it. He wasn't supposed to work today, but his boss called right before class. Wilder didn't tell me exactly what he said, but seeing Wilder's expression as they talked was enough for me. I've never been good at watching him hurt, even before I fell for him.

"You do whatever you have to do. We'll be fine."

He turns his head, kissing my wrist. "You know I love you, right?"

A smile spreads wide across my face. I will never get tired of hearing those words.

"I do know that."

"Good." He grins wickedly, one hand sliding down to squeeze my ass and pull me closer. "I promise to prove it later at your place."

I playfully push him off, feigning a frown at his public display, but we both know I enjoyed it as much as he did. We settle the details of my babysitting duty, and he heads off to his next class, and me to mine.

"Tonight," he promises again, but I know my levels are too high to sleep with him tonight. Not unless I find some time in the day to meet up with one of my artists. A night together typically raises my energies by four levels, more if it's, *um,* a *long* night, and that's only if I can manage to sneak out of bed in the middle of the night and sleep on the couch for while, and then return before he wakes. If I actually spend the night in his arms, it can raise as much as six levels.

But since I'm picking up Gwen from school after my classes, I doubt I'll be able to find an opportunity to release any of the energy before I see Wilder again this evening. I'll have to make some excuse. Pretend to not be feeling well or something similar.

It's not an ideal situation, but I'm managing better than I could have ever hoped. In the few weeks we've been seeing each other, I've only had one close call, and that was when Wilder showed up unannounced while I was supposed to be "working." But even then, I managed to keep a tight rein on my ability until I could get him out of my apartment and squeeze in some time with Lennox.

All in all, I'm cautiously hopeful for my new life.

I know eventually I'll have to think about the future. There will come a point where he will begin to age, and I won't. But that's years away, and there's time enough to stress over that. For the moment, I just want to enjoy what I have. I reach for the familiar pressure of the fate thread that binds us, and the steady buzz of it comforts me. I have to believe there's a reason we're connected. I have faith that everything will somehow come together.

After one more class, I run home to quickly grab a few things and then head to the address Wilder gave me for Gwen's Kindergarten. I park my car and wait outside while teachers begin leading lines of students outside. It takes me a while to find her, but finally I spot her wearing black leggings and a pink cotton dress near the flagpole. I cross quickly and introduce myself to her teacher. Wilder was supposed to call ahead and tell him I'd be picking up Gwen. Her teacher, a tall, lanky man in his thirties blinks a few times when he looks at me, and holds onto my hand for a second too long.

"I'm sorry. What did you say your name was?"

I pull back and smile politely. "I'm Kalli Thomas." I remind him, "I'm here for Gwen. Her brother called to say I'd be picking her up."

"Right. Right, of course. I remember."

He calls out Gwen's name, and she looks away from the small group of kids she's been talking with. She squeals when she sees me and runs forward to launch herself at my legs.

I laugh, and bend awkwardly to squeeze her shoulders.

"Good to see you too, kiddo."

She leans sideways, looking behind me. "Where's Wilder?'

"He had to run into work to take care of a problem. He asked me to pick you up for him. Is that okay?"

She squeezes my legs again in answer, and I marvel for a moment at the sight of her small hand just above my knee. Her short little fingers and tiny palm reveal just how young she really is. I smile down at her.

"You ready to go? I thought you and I could go have some fun."

She pumps her fist in the air. "Yes! Let's go."

Grabbing my hand, she tugs me toward the parking lot as if she knows exactly where she's going. I call a polite goodbye to her teacher, even though he's still staring at me.

"Slow down, princess. My car is this way."

She calms, if only slightly, and lets me lead her in the right direction.

"Where are you taking me? What are we doing? Can we get ice cream?"

I laugh.

"Well, I remembered that you said you loved to swim." They had a pool at the house they lost, and it's one of the things Gwen talks about the most.

"*We're going swimming?*" she yells, drawing a few stares from parents walking their children through the parking lot.

I chuckle. "It's still a little too cold to swim outside. But there's an indoor pool at the university rec center. We can get you a guest pass, and yeah…go swimming."

She screams a little more, hugging my legs again, and my heart feels full enough to burst at her excitement. We make a quick trip to the Bell apartment to get her bathing suit, and then head back to campus.

I take care of her guest pass, and we get changed in the women's locker room. I hold her hand as we walk past the lap pool where a few swimmers are training in the lanes. We bypass it for the regular pool on the far side of the complex, and I have to keep a tight hold on Gwen's hand to keep her from running off. At its shallowest, the pool is still four feet deep. So we brought arm floaties in addition to Gwen's swimsuit. She insisted she didn't need them, but I made her wear them just to be safe. Wilder trusts me with his little sister, and I have no intentions of damaging that. We play for an hour or so, and I find myself sticking close to her even when she proves to be as competent a swimmer as she promised. At her suggestion, we pretend to be mermaids, and I play along as she invents a wild, fanciful story about our life under the sea as mermaid sisters.

I eventually drag her out of the pool for a break to make sure she drinks some water after playing so hard. I know I'm probably being paranoid, but I can't help wanting to protect her. While we're on our break, Wilder calls to let me know he's home. I explain where we are and tell him to take a break and relax, that I'll take care of Gwen for a little longer.

I only intend for us to stay another hour tops, but it's two hours before I finally manage not to buckle under Gwen's begging. We dry off and change, and then hop in the car to return to Gwen's home.

The front door is open when we arrive, so Gwen pushes in before I knock or ring the doorbell. Cautiously, I follow her inside the living room, my eyes scanning for Wilder. Instead, they find his mother, leaning against the wall right outside the kitchen, smiling.

There's music playing, something acoustic.

"Mrs. Bell, we're—"

Her eyes snap to mine and she holds a finger to her lips, shushing me. I press my lips together, and she beckons me toward her as the music quiets. I cross toward the kitchen, and when I'm standing right behind her, I see she has a foot keeping the door from swinging closed. She pushes her foot out, widening the crack a little, and my whole body turns to stone when I glance inside.

Wilder is sitting on a tall stool, guitar laid over his lap as he bends to write on a piece of paper on the island counter. He scribbles for a moment, and then pushes the pen behind his ear, returning to the guitar and starting the music that I'd heard when I entered.

He closes his eyes, and his fingers move quickly over the strings. Sound pours off the instrument, and even though I hear it, it's somehow silent in my head at the same time. Something divides inside of me, peeling apart. Half of me stays here in the moment watching him, and the other half retreats, pulling deeper and deeper into myself, trying to hide.

No. Gods, no. Please.

Wilder opens his mouth and begins to sing, and at the sound of his deep, raspy voice, the dizziness implodes and I don't know which way is up or down or in or out. I don't even know if there's still a world beneath my feet.

There was a moment when you laughed and your eyes met mine
Your cheeks were flushed, eyes bright from the wine
That's when I felt it start, not quite a twist in the heart
But a step, a leap, over some imaginary line

Is this how it feels to fall?
Not so complicated after all.
I expected a tempest. Relentless. Maybe even senseless.
Is this how it feels to fall?

Inevitable. Immeasurable. Unforgettable.
But born in a moment so small.

The music picks up speed, and I swear I can feel every pluck of the string like a whip against my skin. I flush cold and then hot, and my insides feel like they're being wrung out, twisted and pulled inside by some imaginary grip.

"It's been nearly a year since he's played," his mother whispers to me. "He had a band and everything. I told him he didn't have to give it up for us, but he wouldn't listen. He was working so hard to care for Gwen and me. I only wanted him off the road. I didn't want him to give up music completely."

I lose all my words when I'm with you
It might frighten you baby, if you knew
How you own my heart, have from the very start
And it's yours til time is through

Is this how it feels to fall?
Not so complicated after all.
I expected a tempest. Relentless. Maybe even senseless.
Is this how it feels to fall?
Inevitable. Immeasurable. Unforgettable.
But still so small.

"It's you," his mother continues, unaware that I've forgotten how to breathe, how to speak, how to do anything but stand here and listen to my heart break between gentle thrums. "He's been so different since his father's arrest. He was here and supportive and wonderful, but there was always something a little hollow in him. I thought it was the music. But he's been different since you came along. I've never seen him as happy as he is with you. He's become stronger and more vibrant these past few weeks, like you've opened his eyes to a whole new world, and he's finally learning to move on. He loves you." Her hand touches my shoulder and slides over my back as she pulls me into a hug. "Both my children love you."

I should be rejoicing at her worlds, at her acceptance of me (especially considering how we first met), but the weight of the moment slams into me, pressing down on my shoulders. Everything about my time with Wilder that lifted me up—the love, the joy, the hope—those things turn to stone. And I want to them to crush me, want to die beneath them because I don't know how to live with *this*.

His mom is still talking. Her mouth is moving, and so is Wilder's, and I want to hit pause. I want to stop and rewind. I want to never know this about him. I want to never…gods, I want—I want—

I want everything to stop.

"I'm going to be sick."

I don't know how I move, but I do. It feels like I should have to learn how to walk all over again. Like my body should be as crippled as I feel. I don't understand how gravity still exists, and the sun is still in the sky, or how my heart is still beating.

How is my heart still beating?

I throw open the bathroom door and dive to my knees moments before my stomach convulses. Everything is stripped out of me then. Not just from my stomach, but from all of me. I lose my hope in that bathroom. My faith. My future.

This is what it is to die.

Maybe not in body, but in spirit.

"Kalli?"

Oh gods, please no. Please don't do this to me.

I don't realize I'm sobbing until he kneels beside me and says, "Sssh, sweetheart. It's okay." Then I hear it, the awful noise coming from my chest, and *finally* something in this world matches how I feel. His hand touches my back, and I throw myself sideways, slamming into the hard porcelain of the tub. I don't feel the pain. I've got too much of that already in me.

"Kalli? What's wrong?"

"Don't touch me." The words break up as they leave my mouth, sprinkled between gasps and sobs. *I cannot let him touch me.* All this time, I thought I had it under control. I thought I was keeping him safe.

"Kalli, you're shaking. What's wrong? Does something hurt? Mom, call 911."

"No!" I have to get out of here. I have to get far away from Wilder. From his family. I climb to my feet, and he's right. I am shaking.

"I need outside. I need air."

I flinch away from first Wilder, then his mother as they try to help me.

Out in the hallway, I nearly run into Gwen. She's combing out her wet hair, and she looks up at me with wide, confused eyes.

I can't do this. I can't.

I ignore her when she calls my name, pushing through the pain to tell myself to *walk, just keep walking. Get to your car, and you can leave. You can drive and keep driving.*

I stumble over the stairs leading down from the porch, and I hear Wilder shout as I barely manage to stay on my feet. Once I start running, it doesn't seem so hard. In fact, it makes it easier to breathe. So I run down the sidewalk, through the parking lot, and to my car. I throw the thing into drive, and slam on the gas.

Just keep running.

And if I look in the rearview mirror and see Wilder jogging after me, I don't let myself acknowledge it. I scream to fill up the small cab with sound so I don't have to hear him yelling. But I keep screaming long after I'm out of the parking lot, out of their neighborhood, out of the city. I scream until my throat is too raw to make a sound.

PART FOUR

"Behind every exquisite thing that existed, there was something tragic."
Oscar Wilde

Chapter Twenty-Two
Kalli

Three months later

My apartment smells musty when I push the door open. I flip on the lights. Or try to anyway. They don't work. I knew I should have set up auto-pay billing. The floor creaks beneath my feet, and it feels both odd and normal to push the door closed with my heel. There's a sweatshirt on the couch, still pulled inside out from the last time I shrugged it off as I sat there working on homework. Books are piled on the table. My laptop is still plugged in and open, the screen dark.

This place is a museum for the life I lost.

A trip through the kitchen reveals more reason for the smell. There's a moldy bag of bread on the counter. Unwashed dishes in the sink. I don't even want to open the fridge to discover what the last three months have done in there.

I drop my purse on the floor, and lean against the counter. I thought it would hurt more coming back here. I'd anticipated it being like a knife to the chest, which is why I'd gone to a bar first. Maybe I had a little more to drink than I thought. That would explain the numbness.

I'd never had to be drunk to face my past before.

"To new experiences," I mumble, raising an imaginary glass.

Exhausted, I sink down onto the floor right there, leaning against the kitchen counter. Specks of dust float in the beam of light coming in through the window, and I watch them through dry eyes.

Three months ago, I left this apartment behind. I cut ties and ran because I couldn't face him. I knew if I came back to my apartment, he'd follow me, and what could I have possibly said?

I knew if I saw him, if I talked to him, I would be tempted to stay. I told him once that I was selfish enough to want him despite the risk, and that hadn't changed. Still hasn't. Three months, and I still wake up thinking about him. Go to sleep wondering what he's doing. I pick up my phone, hovering over the screen. I can't even put a number on how many times I've thought about calling him, hoping I'd get his voicemail, just so that I could listen to words, *any words*, out of his mouth.

I spent the first week after I left practically catatonic. I checked into a hotel, and I never even left it long enough for them to clean the room. I stayed in bed, raiding the mini bar or ordering room service when the hunger pains got strong enough to break through the haze I was in. The next week I spent driving. I'd head back toward Austin one day, and then change my head and drive in another direction the next day. It wasn't until the third week when I sat down and began to think.

First, I wrote down as much of Bridget's prophecy as I could remember. She said something about my keeping secrets, and that I would lose *him* to them. That I knew well enough already. But she'd also said something else about a *reunion*.

And the line I clung to, even though I knew it was foolish and harmful to hope:

To be made whole, all must first be lost.

I was intimately acquainted with the all being lost bit. It was being made whole that I wanted to know more about.

Because as hard as I tried to leave this place behind, as many times as I've told myself that Wilder is better off without me, that we're both better off, there's one thing I just can't shake.

The thread.

Fate.

It didn't fade. No matter how far I drove. Not with time. Not with distraction. Not for anything. We're still connected, our futures tied together for better or for worse.

So I spent another week traveling, popping into dive bars and art galleries and coffee shops for the occasional inspirational quick fix. And I thought about being made whole. And what that might mean.

Whole.

It wouldn't be enough to just be with Wilder, though I did feel like I'd lost half of myself to him. *To be whole* would be to be normal. To live without secrets. Without this curse or gift or whatever it may be.

For me, to be whole is to be *human.*

Throughout history there have been humans deified by the gods. Heracles. Ariadne. Psyche. Io. Some earned their spot in Olympus through accomplishments. Others were gifted it due to love. Still others found immortality through bargains or accidents or manipulation.

But the other way around? That is not a common story. There had been a centaur that was said to have given up his immortality when he suffered a wound that could never be healed. Some of the myths say he made a bargain and gave his immortality to free Prometheus, and agreed to take his place in the underworld. Instead, he was honored and placed among the stars as the constellation Centaurus.

But the way the myths have been told and twisted and fictionalized over the years, it's impossible to know the truth of the past unless you were there. And even so, I have no wish to give up this world for the underworld or the stars. Not yet anyway.

I would gladly take death at the end if I could have a true life first.

But I don't have the power to grant myself that kind of choice. Only a greater god, perhaps only Zeus, could make that kind of bargain. And it would be a deal, no doubt about that. I'd have to give something up or make a promise or complete a task, but as soon as the idea took root in my mind, I was unshakeable. I would make any bargain, do *anything* to have the life with Wilder that my gut said it was possible to have.

But you can't make a bargain with someone you can't find. I don't exactly have the greater gods on speed dial. And my attempts to find the few other minor deities that still inhabit the earth in the hopes that one of them might have some clue, some connection to help me…well, those had been nothing short of a disaster so far.

Just like me, they learned long ago how to hide and survive among humans. I started with my sisters, trying to track them through historical records from identity change to identity change, inheritance to inheritance, assuming that they must live the same way as me. But one by one, I lost the thread on each and every one of them. They'd hidden their tracks too well. I tried researching artists with a quick rise to fame, but in the Internet age, there are more of those than I can possibly count. I watched YouTube videos and scrolled through hundreds of thousands of event photos hoping to catch sight of a familiar face in the background of just one.

Nothing. If my sisters are anything like me, they stay away from fame, from anything that might get them too much attention.

I visited cities known for their artist populations. New York. Los Angeles. New Orleans. Las Vegas. I tried smaller creative-friendly cities. Providence. Santa Fe. New Bedford. Nashville.

Nothing. I didn't know what else to look for. I could leave for Europe, I suppose. Or Asia perhaps. But it's a big world to try and find seven people who have spent centuries learning how to hide.

And even if I found one of my sisters…what then? Odds are they're just as clueless as me. I could try the furies next. They mete out justice among both mortals and immortals. They're more likely to know how to contact the greater gods, but they're even more difficult to search for than my sisters.

It's hard not to feel hopeless. Like I'm clinging to a solitary life preserver in a never-ending ocean. I could search for months. Years. And in all that time, Wilder will continue to age. He'll meet new people. He'll start dating again. What if he falls in love with someone else?

I drape my elbows over my knees and drop my head against my arms.

Where did my numbness go?

As I work to get it back, something slams into my front door. I jerk my head up, and it happens again. Repeatedly. It takes my inebriated brain a few seconds to understand that it's not something running into the door.

It's someone *knocking*.

"Kalli! Kalli, are you in there? I see your car! Open the door."

I cover my mouth to stop the sob that jerks up from my chest.

Wilder. How is he here? I've been gone three months. There's no way he's still looking for me.

Is there?

"Kalli, please." His furious knocks slow. The sound changes, grows more hollow, and I'd guess it's his palm against the door instead of his fist. "Just open the door for me, please. I'll do anything if you'll just open the door."

Another voice joins his outside. Deep and hesitant. "Come on, Wild. It's dark inside. She's not here."

That's Rook. Oh gods, what are they doing here?

"That's her car. She's back."

"You know, they do make more than one of each kind of car."

There's a thud and then shuffling feet, like one of them shoved the other back.

"I drive by here every fucking day, Rook—"

"Yeah. That's definitely an issue we should talk about."

"There's never been a car like that in this lot since she left. Not once."

"So maybe someone has a friend visiting. Or maybe they rented out her place to someone else."

Wilder ignores him and begins knocking on the door again, hard and fast once more.

"Kalli. I don't care that you left. I don't care why. Please just open the door."

He keeps knocking, and before I can help myself, I'm crawling across the dusty floor on my hands and knees. Sliding carefully so as not to make any noise.

"Wild, Bridget is waiting—"

"I don't care. You go. I'm staying here."

"Damn it. We've done this before. You said it would be different this time."

Wilder doesn't answer, and the desire to see him is burning me up from the inside out. I can't breathe around the heat of it.

"Fine," Rooks says finally. "Torture yourself a little more if that's what you want. Call me when you get tired of the pain."

I kneel before the door and press my hand against it. Numbness is long gone, and tears are falling so fast that I can't see through the blur. But I know he's little more than a foot away from me now. I listen for his breathing on the other side, scared now that his knocking has stopped. Maybe he went after Rook after all.

A thump follows, and I hear what I think is him sliding down my door, sitting down on the other side.

"Where are you?" he says, quieter this time, and I don't think he's talking to me anymore. Or rather, I don't think *he thinks* he's talking to me anymore.

"I just wish you'd call. Or write. Or anything. I just want to know you're okay. You—that day…" He sighs. "I've never been so terrified in my life. The look in your eyes. The way you were crying. Goddamn it, Kalli."

He quiets then, and as slowly as I can, I shift so that my back leans where I believe his is on the other side. I close my eyes and wonder how I can feel so far away when he's this close.

He doesn't speak again. Nor does he knock. But when I stand and chance a look through the peephole a few hours later, I can still see his legs stretched out in front of him on the concrete. I stare for a long while. Until I can close my eyes and see the image from memory, right down to the worn patch on his knee and the scuffs on his shoes.

Then I settle back down against the wall. Eventually, I fall asleep there, slumped over on my side, and when I wake in the morning, my porch is empty.

∞

It takes me two days, but after more research, I put a new plan into motion. A little poking around online reveals the name of Wilder's old band. *Wild Roots*. There was a tree tattoo with intricate twisted roots on one of Wilder's arms, and now I know its story. Or part of it anyway. I find a picture of the group, and just as I suspected…Bridget was part of his band.

From there, I find out her full name, which I then take to social media. And after a little light stalking, I see that she's checked in at a hair salon. So I park my car outside, and wait for her to leave.

It's a gods-awful, creepy move. But she's the only person like me that I know how to find. And sure, she's not going to be able to put me in touch with another god (hell, I'm not even sure she knows what she is), but another vision from her could give me some insight, *anything,* into the future. And this time, I'll be paying attention. I'll get every word.

It's nearly an hour before she leaves, her hair shorter and a darker blonde than the last time I saw it. I decide it's best not to approach her in public, so I swallow down a little more guilt over my stalking and follow behind her when she gets into her car and pulls away.

I'm relieved when she pulls into a parking lot outside an apartment building instead of going somewhere else. Unfortunately, it's an old loft style building, so there's one main entrance that's keyed, and all the apartments are inside. I park quickly, and pull the baseball cap I brought down low on my head.

I have to get into that building right behind her. If I have to wait to get buzzed in or for someone else to come, there's no way I'll know which apartment is hers. With my heart hammering, I walk up behind her as she turns her key in the lock.

Thankfully, she doesn't even look back as I catch the door. She just keeps right on going. I hang back then, pretending to search for something in my purse. I stay just close enough to keep an eye on her and catch which apartment is hers. It's like a maze in here as I glance after her around corner after corner.

Finally, she stops at a door. Once she's inside, I take a deep breath and wait a minute or two. Then I step up next to her door, just out of sight of the peephole, and I knock. The door opens, but I'm off to the side so she can't see me. I want her to be in a vision before she sees me. Otherwise, she'll tell Wilder. And I don't want him to know I'm really back. Not until I know if any of this is even possible. Nothing happens for a moment, and I'm scared she'll close the door without looking further. But then just as I'd hoped, she takes a step outside her door, glancing down the hallway back in the direction we came.

I reach out and snag her wrist, and by the time her head whips around to me, the white is already creeping over her eyes. She sucks in a breath, and I bite down against the swirl of energy in me.

Daughter of Zeus, Eldest muse
Erebus draws near. A reunion calls.
To be made whole, all must first be lost
The eyes are on you, the eyes will come
First shall meet last on death's breath
You will lose him to your secrets
The eyes are on you, the eyes will come
The eyes are on you, the eyes will come
The eyes are on you, the eyes will come

Her body shakes harder and harder as I hold on, her eerie gaze transfixed on mine. When I can barely hold onto her, I loosen my grip and she slumps into the doorframe. I sprint around the nearest corner, hoping to disappear before she comes back to herself. I keep going, turning a second time before I stop and settle against the wall.

I lean over, my hands on my knees, and struggle to breathe. Again and again, I repeat her words in my head until I have them committed to memory.

I don't understand. I hadn't expected to hear that line again...*you will lose him to your secrets.* I've already lost him, haven't I? I'm trying to get him *back*.

Erebus draws near.

Erebus is the god of darkness. Could he be the one to help me? Am I supposed to find him or will he find me? Or maybe she didn't mean the god. Erebus also just means darkness. She could mean that a dark time is coming. Hell, the darkness is already here. Or it could be that...*hell.* Erebus is the region in the underworld where the dead first go when they pass. Could that mean I will become mortal? Things aren't always so linear for an oracle. They see what they see, and it doesn't necessarily happen in order. If I became mortal, I would be far closer to the underworld than I am now. It's also said that the furies once resided in Erebus. They guarded the entrance to Tartarus, the lower level of the netherworld reserved for those deemed worthy of punishment, even sought out offenders and brought them there to their fate. They might have even been born of the god Erebus, or just born out of erebus, out of darkness.

Gods. Now I remember why I didn't put much stock in her prophecy in the first place. It could mean anything. A god could be coming or I could be dead or the furies could come for me.

My stomach goes icy cold.

They eyes are on you, the eyes will come.

That has to mean the Argus. He's still watching me.

A reunion calls. Could that be about the watcher? Or worse...one of the furies? Perhaps the one who put an end to my sister's life when she tried to resist what she was?

And now I'm back to dying. *Great.*

But there has to be a reason she repeated the line about the watcher so many times. *That's* the sign I was hoping for. I could spend decades searching out other immortals who may or may not be able to help me. Or I could get an immortal to come to me. He's one of the watchdogs of the greater gods. If anyone would know how to get me an audience, it would be him.

So, that's it then. I straighten, my heart curiously calm. I push off the wall, and start back down the hallway. I've got to get the Watcher's attention.

I head back to my car, contemplating the other pieces of the puzzle.

To be whole, all must first be lost.
You will lose him to your secrets.
First shall meet last on death's breath.

Whether I understand the oracles meaning or not, one thing is abundantly clear. None of this will be easy. My future is darkness under more darkness.

I push open the glass door to head outside, feeling sluggish and afraid. Is there even a point? Everything about that prophecy points to bad things and worse things. Maybe I should let it all go?

"Kalli?"

I had my head down. I wasn't paying attention to anything as I left Bridget's building, and now two large, *familiar* hands take hold of my shoulders. The touch is a shock to my entire system. I moan. Maybe in relief or sorrow or regret.

The baseball cap is pulled off my head, and my hair tumbles down around me, and then Wilder's face is in front of mine.

"It's really you."

He's pale. His glasses sit on his nose, and behind the lenses, I see bags under his eyes. This can't be happening. How could I be so careless?

"Where have you been? What are you doing here? What's wrong?"

I'm crying again. I can't even control it. His closeness burns like a cold frost against a wound.

"I can't," I whisper, trying to fight his hold, but his grip is tight.

"No," he says, so close I feel his breath on my face. "You *can*. You just fucking left Kalli. You've been gone for so long, and I didn't know what happened to you. I filed a goddamn missing persons report. I drove around day after day looking for your car. I was worried you'd gotten in a wreck. You were upset and in pain, and anything could have happened to you."

"I couldn't do it anymore."

"Couldn't do *what*?"

I lift my chin to meet his gaze, and the pain in his eyes makes it hard to breathe.

"This. *Us*. It's dangerous for us to be around each other. Please, *please* let me go."

He doesn't let go, but he does loosen his grip a tiny bit.

"What's dangerous? Is someone after you? Does this have something to do with all the things about your past you won't tell me? Or your family?"

I shake my head, squeezing my eyes shut. I wish it were that simple, that I could just close my eyes and make this entire situation disappear. I fist my hands in his shirt and try to push him back, but he won't have it.

"It's not any of that. You just have to trust me."

"How am I supposed to trust you when you don't tell me anything? When you left, I went to everyone who knew you. Lennox. Jack. He told me about all the time you two spent together. That you asked him not to tell me. How the hell am I supposed to trust with that hanging over my head? When you leave without a word even though you're supposed to love me. Was any of that even real?"

Without thinking, I cry, "Yes! Of course, I love you."

Wilder slams his lips down onto mine in answer. My mouth is hanging open in surprise, and his tongue sweeps in immediately. All the fight leaves me at the first taste of him, and even though I know somewhere in the back of my mind that I shouldn't let this happen, that it's cruel to give us both what might be fruitless hope, I can't help myself.

I love him.

I love him. I love him. A thousand times, I love him.

One hand cradles the back of my head, fingers threading through my hair, and my back meets the brick wall behind me. I tighten my fists on his shirt, but instead of pushing him away like *I know* I should, I end up pulling him closer. His body pushes so tight against me that the brick scratches at my back and my arms and legs. His mouth is hard and frantic, and I can feel his sadness and his anger in every desperate thrust of his tongue. His other hand grips my waist so tightly that his fingers are likely to leave a bruise. It's punishing, this kiss. But it's not a punishment. Or it doesn't feel like one to me. It's the first time I haven't been in pain in months.

And that's why I have to stop.

I tear my mouth away, turning my head to the side on a gasp. But Wilder doesn't stop. His mouth drags down to my neck, sucking soft skin into his mouth hard enough to leave a mark.

I try to say his name, but nothing comes out. Then his hand leaves my waist, and his fingers wrap around my thigh, tugging it up against his hip. He pauses his assault on my neck long enough to push his lower body against mine, leaning all of his weight until I'm pinned completely between him and the wall. I can feel his arousal against me, even through our clothes, the weight of it pushes deliciously against my core.

"Come home with me," he pleads. "We can talk about everything else later. But I need to be inside you, need to feel your skin against mine. It's the only way I'll know for certain I'm not crazy right now. That you're really here."

Everything snaps back into place, and all my objections and fears come roaring back so loud, like they'd been on mute with the volume turned up high. Finally in control again, I push him back. He loses his grip on me, caught by surprise, and I take off for my car.

After a few moments, I hear him behind me. And gods, how must we look? Like two actors playing out our own tragedy on stage. I make it to my car, but he catches the door before I'm able to tug it closed.

"Please," I beg. "I know it's not fair. I know you're confused. And I'm sorry. More sorry than you will ever know. But if you love me, you need to let me go."

He falters, his grip going slack, and I take advantage and push his hand off the door long enough to close it. I flip the lock and start the car. He's still right there beside me as I start to pull away. His hands braced on the hood, he moves with me, saying, "Kalli, stop. At least tell me where you're going. Are you going home? Can I see you again? Will you fucking tell me anything?"

So I tell him the only thing I can. The truth that threatens to slice me down the middle. "We can't be together. Not anymore. I'm sorry."

This time, I let myself watch him through my rearview mirror. He doesn't run after me. Instead, he stands staring in the road, his hands clutching his head as I go. I don't breathe again until I turn the corner and he's out of sight.

Chapter Twenty-Three
Wilder

I don't know how to let her go.

Even though she asked me to. Even though I know it's not fucking healthy to hold on to this. I can't. It's not like we had a fight and broke up. It's not like either of us lost interest. Something is wrong, and she's hurting, and I *cannot* let that go.

I stay staring after her car for a while after she leaves, trying to decide whether I should get in my SUV and go after her or not. Last time I did that, I went to her apartment, and she never came back. If she's running again, there's not much I can do about it. So, I do what I came to do, which is apologize to Bridget for skipping our gig the other night to camp out on Kalli's porch.

After she left, I had to go back to the music. It was the only thing that could get me out of bed in the morning. That and the marketing class that Kalli and I shared that I kept irrationally hoping she'd return to.

I still don't have the time to play as often as we used to, but I was managing. Then I drove by Kalli's apartment, a habit of mine every time I go near campus. I saw her car, and nothing else mattered.

I hit the buzzer for Bridget's apartment number, and after a few moments, she buzzes me in. I shove my hands in my pockets, and tell myself just to get this over with. One thing at a time. That's how I'd been living the last three months.

I knock on Bridget's door, and it opens almost immediately.

"Were you just here?" she asks.

I frown. "No. I just buzzed up."

"I know. But there was a knock at my door a few minutes ago, and I opened it and no one was there, and…" She trails off.

"And what?"

"Nothing. I don't remember. It's like I blacked out or something. You weren't at the door?"

My guts twist as I think about Kalli walking out of the building, a baseball cap hiding her face.

"You're okay?" I ask.

"Yeah. I'm fine. It's just…weird."

Weird. Right. What could Kalli have been doing here? Is it some bizarre jealousy thing? Did she come back into town and think that I'd started seeing Bridget again in her absence? How could she think that? And if she wants me to let her go, what the hell does it matter?

She opens the door a little wider and gestures for me to come in. I step inside, and my anxiety kicks up a notch. What if that's why Kalli pushed me away? She came here to make sure I wasn't with Bridget, and then I go and show up. What must it have looked like to her?

Bridget crosses to the couch, but when I don't follow, she stops and crosses her arms over her chest.

"Listen, I can't stay long," I say. "But I just wanted to apologize for bailing the other night."

"What happened? Rook said something about the girl."

The girl.

"Kalli is back in town."

Bridget scoffs. "She is, is she? What was her excuse for leaving you high and dry?"

I swallow and purse my lips. I don't know if I'm upset she didn't give me an excuse or relieved. Nothing she could have said would have made a difference. Except to promise she's back for good.

Bridget's eyebrows lift. "Fine. Don't tell me."

I sigh. "Bridge—"

"No, it's fine. I realize that I'm probably the last person you want to talk about relationships with."

"I don't know. Rook gives pretty terrible advice. It's a tight race."

She laughs, and drops her defensive posture. "Are you...are things better?"

I've been miserable to be around lately. I've been wavering between writing and playing love songs and depressing heartbreak songs. But music was the place I could get closest to her, whether I was singing about the good or the bad she made me feel.

"I don't know. There's just a lot I don't understand, and I have no idea what happens next."

What if she's gone for good this time? How long can I make excuses to drive through her neighborhood? How long can I drag up the pain and write about it before I forget how to push it back down when I'm done? Or worse...how long until I'm numb to it? Until it becomes harder to remember her altogether.

"Will you at least be at the gig tomorrow?" Bridget asks. "I get that playing rock songs isn't exactly your vibe at the moment, but this one pays really well."

It goes unspoken that it's money she needs. Hell, we all need it. It's not one of our usual jobs. We're filling in for another band we know at one of the bigger bars in town. If we could get a permanent spot on their roster, it would be a good break for us.

"Yeah. I'll be there."

When I go by Kalli's house, her car is nowhere to be found. I knock on her door just in case, but no one answers. Not that I'm surprised. I stay for a while, scratching out lyrics on an empty page in one of my class spirals.

It's always push and pull with you, push and pull
And it's hard, baby, not to feel like I'm the fool
I'm fighting battles in a war I don't understand
I'm losing speed, honey, here's where I crash land

I just want to know you, honey. Let me know you.
There's not a thing I wouldn't go through.

I shake myself. Scared I'll break myself
But I can't shake you. I don't want to.
I'm caught up, turned around
Inside out, and upside down
Just to know you, honey. All to know you.

I'll spin a little faster. Dive a little deeper.
Crash a little harder, anything to keep her
Her taste is my drug, and her lips are my dealer.

I shake myself. Scared I'll break myself
But I can't shake you. I don't want to.
I'm caught up, turned around
Inside out, and upside down
Just to know you, honey. Let me know you.

I don't know how to win this war I'm losing
I'm swinging at air, babe, and come back bruising

I'm outnumbered in a fight against none
Planting my feet just to watch you run

I'm caught up, turned around
Inside out, and upside down
You're the last thing I see as I hit the ground
Oh, I know you, honey. Too late to show you.

Eventually, I climb back into my car and leave. But I don't think I can spend the night in my bed. Not with the memories that are there. I need a break from the fight. So I head to my mom's place. It's late, and both she and Gwen are already asleep by the time I come in.

I bypass the couch because it belongs to Kalli in my mind, too. Instead, I head for Gwen's room. She's taken Kalli's absence almost as hard as I have. In the beginning, I told her that Kalli had just taken a trip. But the longer she was gone, the harder it was to tell that lie. When I finally broke down and told my sister that she was gone and might not be coming back, Gwen had cried uncontrollably. Harder even than losing dad. I don't know if it's because she'd grown to love Kalli too, or if it was just the toll of losing another person.

I nudge her door open, and she's curled up into a tiny ball on one corner of her bed. I take a weary breath and kick off my shoes before climbing into bed beside her small frame. She wakes when the mattress jostles, and blinks up at me. But she doesn't say anything, just rolls over and lays her head on my stomach instead of her pillow.

I rub her back until her breaths even out again, and I'm sure she's asleep. Then I stuff my arm beneath her pillow, and let myself fall, too.

"You ready?" Rook thumps a hand against my back, and I shrug in reply. He sighs. "I won't pretend to know what you're going through. I don't know shit about getting my heart broken. But I do get what it's like to feel like all the things that are supposed to be good have rotted around you."

Fuck. Rook never talks about his family. If he's bringing that up, I really need to pull my head out of my ass. "I'll survive," I tell him, even though it sure as hell doesn't feel that way. I don't know the timeline on a broken heart, and mine is well past broken. It's been cracked and pummeled and ground down into dust, and all I've got left is the empty hollow where it used to be.

"Bridge and Owen ready?" I ask.

"Yeah. Bridge is decked out like some kind of erotic cat woman." I laugh. Great. "Owen is in a bow tie."

"So, relatively normal?"

"Exactly. It's not too busy yet. The weather is keeping people from coming out, I think."

Thunderstorms have been moving through the city for most of the day, and as a result the streets are wet and the sky has been dark since mid-afternoon. Maybe it will let up, and some more people will decide to go out for the night. Or maybe it won't. I'm having trouble caring, even though I know this gig is a big deal for us.

"You feel okay with the set?" Rook asks.

Normally, I would have done that. But Rook said I wasn't to be trusted with picking music that won't make people want to dive headfirst off a building. So I let him take it this time. "Yeah, I looked through it last night. We should be good."

"Well, I added a few extras on there to be safe. So, if you get to one, and there's something you want to skip, just let us know."

"Got it."

"That song you sent me last night…"

"What about it?

"We could give it a try."

I lift an eyebrow. "I thought depressing stuff was off limits."

"The way you imagined it, I'm sure it was a downer. But there's some grit to it. We could rough it up a bit. Get a little angry. Do it a little like that song we wrote in high school. What was that poetic title we gave it? Oh yeah, *Fuck It All*."

I laugh. "That song was awful."

"Hey speak for yourself. The words sucked, yeah." I punch him in the arm. "But the music wasn't bad. It could work."

When I continue to stare at him skeptically, he sings a couple lines. His voice is gruffer than mine, deeper too.

"*I don't know how to win this war I'm losing. Swinging at air, babe, but I come back bruising.*"

He's right. It sounds more like a pissed off rock anthem when he sings it.

"I don't know."

He holds up his hands. "No pressure. I just thought if the place doesn't get too busy, we might have some freedom to play a little bit. And it wouldn't hurt you to get a little angry."

I could admit to myself that I'm afraid to let it get that far. If I dive into the anger, I'm not sure I'll be able to break the surface again.

"I don't know," I say again.

"Well, if you want to try it, I think I can follow you."

Ten minutes later, we make our way up to the stage that's been set up in a corner upstairs. There are maybe a dozen people here, probably a few more downstairs that will hopefully come up when we start to play.

"Just like old days," Owen says as he picks up his bass guitar.

"What?" Rook asks.

"Playing to an empty room."

"It's not empty," Bridget cuts in. "There's a cute bartender at the back."

Rook laughs. "Great. We get to play for the guy who gets paid to be here."

"We're getting paid too," she points out.

"Not if we don't start playing soon," I say.

I don't bother with introductions, not to a practically non-existent crowd, most of whom are standing or sitting in small groups, talking or drinking or eating. I look down at the set list. Rook has us starting right off the bat with a fast song. I decide we probably need to ease people into it. So, I pick a different song to start.

"Let's start with number twelve," I say. It's a less well-known song by a Swedish singer. Still upbeat, but people will be able to keep talking over us if they want.

We jump into the music, and I block out the empty spaces in the room. I just let myself enjoy the feel of a guitar in my hands, the pressure of the strings against my callused fingers, the smooth pick in my hand. For a little while, I put off my issues and worries. I shed them like dirty clothes, and put on a different costume for the night. I let myself pretend that I'm the old Wilder, the one before Dad went to prison and I came back home. The Wilder before Kalli.

It feels like a different life. A simpler one. A little two-dimensional, like I'd been living a flat life and didn't even realize it. But flat feels good now. It's easy. I let someone else's lyrics fill up the empty space, and for a while it's almost like being whole again.

Eventually, I notice that the crowd has grown. People are filling the floor in front of us, some even dancing. So, I skip to a few songs on the list with a better beat, and I watch the people move in front of me. There are probably people out there who've been through this same thing. And they've gotten past it. They're dancing again. It's not like a broken heart is a new invention.

Feeling reckless, I look back at Rook between songs, and say, "Let's do the new one."

He smiles. "Hell yeah."

He motions Bridget and Owen closer to explain, while I talk to the crowd.

"How's everyone doing tonight?"

A cheer goes up in response.

"Thanks for coming out. I see a couple familiar faces out there. We appreciate it. We've mostly got covers for you tonight with a few of our songs sprinkled in between. But there's this new one I just wrote, and it's probably a really dumb idea to do this without any practice, but well...I've done stupider things." I glance back at Rook and the others, and they give me a thumbs up. Rook and Owen have switched places, and they smile when I raise my eyebrows. Hopefully we can pull this off. "So, this song is called, well, damn...I don't even know what it's called. Probably *Just To Know You*. Or something. I'll let you guys decide."

I start off with my guitar, playing the old song that Rook mentioned. It takes me a second to get into it, but then muscle memory kicks in and the music comes back to me. Rook joins in on bass, and he grins at me, and I know we're both thinking of that truly terrible song we wrote back in high school. Owen keeps up a basic rhythm behind me.

"Here goes nothing," I say to the crowd.

It's always push and pull with you, push and pull
And it's hard, baby, not to feel like I'm the fool
I'm fighting battles in a war I don't understand
I'm losing speed, honey, here's where I crash land

I just want to know you, honey. Let me know you.
There's not a thing I wouldn't go through.

So far so good. I stick with the melody I remember, throwing in a few improvisations here and there. Rook really gets into the bass, and Owen throws in a flourish on the drums.

I shake myself. Scared I'll break myself
But I can't shake you. I don't want to.
I'm caught up, turned around
Inside out, and upside down
Just to know you, honey. All to know you.

I'll spin a little faster. Dive a little deeper.
Crash a little harder, anything to keep her
Her taste is my drug, and her lips are my dealer.

It's coming easy now, so I let myself relax a bit and go with the flow. I look out at the audience, and they're definitely with us. At the back of the room, right in my line of sight is girl who looks like Kalli, so much so that it knocks the words right out of my mouth, and I miss my cue. Even my fingers forget how to work for a moment. My eyes shoot to Rook, and he nods, sticking with me. We repeat a few chords, circling back around, and when I glance back at the crowd, the girl who caught my eye is gone.

She was probably never there to begin with.

I force myself to smile. "Sorry about that. Like I said this one is really new. I mentioned this was a stupid idea, right?"

A bunch of the crowd laughs, and a few cheer their encouragements, so after one last sweep of the room with my eyes, I jump back in.

I shake myself. Scared I'll break myself
But I can't shake you. I don't want to.
I'm caught up, turned around
Inside out, and upside down
Just to know you, honey. Let me know you.

I don't know how to win this war I'm losing
I'm swinging at air, babe, and come back bruising
I'm outnumbered in a fight against none
Planting my feet just to watch you run

I'm caught up, turned around
Inside out, and upside down
You're the last thing I see as I hit the ground
Oh, I know you, honey. Too late to show you.

We end the song to cheers, and I sneak a glance at my watch. Sure enough, we're due for our first break, and I gladly put up my guitar and hop down off the stage.

Then I see her again, and this time I know I'm not going crazy. She's heading for the stairs, and she flicks her head around to look at me, her hair spinning with her. She freezes when our eyes lock, and once again starts to run.

Fuck it. She's not doing this to me again. Once and for all, I'm going to get my answers or I'm going to put this to an end for good.

We're not playing by her rules anymore.

Chapter Twenty-Four
Kalli

I thought I could do it.

Just a little push. I wouldn't even have to go as far as last time. If I just opened myself up and poured a little energy out on the crowd, I felt confident that the watcher would find me. He'd been stern in his last warning. Any reckless behavior, anything that put the secret of our existence at risk, and he would come for me.

And considering I didn't want him to come with a fury on his heels, just a small amount of energy is all it would be.

But I couldn't get myself to do it. I couldn't even get myself to go inside that club again. So instead, I go for a place down the street where I hear music streaming out of the door.

And fate has a cruel sense of humor because when I follow the strains of music up the stairs to the crowd, it's Wilder on the microphone. His hair is damp with sweat, curled and sticking to his forehead. His lips hover over the mic, and he sings with abandon, making it hard to look away.

When I'd seen him playing in that kitchen, I'd been so horrified, so distraught that I hadn't *really* heard his voice. I'd taken in the words. I remember that his voice was low. But now…he's stunning. His tone is warm and deep with just enough of a rasp that he sounds uniquely like himself. And I can't do anything but watch the way his mouth forms the words, the feeling he infuses into each syllable.

How did I miss this? How could I have loved him so completely and yet not known this integral piece of him? If I didn't know him, and I'd just walked into this bar by chance, he's exactly the kind of artist I would have gravitated toward. The passion pours off of him in waves, and he could be really great. More than great even. He's gorgeous, and he looks so incredibly good up under the lights. His movements are magnetic. He's the kind of musician that people would fall in love with.

I fall in love all over again just *watching* him. Then his eyes meet mine, and he stumbles. His fingers strike the wrong chord, and he glances at Rook, who picks up the slack. I shift behind a group of people standing and chatting nearby, and I watch his face fall when he looks back and can't find me.

He apologizes to the crowd, and reminds them that it's a new song. I press a hand to my chest, feeling like all the air has been sucked out of lungs. *This is* his *song. He wrote it.* He must have mentioned it before I came upstairs, and now I run through my memory, picking out the lyrics that I remember, and I know with a sickening certainty that this song is about me.

I'm outnumbered in a fight against none
Planting my feet just to watch you run

I shuffle backward, and I run into someone waiting at the bar.

"Sorry," I mumble.

My heart pounds in time with the song, and I know I should leave while he's distracted. But I can't bring myself to walk away from his voice. From this song that beckons me even as it heaps grief atop my head.

Somehow, despite how careful I was, I still let my ability affect him. Maybe the energy leaked out in an unguarded moment. During sex or while I was curled up sleeping against him. Maybe my control isn't as good as I thought it was. Whatever happened, this is the result. His mother said he'd stopped playing after everything happened with his father, and it was only after me that he started again. As sorry as I am, as awful as it is to have envisioned a future with him only to feel it slip from my grasp…I can't be sorry that it brought out this.

It's perfect. *He's perfect.*

He clearly needs music. So I stay and listen through the end of the song, and I fight my watery eyes as it ends.

Oh, I know you, honey. Too late to show you.

Too late. Too far. Too much.

There was never anything about my relationship with Wilder that fell within normal levels. It was always bigger than it was supposed to be. Scarier. Harder. Better.

The band starts removing their instruments for what I assume is a break, and I panic. What if they come this direction? Back to the bar to get a drink? I abandon all thoughts of catching the Watcher's attention, and just try to escape Wilder's notice again. I glance back once. Maybe to make sure he's not watching. Or to get one more look. He's looking in my direction, but I don't know if he sees me. I don't stop to find out, breaking for the stairs as fast as I can.

I make it downstairs, and through the long room, but there's a back up of people at the door.

Damn. It's pouring outside.

"Kalli!"

I don't look back. I don't have to. I would recognize his voice anywhere. But there are half a dozen people in my way, and two more have just stepped inside, trying to escape the rain.

"Excuse me," I say, not bothering to wait before I start squeezing my way through people. "Excuse me, I need out."

I hear my name again, and I give up being polite, pushing my way through. Someone calls me a bitch, but I couldn't care less when my hand reaches the door enough to push it open. I throw myself outside, and the wind hits me so hard I stumble back. The rain pelts sideways, and the bouncer reaches out to tug the door closed. My clothes are soaked through to the skin in seconds. I try to wipe my eyes, but it's raining too hard to make much of a difference. It runs over my eyelids and into my nose and mouth, and it's like I'm drowning on land. So I put my head down, and start walking, trying to cover my face enough to see my feet. I don't even know what direction I'm walking, if I'm getting closer to my car or farther away.

"Kalli! Damn it, come back inside."

I don't know whether I loathe or love his persistence.

Love. Where he is concerned, the answer will always be love. But that doesn't mean I want to face him. Not yet. I just need to get the Watcher first. Maybe then. When I hear his feet slap through puddles in the pavement behind me, I start to run. My sandals slip on the rain-slicked concrete, and I can hear him gaining on me.

I can't survive another run-in with him where all I can do is lie and avoid. I'm tired of hurting him. Tired of pushing him away. Tired of not knowing what to do. All I can do is run. If I can just reach the corner, I can turn north. The street slopes uphill, and maybe I'll be able to run faster without the puddles of standing water. I look over my shoulder. He's so close. Soaked to the bone just like me.

I face forward again, just feet away from the corner, and I see something dark in my peripheral vision moments before it plows into my shoulder. It's a man, jacket held above his head trying to stave off the rain. Maybe running toward one of the bars for cover or trying to find his vehicle. He reaches a hand out to me, but my feet can't find purchase on the flooded ground, and I'm falling too fast. Too hard. I try to twist to catch myself with my hands, but before they even reach concrete, my head connects with something hard, and the storm, *everything*, disappears.

∞

Pain comes back first. Sharp and bright. I can't feel anything beyond the throbbing too-fullness of my head, like the rest of me doesn't even exist. I groan, and my whole body jerks of it's own accord.

"Shit."

Something presses hard on my head, and I try to push it away, but my arms don't listen.

"Hang on, Kalli. We're on our way. You're going to be okay."

I force myself to drag open my heavy eyes, but everything is shadowy, indiscernible shapes.

"W-What?"

"You're awake. Thank God. Oh thank God."

Something pushes on my head again, and this time I manage to jerk back from the pain. My body lurches forward against something I hazily identify as a seatbelt. Then the pressure is back on my head.

"Don't, baby. You're bleeding. I'm taking you to the hospital."

"What? No."

"I couldn't wait for an ambulance. It was pouring outside and you were soaked. And there was all this watery blood around the lamppost where you hit your head. I was so goddamn scared. Tell me what you feel. Can you see all right? Can you move everything?"

My vision sharpens, revealing the inside of Wilder's vehicle, and the dashboard clock that reads 11: 51 P.M.

"You can't take me to the hospital."

I can't walk into the emergency room with a bleeding head wound only for it to heal right before their eyes.

"What? Don't be ridiculous."

The car jerks again as he tries to keep one hand on the wheel, and the other pressing what I now realize is his wet shirt against my head.

I push his hand away, taking hold of the shirt myself. "Listen to me, Wilder. *You can't take me to the hospital.*"

"I don't care about whatever the shit is you're running from. I don't know if you're in trouble or scared or what, but none of that is worth your life, Kalli."

"I'm not going to die. I promise you. Take me home, and I'll be just fine."

"No—"

"Take me home!" I yell.

His wild eyes snap to mine, and I can see how afraid he is. We're both drenched, and he's shirtless. There is blood on his hands and some smeared on his cheek, and I'm sure I look far worse.

Softer this time, I say, "Take me home, Wilder." I glance at the clock. "And in seven minutes, you'll get all the answers you've been wanting from me. I'll tell you everything."

I can see him warring with himself.

"I've kept things from you. But I wouldn't lie to you. Not about this. Take me home, and I promise I'll be just fine. You'll see."

"I can't lose you." His voice is gruff. Raw.

"Things are…complicated. But you're not going to lose me. Well, not unless you decide you don't want anything to do with me after you hear the truth."

He reaches over to grip my thigh, his fingers desperate against my flesh. "That will never happen."

"Then trust me and take me home."

With a sound somewhere between a sigh and a growl, he switches lanes, abandoning his route toward the highway, and instead turns left toward my place.

That immediate catastrophe avoided, I sink back into the seat and close my eyes. I hadn't realized how much the streetlights and passing cars had been paining me, until the relief of darkness washes over me.

"Kalli?"

"Hmm?"

"Don't fall asleep on me."

The ragged terror in his voice makes me open my eyes. I hold his shirt against my head with my right hand so that I can reach over and lay my left on top of his forearm. He immediately shifts to lace his fingers with mine, and I close my eyes.

He squeezes my hand every few seconds as he drives, and I squeeze back. And I can't bring myself to feel anything but relief at feeling this close to him again. I must fall asleep even though he asked me not to, because I come to with my door open and his hands on my face.

"Damn it, Kalli. I'm taking you to the hospital."

"No. I'm up. Sorry. Just…just take me inside."

He helps me from the vehicle, his arm wound tight around my waist, and I lean my weight into him. Even through the rain, he smells familiar. Like Wilder. I fish my keys out of my pocket and hand them to him, and he pushes through the front door and leads me straight to the bathroom that sits across from my bedroom.

"What time is it?"

"Midnight."

No, not quite.

"What time is it exactly?"

He glances at his watch. "Two til."

One look in the mirror reveals his white shirt is tinged pink by water and blood. I drop it in the sink, knowing it's well past its usefulness.

"Hey!" Wilder grabs a hand towel off the holder by the sink and tries to press it over the wound on my forehead, but I put a hand out to stop him. It's still bleeding, but just a slow trickle. The rain washed away most of the blood from before, but there are still a few marks and stains.

Two minutes.

I kick off my shoes and hold out my hand to Wilder.

"What's going on?"

"We're getting in the shower."

"Kalli." He still doesn't take my hand, so I turn and push aside the curtain instead. I step in the tub, still wearing my dress, rust-colored stains splotched down the front. It's a barbaric replay of our first night together, but this time we're at my apartment, and instead of kissing him, I'm about to change everything about the way he sees me. About the way he sees the world, too. I start the water, letting the faucet run and the water warm up for a few moments, and Wilder steps inside. I turn to face him, and I mentally estimate, "One minute."

I pull the knob to switch the showerhead on. I wait, letting the water run down my back, and I know the second it hits midnight. The dull throbbing in my head disappears, and the overhead light in the bathroom no longer makes my eyes water from the sensitivity. I lean back, letting the water run over my head. I lift my hands, intending to rub away at whatever blood is left on my now healed forehead, but Wilder grabs my arms and pulls them away before I can do more than smudge it.

I meet his eyes, pulling one wrist free from his grasp, and with him watching, I rub my fingers over the spot where my head had apparently hit a lamppost earlier as I fell. I don't just hear him suck in a breath; I feel it too. His grip tightens around my arm, and his body locks up next to mine. He starts to step away, but it's my turn to grab hold of him this time.

"Wait. Don't go."

He stares at me for a long moment, and I can feel tears welling at the corner of my eyes. This could be it. This could be the moment he walks away from me.

His fingers graze my cheek, and he steps in closer. His height puts him looking down at me, and he rubs his thumb across the skin just above my eyebrow, just below my former injury. His eyes dip down to mine briefly before returning to my forehead, then he tilts my head back, leaning me into the line of the water again. It sprays against my hairline, smoothing through the knots and clumps left by the rain and blood. He runs his thumb over the unblemished skin there—back and forth, back and forth—as if he needs to touch it to believe his eyes.

"How?" he finally breathes.

Here goes.

"I'm—" Not human. Not like you. Not normal. "Immortal."

He doesn't react. He doesn't call me a liar or crazy. He doesn't ask me any questions. He doesn't say anything at all. So I keep going.

"I'm a muse."

Chapter Twenty-Five
Wilder

I can't stop staring at the smooth olive skin on her forehead. There was a cut there. Not just a cut. The skin had been *broken*, and it had bled and bled.

It bled so damn much.

But now there's nothing there.

I can't decide if I want to be afraid or worried for my sanity or to pinch myself to wake up. Maybe that was it. Maybe I missed Kalli so goddamned much that this was some elaborate fantasy dream gone wrong

"Wilder, say something."

Her arm smooths over my bare bicep and presses hard against my chest.

"You feel real," I mumble, more for me really, than her.

"Of course I'm real."

She's always felt too good to be true. How beautiful she is. The pull I felt to her from the very first moment I saw her. The way we both fell so quickly and so hard.

Am I crazy? Is that what's happening here?

"Wilder, did you hear what I said?"

"Yes. No. I don't know."

How the hell is this happening?

I touch her forehead again. "How?"

"I told you. I'm immortal."

The word doesn't really register in my head. And if she told me, I must not have heard her. Maybe I really am going crazy.

"Immortal…like live forever immortal? Like a vampire or something?"

She grabs my wrist, pulling my arm down in front of her. Her index finger traces over my forearm, down the form of Atlas tattooed on my skin.

"Like this. When I told you that my name is Kalliope, you mentioned that you remembered a goddess by that name." She pauses, her eyes searching mine. "I'm her."

Water is still spraying around her head and shoulders, and maybe it's a trick of the light or maybe it's part of my delusion, but she does look ethereal all of a sudden. The spray creates a halo effect around her head, and the water sluices down over her perfect skin. Her clothes cling to her form, and she's a modern day statue. Fabric draped against her breasts, revealing beautiful curves and lines.

One second I'm standing up looking at her, and the next my knees have given out and my back is slamming into the shower wall as I fall down into the tub.

"Wilder!"

Kalli kneels over me, cupping the back of my head, easing me down until I'm laying back against the wall and my legs are stretched out in front of me.

Everything feels like it's spinning out of my control, and as often as I look at her, as I touch her, there's a shrill, shouting fear in the back of my mind that this isn't real, and I'm going to lose her all over again. But it will be so much worse because I won't be able to win her back, to find her. She just…won't exist.

I clutch her waist, pulling her closer until her knees are over my thighs and she's straddling me. I take hold of her neck and pull her face down to my level. Her forehead rests against mine, and she feels so solid and good in my arms. But there's still a spot of blood on her neck, and more on my hands, and *I don't fucking understand.*

"How is this real?"

Her fingers drag through my hair, holding me tight.

"It just is. I was born several thousand years ago. I'm the daughter of Zeus, the god of gods, and Mnemosyne, the deity of memory. The rest of the gods have withdrawn from the human world, but my gift as a muse, my ability to inspire artists, is just as much of a curse. I *have* to use it."

She starts talking about poisonous energy and influencing humans and the madness she'll experience if she doesn't do it.

"The night you found me downtown—when I ran out of that club and you came after me…I'd thought I could fight the energy. I'd thought I could live without doing what I'm supposed to do, without affecting mortals. But the energy had a will of its own. My mind…I lost control and did a terrible thing. I put a lot of people in danger, and I was running from it when you found me."

"What terrible thing?"

Her hand trembles, releasing her grip on my hair.

"There's a fine line between genius and madness. A little time with me can open up a person to their potential, move them to greatness. But too much time with me…and that balance can be damaged. That fine line can be crossed. I…before we met, there was an artist I was *seeing*. He became obsessive. He couldn't let go. Of me or what my abilities did for him. I stayed too long, and he tried to kill himself. It's why I pushed you away at first. Why I ran the morning after our first night together. I'm dangerous. Being with me is *dangerous.* And you were better off never knowing me at all than risking the same fate as him. But—"

"But I kept coming back. Kept pushing you."

"But I *fell in love* with you. And even more than that...you and I, we're connected. I can feel it, like our fates are tied together."

That's it exactly. From the moment we met, I'd felt like there was something that tied me to her. I couldn't let go even when she told me to. I couldn't give her up even when she disappeared for months on end. Because something deep in me, buried beneath tissue and muscle and bone, something told me that we belonged together. I clung to that, knowing that regardless of what was happening in that moment, somehow we'd be together in the end.

But I'd thought that was love. Faith, maybe. Stupid, blind stubbornness.

Not something *more*. Something supernatural.

"So when you left," I begin, trying to piece everything together.

"I saw you singing in your kitchen. Writing music. You never told me you were a musician. The whole time we were together, I thought I could keep you safe because you weren't in any way connected to my ability. I would burn up the energy with Lennox and Mick and—"

"Jack?" Shit. Oh shit. Am I crazy that this is actually making sense to me? That I believe her?

"Yes. Him, too. It was the only way I could spend time with you and keep you safe. I thought..." She laughs darkly. "I thought I had everything figured out. I thought I'd finally found a way to have a normal life. To have all the things I'd never been able to have...love, family, a home. A future. Then I saw you in your kitchen, and I knew I had only fooled myself into believing what I wanted to be true. I was just as dangerous to you as I had always been. And I'd been so incredibly selfish. So...I left. It was the only way I knew to guarantee your safety.

If I hadn't…" She looks down at my fingers curled around her hips, her body pressed against mine. "Well, I'm not very good at staying away from you."

"Good." It's the first thing that comes to my mind, my gut reaction.

She shakes her head and starts to peel my hands away from her hips. I let her, but she's not about to move away from me now. The only thing keeping me together, the only reason I'm not completely *losing my mind* right now is because I can touch her, feel her, know she's real. My hands migrate to her neck instead, gently pulling her toward me. She doesn't hesitate until her mouth is almost on mine.

"Wilder, don't. Are you even listening to me? Spending time with me could ruin you. It's not safe."

I keep pulling her, until her mouth is a breath's width from mine.

"Did you ever stop to think that maybe I started writing music again not because of any magical ability on your part, but because I love you? Is that not reason enough to be inspired?"

She exhales against my lips, and when her eyelids fall, they send a few tears down her cheeks.

I kiss her then, and she doesn't fight me. Her body melts into mine, each soft curve tempting me to pull her closer, hold her harder, until the only thing I can feel or see or hear or smell or taste is her. I coax her mouth open, weaving my fingers through her wet hair, and let her become my everything.

It's easy, really. To get lost in her.

Our clothes are cold and wet, but I can feel the hint of her hot skin beneath. I drag my fingers up her spine, introducing myself to her body again, trying to swallow all this new, strange information she's given me.

A muse.

My brain conjures an image of marble. A lifeless portrayal of wavy hair, barely hidden breasts, holding an instrument maybe. Are there figures of her out there like that? Paintings? I know Jack painted her. And suddenly my mind is filled with hundreds upon hundreds of imagined paintings and photographs and sculptures. I think of all the eyes that have looked at her, hands that know the warmth of her skin, mouths that have kissed where I'm kissing now. *She's immortal.*

I burn with the need to erase every single person who came before me. To know the shape of her body better than anyone has. To own more of her. To wrap her up in whatever it is that binds us together until she's as helpless without me as I am with her.

I reach for the hem of her dress, pushing it up her thighs, and she stills.

"I heard you," I say before she can protest again. "I know who you are. I know the risks." I wait until her eyes are on mine before continuing, "But I don't care. I have never been so scared in my entire life as I was when I saw all that blood tonight. When you left three months ago, I thought that was the hardest thing I'd ever faced. And I *was* absolutely miserable without you. But a part of me always knew you wouldn't stay away forever. I believed that you would come back because we belong together. I couldn't see any other future for myself but with you. But tonight...everything happened in slow motion. You were running from me, and you were so damn close. If I'd been a little faster, that guy never would have hit you. Or maybe I could have caught you. Or if I'd listened to my brain the first time I thought I saw you in that bar, maybe I wouldn't have chased you outside in the first place. I thought of all the dozens of things I could have done differently. They flashed through my head faster than I could get to you. And I thought...Christ, Kalli. You were unconscious and bleeding, and I thought I'd lost you for good. Not for a few months. But permanently. If it's addiction you're worried about, too late. I already can't live without you, but I swear it has nothing to do with music or energy or any of those things. And if you think I'm going to walk away because of all of this, you're wrong. We'll find a way to make it work. I'll never play music again. You can hang out with fucking Jack as much as you need to. And if that's still not enough, then we take our chances. I don't give a fuck about genius. But I'll take madness if it gives me you first."

She starts to speak, but I cut her off again. I'm done letting her take all the responsibility on herself, letting her make all the decisions.

"There's still blood on you. I can't concentrate on anything else but how I almost lost you tonight when I see it. Let me wash it off. Then you can say whatever it is you have to say."

After a moment, she nods.

"But just so we're clear, it won't change anything. I love you. Fuck everything else."

She laughs under her breath. Or at least I think it's a laugh. There are still tears in her eyes, and her lips are drawn in a tight line, so it's hard to tell.

She braces her hands on the sides of the tub and lifts herself up off me. I grab hold of the bar on the tile wall, and pull myself up after her. Then it's just the two of us, standing before each other in a too small space, and it feels like things have come full circle. There's a weight to the moment that I can't describe, beyond the fact that I love her and she loves me. More than the importance of her secrets. I've never really been the type to believe in fate. I couldn't stand by while my father dismantled the family he was supposed to love and provide for and say, 'Things happen for a reason.'

But now?

I know in my heart that we're exactly where we're supposed to be. And if there were ever a reason to believe in a bigger plan, Kalli is it. She's the only fate I want any part of.

I take the hem of her dress again, and this time she doesn't resist when I begin to pull it up her body. She raises her long, lithe arms, and I keep dragging until the fabric is completely over her head. I ball it up and throw it on the bathmat just outside the curtain. As soon as we're out of here, I have every intention of tossing that blood-stained thing in the trash.

Kalli stands before me in her bra and underwear. I turn her around, and when I run my fingers from her neck down to the clasp, she trembles in front of me. I drop it outside the curtain too, and then tuck my fingers under the fabric around her hips. Then she's standing in front of me bare, and there's a smudge of dried blood where her shoulder meets her neck.

I grab a bar of soap and work up a lather between my hands. Gently, I rub at the skin there until it's nothing but smooth, unblemished perfection. I keep going, cleaning her shoulders and her back, then down her arms. Even when I don't see any hint of blood on her. When I turn her toward me, she doesn't hesitate. She lifts her chin as I take in the faint trail from where the blood had run down her face and neck until it met her clothes. My stomach clenches, but I force focus and calm, gentling my touch as much as I can.

I start with her hair, trading soap for shampoo, and gently work at the blood that's still clumped along her hairline where the wound had been. I focus there for a little while, then add shampoo to the rest of her hair, watching carefully to make sure none drips down her forehead. She tilts her head back, making it easy for me, and I loop one arm around her middle before nudging her to slant her head back farther, into the spray of the water. Her bare stomach presses tight against mine, and I can't do anything to control the hard-on that presses at her through my wet jeans.

I use my free hand to angle her head back and help rinse the shampoo from her hair. It's thick and long, and it takes forever for the shampoo to wash out. I can tell she's tired, so I cup my hand around the back of her neck, so she doesn't have to hold the weight up anymore. When her hair is fully rinsed, she lays her cheek against my chest and laughs softly.

"What's so funny?" I murmur, scooping up water in my hand to pour along her shoulders and collar bone as I hold her.

"I think you used a fourth of a bottle of shampoo in my hair."

I frown. "You have a lot of hair. And I wanted to make sure all the blood was out."

She laughs again, a little harder this time, and it feels so damn good to have her in my arms again. I missed that laugh. "You only really need to put shampoo at the top. The rest gets clean enough as you rinse it out."

I take her long hair in my fists, squeezing out the excess water.

"I'll remember that for next time."

I use a finger against her chin to tilt her face up so I can clean the rest of the blood off, but her eyes have gone vacant at my last words.

"There *will* be a next time, Kalli."

I pull away from her long enough to poke my head out of the curtain and snag a washcloth from a shelf on the wall outside. I wet it with warm water and a little soap, and begin cleaning off her face and neck with as much care as possible. When I'm done, I let out a relieved breath and hang the washcloth over the bar on the wall.

"How is it that I always end up fully clothed in a shower with you?" I ask, trying to find at least a little levity in this heavy day.

"You're not technically *fully* clothed."

I'd taken my shirt off to use as pressure on her head out in the rain. And I'd at least lost my shoes and socks before stepping in after her this time.

"Wet jeans are wet jeans, sweet."

She bites her lip, her eyes trailing down over my chest. She lingers for a moment at the tattoos on my arms, even reaching out to span her fingers over the Atlas figure. Her fingers tighten around my forearm, and her gaze travels the rest of the way down.

I see the moment she comes to a decision, releasing that bottom lip and my arm, reaching for the button of my jeans instead.

Maybe I should have stopped her. Maybe that would've been the gentlemanly thing to do. But the need to touch and claim her rides me hard. It's not just the supernatural stuff or the thought of all the relationships she's had in her past or the scare we had tonight.

I also just fucking missed her.

Like I've been living blind for the last three months, I don't want to blink for even one second as I soak up everything about her.

She pushes my jeans and underwear down over my hips, and I take over dragging them the rest of the way off. The wet material sticks stubbornly to my skin, but soon enough, I toss them out of the shower to land with her clothing. Her fingers graze along my hip before trailing up my side to my ribs. Her eyes follow her movement, still hesitant, so I keep my hands at my sides, waiting for her move.

She swallows and whispers, "I missed you."

I smile. "You took the words right out of my head."

With her face still tilted down toward my abdomen, her eyes lift just enough to meet mine. I can read the longing in her plain as day, but she's still scared. If she needs me to be the one to make that final push, I will. And I won't regret it for a second.

I touch my thumb to her bottom lip, tracing the fullness, feeling the tease of breath on my skin.

"Three months was too long to go without kissing you."

I bend, replacing my thumb with my mouth to suck her bottom lip between my teeth. The hand on my ribs slides around to my lower back, and her body falls against mine. When I cover my mouth with hers, whatever hesitancy she felt is long gone, and she kisses me back fiercely. Her fingers dig into my back, and the feel weights me in the moment at the same time that it sends need barreling down my spine. I pick up her other hand and drag it up to wrap around my neck.

"Too long to go without holding you," I tell her. "I would dream about having you in my arms. Ache for it. Only to wake up back in a world without you. I would have given anything. I'll *still* give anything."

Her face scrunches up as if she's in pain. "Wilder, every time you say something like that…it makes me want to run in the other direction. Don't you understand that the last thing I ever want is to see you hurt."

"I do. And the feeling is very much mutual. But I don't want you here with me because I was able to distract you. Or because the way you feel about me made you give into temptation. I don't want you to step out of this shower and decide you've made a mistake and try to leave me again. You've trusted me with your secret. Now trust *me* to know what's best for me. You've done the worrying from the start.

Hand it over to me for a while. The only thing you need to think about right now is whether or not you love me."

"You know I do."

"Then let me show you."

I dip my mouth to hers, but before our lips touch she murmurs, "Your song. The one you sang tonight."

"That was Rook's idea."

I kiss the corner of her mouth, then her jaw, and I brush my fingers up her side, mirroring what she did to me. I keep sliding up until my palm meets the curve of her breast, and then I put my lips to her ear and sing her the song how I wrote it. Not angry. Not hard.

I'm caught up, turned around
Inside out, and upside down
Just to know you, honey. All to know you.

Her hand slips up into my hair, and her lips meet my chest as I sing. I drag her closer, and our bodies rub together, wet and wanting. I let my hands do what I've been dreaming about, cupping her breasts, tweaking her nipples. I slide another between her legs, and she's already hot and wet when I run my fingers through her folds.

She gasps, her mouth opening wider against my chest, tongue dragging over sensitive skin. She works her way farther up my body, and when her teeth bear down just for a moment at the base of my neck, I lose every ounce of patience in my body.

"Fuck, Kalli. I need to be inside you."

"Yes," she breathes, her mouth moving along my collarbone.

I grit my teeth. "I don't know if I can be gentle. Not right now. Not with you wet and up against the shower wall."

"So don't be."

I hiss out a breath when she sneaks a hand between us to circle my cock.

"You can still say stop," I promise.

"I'm not going to."

"But I'm in control this time. And I'm going to touch you. Every single inch."

She pumps her hand along my shaft, squeezing tighter when she gets to the tip, and I decide she's had enough warnings. I pull her off the wall and spin her so that her back presses to my chest. My erection presses into her lower back, resting just along the upper curve of her ass. I circle my index finger around the tip of one breast while my other hand dives between her legs. Her body arches against mine, and she rises up on her tiptoes, a soft cry escaping her mouth. I bend my knees and my cock slides down to the valley between her thighs.

"Put your hands on the wall."

She does, pressing her ass back into me, while curving her back and tilting her head to look at me.

Fuck, she's gorgeous.

"You're mine," I say, unable to control myself. "I don't care if you are immortal. As long as we're alive, it's you and me."

"You and me," she promises.

I reach down and adjust myself so that the tip teases at her entrance. She moans, rising on her tiptoes again and pushing back against me. I press into her slowly, and each tight inch makes me lose my breath. I curve a hand around her, stroking her clit, and she tilts her hips, opening herself up a little more. I pull out halfway, and then drive forward until her body is flush against mine.

Kalli's hands slide on the wall, her body lurching forward so that she's almost standing again, and the change in angle makes me shout. She's squeezing the life out of me in the best possible way, and I lean forward, laying my hands atop hers on the tile. With my mouth at her ear, I say, "I'm going to fuck you now."

She nods, whimpering slightly.

"I need to hear you. Tell me you want me to fuck you."

"Please." She wiggles her hips, but I've got her crowded too close to the wall to move beyond that. "I want you to fuck me."

I grind my hips into hers, and her head falls back against my shoulder.

"Oh gods."

I laugh. She's said that before. The night we had our last shower together. I thought she'd just misspoken.

I must pause too long in thought because she wiggles against me, making a noise low in her throat. I trail my hands from her hands all the way up to her shoulders, then I follow the shape of her back until I get to the slight indent of her waist. My hands fit perfectly there, like we really were made for each other. I pull her back a little more, so that I can slide in and out of her easily. With my grip tight on her waist, I withdraw until just the head of my cock is inside her, and then shove forward. My legs slap against the back of her thighs as I repeat the motion. Kalli's arms waver under the force until she starts to rock her body back to meet me.

It's fast and hard, and Kalli meets me every second, right there with me. I whisper to her as we move, snippets from songs that I'd written for her, about her, because of her. Her body clutches at mine, reminding me again and again that this is *real*. She's here.

Too soon, I feel my body tightening, on the edge of release, and shorten my thrusts, keeping my body close to hers. I bend, tasting a drop of water that sits in the valley of her spine, slipping my hand down again to press at the bundle of nerves to bring her with me. I circle my fingers softly as I rock my hips into hers. She clenches tight around me, and I curse, just barely managing to hang on.

"Come on, baby. I need you to come with me. You feel so fucking good around me. I can't hang on much longer."

She bucks into me, trying to get there.

"Don't think I'm done with you. Once you come around my cock, I'm going to take you across the hall and lay you out across your bed. I'm going to drink every drop of water from your skin." I curl a hand over her breast, squeezing in time with my thrusts. "I'll start here," I promise. "I'll use my tongue and my teeth, and I make sure your tits know how much I missed them. Maybe I'll tie you to the bed like I promised, so that I can have my fill of tasting you. I'll push your thighs to the mattress and make you come with my mouth until you can't anymore. Then I'll push inside you again and work on proving you wrong."

Her arms start to shake, drooping again until her body falls closer to the wall. I pick up the pace, pressing more firmly against her clit as I go.

"Wilder, oh, Wild—" she gasps, almost forming my name again. "I love you," she whispers, and then her body grips me hard, pulsing around me tighter than I've ever felt. I push in deep, and when I circle my fingers on her again, she cries out, begging for something. Whether it's to keep going or stop, I'm not sure. Her muscles contract again, and I give in to my release. I let out a hoarse cry as my body jerks forward, and for a moment, everything blanks out except the feel of my body inside hers. It feels like a miracle, and I know what she meant our first time together about never wanting me to not be inside her.

We just fucking fit.

I ease off that bundle of nerves, and her body pulses in time with mine, slower now, but each one curls around me, sending a rush of heat through the rest of my body. I lay my forehead against her back, slipping out of her as she leans more fully against the tile. I kiss up her spine, until I push her hair over her shoulder, and find the back of her neck. With my lips resting there, I say, "I love you, Kalliope."

She starts to turn, and I lift up my sluggish body long enough for her to maneuver around to face me. Wrapping her arms around my waist, she places a kiss on the center of my chest. "We're going to be okay."

I don't know whether she's saying it for her or me, but either way I'm glad to hear those words from her mouth. I lace my fingers through her hair, and pull her in until she rests against my chest.

"We're going to be better than okay."

When our heartbeats slow back to normal, we step under the showerhead again. The water has gone cold, so we rush to clean ourselves up. Kalli shuts the water off, and I pull open the curtain.

I take my time drying Kalli off, pausing every few seconds to taste a stray droplet on her shoulder or breast or stomach.

"We're going to need another shower if you keep that up."

I wrap a towel of my own around my waist, and follow her out the door. "I wouldn't mind another shower. After a couple hours in your bed."

I run into her just outside the bathroom and have to wrap my arm around her waist to keep us broth from falling.

"Kalli, what—"

Her posture is stiff against me, and I follow her gaze to what should be her empty living room.

Instead, an old man is standing there, long gray hair, gnarled beard, and the strangest pair of eyes I've ever seen.

Chapter Twenty-Six
Kalli

"Wilder, go in my bedroom."

His hands settle over my shoulders, long fingers covering the bare flesh above my towel.

"Who are you? What are you doing in here?" he asks the watcher, and I wince at his growled tone. I turn to him, even though putting my back to the watcher makes me queasy.

"Please, Wilder. Go dry off. See if you can find something to wear."

His hard eyes meet mine. "And what about you? Come find some clothes with me."

The man behind my back speaks for the first time, and I whip around to face him.

"I was kind enough to wait for you before," he says, gesturing in the direction of the bathroom, and my cheeks flush. "I find that I'm not much interested in kindness anymore."

I'd wanted to attract the Watcher's attention, but now that I had it I was terrified. I never intended for Wilder to be anywhere near him. It was one thing to risk myself, but the man I love? My focus from the very beginning has been about keeping him safe.

"You know why I'm here?" he asks, his dangerous eyes flicking to Wilder.

I'd thought I would have to make a big splash to bring the son of Argus to me. I should have known better. Known he would see even something small like my confession to Wilder.

"I do." I swallow. "If you could just let him go home, there's something I'd like your help with."

He drags a hand through his beard and smiles at me. My stomach turns ice cold. "You know that's not happening, pretty one. And if you think I'm here to help you, you've not been paying attention."

Wilder's hands tighten on my shoulders, pulling me back against his chest.

"What's going on?" he whispers against my ear.

"What's going on," the watcher answers, "is your little muse broke the rules. And I already warned her once."

"This wasn't like last time. There's no one else around. And he'll never say anything. There's no risk."

Those double irises flash. "You and I see risk differently. You can only see what's right in front of you. I see it all. And now I see a foolish goddess who thinks she can keep a mortal. What happens when he grows older and you don't? Will he stay with you then? Will he keep your secret? When he dies, will you find another little pet to keep you from getting lonely? Will you tell that human too? When I look at you, all I see are risks."

"Not if you help me."

His eyes narrow. "Does this have something to do with the little trips you've been making?"

I stiffen.

He continues, "I told you I'd be watching. Perhaps I should have stopped you before it ever got this far, your foolish attempts to pretend you're something you're not. But what can I say? I like to watch."

I force myself not to react to his taunts. I'd been prepared for this. I needed to present my case, try to strike a deal. Before I can get a word out, he snaps, "I see you, mortal. You're even more foolish than she if you think you can slip something past me."

I whip my head around to see Wilder has inched to my side to lean on the kitchen counter, his hand creeping toward a knife. My eyes widen, and I grab his hand. "You can't. He's like me." Scratch that. "He's *more dangerous* than me."

The watcher flashes his teeth at me in a mockery of a smile. "That's right, pretty one. Keep a tight leash on your pet."

"Enough," I say. "If you've been watching me, you know I've been searching for other deities."

He tilts his head to the side. "Is that what you were doing? I thought perhaps you'd gone mad after all."

"I need to speak to my father. Or any of the originals. I'd like to give up my immortality."

He laughs, a low chuckle that crawls over my skin.

"All for a pet?"

"Stop calling him that. He's not a pet."

His eyes scan over Wilder, who I can feel tense behind me. "Looks like one to me."

"We're fated," I say. "Or is that outside your vision?"

He rolls his eyes at me. "I see the strings."

I falter, swaying back into Wilder a little. His hands catch my hips, steadying me.

"You do?" It takes a long moment for me to recover from my shock. "Then you know why I need to be with him. We're bound."

The watcher sighs. "Pretty one, I see nothing but strings. Millions of them. I've seen the strings for the person you were going to stand in line next to as you got coffee, for who sits beside you in your frivolous human classes. I see the fate strings that are too small for you to feel. Every single one."

"But this one isn't small. I *can* feel it."

"True."

I wait for him to say something more, but he doesn't.

"Can you help me? Just get me in contact. I'll do the rest."

"Why should I?"

"Because you won't have to deal with me at all if I'm mortal."

"You'll never be mortal. You've far too many strings for that to be your fate."

I gasp like he's dealt me a physical blow.

"Maybe—maybe that will change. You can't know for certain."

At least, I didn't think he could. He had to only see the present. If watchers saw the future, we never would have gotten this far. Melpomene either. There would be no needs for threats. They could just cut us out of existence before we ever caused problems.

Suddenly, he drops his head down, as if he's praying. But I can see his open, eerie eyes peering at the floor. He makes a humming noise in his throat. Like he's assessing something or agreeing. He stands frozen that way for so long that I consider telling Wilder to run again. Or to shut himself in my room. But in the end, I know it wouldn't do any good. If a son of Argus wanted to find either of us, he could do it in a heartbeat.

I pull the towel tighter around my chest, uneasy about this whole situation, when the watcher's head snaps up once again.

His pale blue eyes are nearly translucent, they're so bright. But gradually they dim, and he focuses on me once more.

"Say I did know a god who might help you."

My heart expands in my chest, so big that my lungs don't seem to work around it.

My voice strangled, I say, "You do? Who?"

He waves my question away and continues, "Would you be willing to make a blind bargain?" His eyes skip from mine to Wilder's. "Both of you?"

I freeze. "Why would he need to make a bargain? It's me. *My* immortality. He has nothing to do with it."

He smiles that fearsome smile again. "Strings, pretty one. He has everything to do with it."

"What kind of bargain?" Wilder asks.

"I know a god who needs something done. But he can't go through…*normal* channels, lest the other gods find out. Complete this task for him, *both of you*, and he'll give you what you want. The two of you can be together."

"No strings attached?" Wilder asks.

The watcher laughs. "Oh pet, there are always strings. It's all life is."

I clench my teeth against that stupid name and snap, "And what do you get out of this? Why the change of heart?"

"I owe this god a favor. If I get you to agree to take his bargain and look the other way as you complete it, we're even."

"And you can't tell us anything more about the deal? What if it's something terrible? Or something we can't do?"

"Risk." The watcher smiles and waves a hand in the direction of the bathroom. "You were willing to take one before." His eyes turn to Wilder. "You were willing to do anything. Are you not willing to do this? Or were those just pretty words by a mortal who wanted a piece of—"

"I'll do it," Wilder growls, stepping toward the watcher.

I cut him off, planting my hands against his chest to hold him back.

"Don't. You don't know this world like I do. Bargains are a dangerous thing."

"You were planning to make one."

"Yes, but I have nothing to lose. You're it for me."

His hands clasp my cheeks, pulling me into him.

"You're it for me, too."

"But you have Gwen and your mother. Rook and Owen and…and Bridget."

"I love my family. I would do anything for them. But Kalli, I consider you my family too. I meant what I said earlier. Whatever we have to do to make this work, we do it. Whatever it is, it can't be worse than losing you. Nothing can."

He kisses me, and his mouth is painfully sweet against mine. Day by day, kiss by kiss, he's winning pieces of my soul. Parts of me weighed down by memories or fatigue or loneliness. He loosens the binds and makes me feel like everything is new, like I'm seeing the world for the first time because it is so incredibly different with him in it.

He pulls back, resting his forehead against mine.

"We're doing this. And when it's done, you're marrying me."

After a moment, I nod.

He continues, "Promise me. Promise that on the other side of this we'll be together for good. I want to wake up next to you every day. I don't want to share you with anyone. Except perhaps Gwen. I want to belong to you and you to me, so nothing can ever come between us. When you…when it's done, you'll be like me. You won't live forever. And I'm sorry for that. But I promise I won't waste one single day."

I blink back tears, and my lips brush against his as I speak. "I don't need immortality. Living a thousand lives means nothing to me when the only one I really want is this one. I promise you. We'll be together for whatever part of forever we have."

"Touching," the watcher says behind me, his tone flat. "Are we all agreed then?"

Wilder looks at me, and together we nod.

"We're agreed," I say.

"I'm afraid I'll need more than your words for this one. Hold out your hands."

I take a deep breath and stick out my hand. Wilder follows. The watcher has us lace our fingers together, and then he wraps both of his large, weathered hands around ours.

"Do you agree to the bargain I've offered you, knowing full well that the terms of the deal that will be set forth by the god in question are non-negotiable?"

My eyes meet Wilder's.

Together we say, "We do."

"And are you willing to do whatever must be done, go wherever you're needed, face any consequence to complete this bargain?"

"We are."

"And will you do this all in exchange for this god's help in securing your future together?"

Wilder's lips quirk up in a smile. It feels a little like we're getting married now.

"We will."

"Then on behalf of Hades, god of the underworld, I declare this agreement binding."

A string of gold light snaps into place around our hands, squeezing so tight it feels like it's slicing into our skin. It glows brighter, and I grit my teeth when it burns hot against our hands. Tears prick my eyes, and when I look at Wilder, his face is screwed up in pain. I want to cry out for it to stop, to say I changed my mind, but before the words can surface on my tongue, the string disappears, and I can feel the weight of our bargain, a heavy cord, settle in next to the one I share with Wilder.

I hold on tight to him and lift my other hand to my chest. I gasp for breath, and try to will my raging heart calm.

"It is done."

The watcher's voice clears some of the haze in my head, and his final words come back to me. Hades. We'd made a deal with *Hades*.

Why didn't I force him to tell me who the god was before agreeing?

I lift my eyes to yell or curse or scream at him, but I only catch the blur as he moves. He ends up on the other side of Wilder. His frightening eyes meet mine from over his shoulder.

"I'm sorry, pretty one. It's the only way."

He raises his hands, moving so fast that I don't have time to say anything, not even a moment to meet Wilder's gaze. A sickening crack reverberates around the room as he grips Wilder's head and snaps it to the side.

I stare, certain that I'm seeing things wrong. Then his body begins to slump to the floor, and I scream.

I reach out, grabbing onto his arms, but his body is too heavy, and he's not moving. All his weight is pulling toward the floor, and my chest feels like it's been cracked wide open. All my strength leaves me, and I can't make my fingers squeeze tight enough or my arms pull hard enough. And he's falling.

"Wilder! No, please!"

I scream and scream his name, but I can't stop his body from hitting the floor. He sprawls, arms and legs thrown wide. I follow, collapsing against his bare chest. My hands shake as they move over him. I reach for his neck, hoping somehow he still has a pulse, that somehow he's alive. But purple splotches have already inked across his skin, and when I run my fingers over his neck, it feels wrong. The skin is tight and twisted, and oh gods.

I bury my head against his chest, and I forget how to do anything but scream. Everything hurts. Beginning with my throat and moving through my lungs and my heart and even my skin. Every second that I don't hear his heart beating beneath my ear, the silence crushes me. My ribs are collapsing, bones snapping, organs being ground to dust.

And I beg for it to move faster. To flatten me so completely that there's not enough of me left to feel.

But it doesn't.

Despite the way it feels, I am completely, horrifyingly whole.

And Wilder is...*not.*

He's not. He's not. Oh gods, he's not.

The floor creaks nearby, and time seems to reel backward. I'm finally able to think beyond the sight of Wilder's broken body before me and remember what came before it.

Watcher.

He stands in my kitchen. His arms crossed over his chest as if he hasn't just ripped the heart out of my existence. I fly at him, needing to break his murdering fingers and claw out his vile eyes. He catches my wrist and for the second time in minutes, my body lets me down. I throw myself into him, pull and tug and swing, but he's strong. And I'm so very weak.

So weak that I let him take the very best of this world. I think of Gwen and Wilder's mom and Rook on the edge of his darkness. This will destroy them. And it's all my fault. I brought him into this world. I was selfish enough to want him even though I am and have always been poison.

"Breathe, pretty one."

I scream again, digging my fingernails into the backs of his hands. But he stands there, stoic and steadfast.

It occurs to me then. What I need to do.

I draw up the energy in me, but even it feels wilted and waning in the absence of my other half. But all I need is enough to be dangerous, enough to affect the other people in my apartment building. If I push hard enough, he'll have to kill me.

He slaps me hard, and then his hand grips my face, squeezing my jaw so hard I feel like the bones might shatter.

"Enough of that. It had to be done. There's only one way for a mortal to get to the underworld, and he just took it."

The fight leaves me, rushing out of me, and leaving only a deep, hollow ache in its place. *So, it was my fault.* I can't even blame it on the deity in front of me. *I* made the bargain. *Me.*

"Are you going to stand here and weep or follow him?"

"You'll do it? You'll kill me?"

He scowls. "Don't be stupid, girl. Hades doesn't want you snuffed out. Were you not paying attention? He wants both of you."

My mind is too sluggish, too fogged by pain.

"Are you—are you saying this might not be permanent? Will Hades let me take him back?"

It's not unheard of. Orpheus went after Eurydice. He would have brought her spirit back with him too if he hadn't looked back as he'd promised he wouldn't. Could that be part of the bargain?

"I'd imagine that rests upon the task he has for you. It's not my deal. I'm just a facilitator. But time moves differently in the Netherworlds. If you don't go and find him soon, he'll have lived lifetimes down there by the time you reach him."

I could attack him all over again for keeping that from me. For keeping all of this from me.

"How? How do I get there if not through death?"

From his pocket, he pulls out a coin. It's ancient and gold, a skeletal man in a ferry carved on the face.

"Charon?"

He nods. "Show him this coin. It will get you across the river. Find your Wilder, then together find Hades. Do not lose the coin or you won't be able to get back. This is not a mere token coin for the dead. It will keep you anchored here in this world."

"And how do I get to Charon? How do I get there from here?"

I glance again at the lifeless body on the floor beside me, and my heart seizes up with pain. How long had I sat there crying? How long has it been since the watcher snapped his neck and took him from me?

I can't think about him in the Underworld. He won't know that I'm coming for him. He'll be alone, wandering, thinking I've forgotten him completely. How much faster does time move there?

"You'll need to put it in your mouth, as we do with the dead. Cut your tongue. Or bite down. When your blood offering touches the coin, it will take you to Charon."

He holds out the gold piece and drops it in my palm.

Quickly, I drop to the floor, laying down beside Wilder. I grab his hand, lacing our fingers together, and lift the coin to my mouth.

But first, "The string. I can't feel it. But I didn't feel it snap either. Not like when my sister died. Can you still see it?"

"Fate is a fickle mistress, Kalliope. Do not think of her as a friend. She will tie you up or cut you loose to reach her ends."

I nod and hold the coin up as if it's a toast.

"To be made whole, all must first be lost."

I place the cold coin in my mouth, and before I can think about the pain, I bite down hard on my tongue.

Blood floods my mouth, and my last thought before I'm ripped from this world is of Bridget's prophecy.

Erebus draws near.

End of Book One

How much can love overcome?
Continue Kalli and Wilder's story with *Inflict*, book two of the Muse series, coming in 2015!

Author's Note:

Thank you SO much for reading *Inspire*. Hopefully you don't hate me too much after that ending. I've had an incredible time writing this story, and I hope you love it as much as I do. If you've read my other books, you know this is something very different for me, but in reality, this is the kind of story I've been writing for most of my life. I just took a detour into contemporary romance. I'm hopeful that I'll get to continue to write both types of stories, and that we'll see more fantasy and other subgenres in the New Adult category as a whole. Because I think they're pretty awesome. But we need your help as readers to expand! If you like fantasy and paranormal and scifi—read and recommend those books! As more people read and buy those books, more authors will begin to write them. So if you enjoyed this book (or any other for that matter), please consider telling a friend or writing a review to leave online to encourage other buyers. I cannot overstate how much of an impact that small action can have for a book. So, if you've got the time, I would greatly appreciate it! And I hope you'll also connect with me online. I always love to hear from readers on Facebook, Twitter, Instagram, and my blog. You can expect teasers and more information about Kalli and Wilder's future there too. Thank you again. And I'll see you in the Underworld!

Acknowledgments

This book very nearly didn't happen. On several occasions. Life tried to get in the way multiple times, but these characters and this story not only managed to rise above that, but they kept me sane when so much around me was falling apart.

To be honest, I'm still not really sure how I survived it. But I know I never would have been able to actually get this book in your hands without the help of several beautiful, incredible people. Lindsay—don't ever leave me. You're the best friend and assistant I could ask for. There aren't words for how much better you make my life. Mom—you are undeniably the best mother in the world. I am a hot mess 99% of the time, but you're always there to help me get back on track, whether it's by reading my stuff, brainstorming titles, or making me a home cooked meal when I've been in the writing cave for daaaays. I owe you everything. Amy—my dedication said most of it, but thank you again for everything. You're always the person I can go to with anything book related, and that makes you the very best kind of sister. Jen—you were there when I first started brainstorming this book, and you helped me mull over that ending, oh, a thousand times. Now, it's your turn to finish that book you've been sitting on forever.

KP and Suzie—I should preface this thank you with an I'm sorry. Thanks for keeping me grounded and not panicking when all my plans for this book went awry. And thanks for not saying I told you so. Next time, I promise not to give us all heart attacks. Maybe. Probably. (Okay, I promise for real). Vania, thanks for working so hard on this cover and for dealing with my pickiness until we got it right. And to all the authors and readers out there who have been pushing for NA speculative fiction for ages—thank you! Keep up the good work! We'll get there!

And to a few of the lovely bloggers and readers who make my life better on a daily basis—Vilma, Amber, Brooke, Kim, Stephanie, Jordan, DJ, Laura, Kayleigh, Jen, Megan, Hannah, Mary, Alana, Lenore, and so many more! And to all bloggers—thank you for doing what you do. I know it's a full time job plus some, and you do it not for money, but because you love books and you have huge hearts. Thank you for supporting books and reading and authors, even when this business is not always good at supporting you. I, for one, owe so much of my career (and the joy I've gained from it) to you all. So, in case you don't hear it enough: You are loved. You are appreciated. You are important. You are powerful. Don't forget it. [Insert cheesy joke about being *inspired* here] :)

About Cora Carmack

Cora Carmack is a twentysomething *New York Times* bestselling author who likes to write about twentysomething characters. Raised in a small Texas town, she now splits her time between Texas and New York City. She spends her time writing, traveling, and marathoning various television shows on Netflix. In her books, you can expect to find humor, heart, and a whole lot of awkward. Because let's face it…awkward people need love, too. Find her online at www.coracarmack.blogspot.com, friend her on facebook (facebook.com/CoraCarmack), or follow her on twitter (@CoraCarmack).

Printed in Great Britain
by Amazon